P9-DFT-720

"You never expected to live out of a van forever.

"That's the whole reason you came here in the first place when you found out about the baby. You wanted a place to belong. You wanted good people around you, and a regular roof over your head, and so you came here, to this place. That's no accident. That's why you started working on the bunkhouse. You wanted a community, a real live flesh-and-blood community that stays in one place."

"Stop doing that."

"Doing what?"

"Talking about me like you know me. Boxing me in."

"Boxing you in? How? By putting a roof over your head? That's bull. You drive away now, you still live in a box. It's just a box on wheels, whose transmission could go out a hundred miles from nowhere."

"That's *my* problem, not yours or anybody else's."

Dear Reader,

Family land. There's a lot of emotional content packed into those two words. It's not easy in today's world to keep land in the family, much less make a living off it. Still, modern-day farmers and ranchers find a way, as farmers and ranchers always have. I'm privileged to live on a farm that's been in continuous operation by the same family since 1852. I'm a homebody by nature, and I love living deeply in a place that has a story to every pasture, fence post and tree.

At the same time, I'm intrigued by the modern van-life movement, and impressed by the dedication, clarity of vision and genius contrivances of those who live it. I wouldn't want to do it myself, but I like looking at the pictures.

So what would it be like if a seventh-generation Texas rancher and a van-dwelling free spirit fell in love?

This is my first book with Harlequin Heartwarming, a line that affirms things I hold dear, like family, community, hard work, friendship and triumphant love.

I hope you enjoy Alex and Lauren's story.

Kit

HEARTWARMING

Hill Country Secret

—

Kit Hawthorne

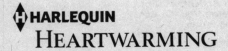

HARLEQUIN
HEARTWARMING

If you purchased this book without a cover you should be aware
that this book is stolen property. It was reported as "unsold and
destroyed" to the publisher, and neither the author nor the
publisher has received any payment for this "stripped book."

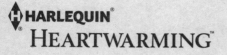

HARLEQUIN®
HEARTWARMING™

Recycling programs
for this product may
not exist in your area.

ISBN-13: 978-1-335-88987-4

Hill Country Secret

Copyright © 2020 by Brandi Midkiff

All rights reserved. No part of this book may be used or reproduced in
any manner whatsoever without written permission except in the case of
brief quotations embodied in critical articles and reviews.

This is a work of fiction. Names, characters, places and incidents
are either the product of the author's imagination or are used fictitiously.
Any resemblance to actual persons, living or dead, businesses,
companies, events or locales is entirely coincidental.

This edition published by arrangement with Harlequin Books S.A.

For questions and comments about the quality of this book,
please contact us at CustomerService@Harlequin.com.

Harlequin Enterprises ULC
22 Adelaide St. West, 40th Floor
Toronto, Ontario M5H 4E3, Canada
www.Harlequin.com

Printed in U.S.A.

Kit Hawthorne makes her home in south-central Texas on her husband's ancestral farm, where seven generations of his family have lived, worked and loved. When not writing, she can be found reading, drawing, sewing, quilting, reupholstering furniture, playing Irish pennywhistle, refinishing old wood, cooking huge amounts of food for the pressure canner, or wrangling various dogs, cats, goats and people.

To Mary and Cheryl, with gratitude, and in hopes of another twenty years of road trips, Cheez-Its, brainstorming, laughter and patient pauses in the conversation as we write down each other's book and movie recommendations. I treasure your friendship as much as your critiquing skills, and that's saying something.

Acknowledgments

Many thanks to my husband, Greg, for making it possible for me to stay home and write; my daughter Grace, for being such an excellent sounding board and encourager; my mom, for not balking at how many titles I used to circle on the Scholastic book catalog in elementary school; and for all the family and friends who have encouraged me and made my life richer over the years.

Thanks also to Isaac Dehoyos for making the Spanish language passages sound right.

CHAPTER ONE

A LOUD CRASH jolted Lauren Longwood awake. The October sunshine, so warm and bright when she'd settled into the porch swing earlier in the afternoon, had faded to an eerie twilight. A hard, straight wind cut through her thin T-shirt and rumbled over the metal roof.

She sat up and pulled the quilt around her shoulders, upsetting the gray barn cat nestled in its folds. Cushions tumbled to the floor, along with a worn copy of *Ghost Stories of the Texas Hill Country.*

She'd fallen asleep reading the sad tale of Alejandro Ramirez: husband, ranchero and soldier in the Texas Revolution. Now *that* was a man. Fearless, faithful, unstoppable. Not even death at the hands of Santa Anna's army could keep him from protecting the woman he loved.

"Durango!"

The wind swallowed her voice. She tried

again, louder. This time the sleek black-and-white border collie came racing up the walkway. He cleared the porch steps with an easy bound and nuzzled Lauren with his pointy snout.

A clenched fist of tension inside her relaxed a tiny bit as she rubbed Durango behind the ears. Dogs made everything better, and these days she was humbly grateful for any shred of comfort.

She'd been hurting long enough to grow used to the pain. Cling to it, even, like a ratty old blanket. She could function well enough, go through the motions of work and meals and personal hygiene, but not much more.

Durango followed her into the house. The LED displays on the electronics and kitchen appliances were blank. Wind must have taken out some power lines. So much for streaming something light and frothy on TV.

She fell to the sofa with a groan, still cocooned in the quilt. She'd been glad, sort of, to have the entire ranch to herself this weekend—as glad as she was about anything these days. Dalia was a good friend, but even her easy company was a burden at present. Lauren needed to get her head on straight, and

La Escarpa had quiet and solitude to spare, with nothing to remind her of Evan.

But she didn't need reminders. Evan filled her thoughts no matter where she went or what she did. She felt beat up inside, and all she really wanted was sleep.

She was on the verge of dropping off again when something creaked.

She opened her eyes. The old wooden cradle that stood before the fireplace was rocking.

Suddenly Lauren was wide-awake. She could feel the stiff spine of the ghost story book in her hand, and she remembered Alejandro's story vividly. Just before leaving to fight for Texas independence, he'd told his pregnant wife, Romelia, that he'd be back in time to place a spray of yellow *esperanza* blossoms in the cradle beside their child.

But Alejandro had been killed by a Mexican musket ball at the Siege of Béxar and buried in a hasty grave far from home. He'd never seen his only son, or returned to the young bride he'd left behind just months after their wedding.

Years later, during a bad drought, wildfires raged through the pastures of the rancho. As Romelia and the vaqueros fought to save the buildings and livestock, she'd seen a shadowy form moving through the smoke, fighting the fire—her husband's form. The house and outbuildings were saved, and not a single life was lost, human or animal.

And ever after, it was said, whenever danger threatened, Alejandro returned to save his family and their rancho.

This rancho. La Escarpa.

Cold prickles ran up Lauren's spine. Could this be the very cradle Alejandro had built with his own hands before leaving home to defend his country?

Durango lifted his head, fixed his ice-blue eyes on the cradle and growled.

In a flash, Lauren freed herself from the quilt and bolted out the door.

An *esperanza* bush stood near the porch steps. Its branches tossed in the wind, scattering leaves and yellow petals as Lauren ran past. She hurried down the walkway, through the gate and onto the long winding driveway. Durango kept pace, stretched out low and sleek at her side. She could feel the crunch of gravel beneath the soles of her boots, but couldn't hear her own footsteps over the wind's hollow roar.

The adrenaline rush lasted about a quarter mile before leaving her to crash and burn. She slowed to a walk, forcing herself to keep moving, keep putting one shaky limb in front of the other. She felt like she was going to throw up.

She laced her fingers behind her head and looked back toward the house. Had the cradle really rocked? She'd been half-asleep; maybe she'd dreamed the whole thing.

Of course she had.

In any event, ghost or no ghost, she couldn't keep running forever. She had to go back sometime.

Vincent Van-Go was parked close to the machine shed, his silver paint looking dim in the twilight. She'd sleep there tonight instead of in Dalia's guest room. Surely no self-respecting ghost of a nineteenth-century ranchero would bother to haunt a Ford Transit cargo van.

"Well, Durango, I guess we might as well go check the stock. Come on, boy."

Durango's ears perked, but he wasn't listening to Lauren. He was staring away from her, away from the house, with that weird fixed look in his eyes. Then he took off like a shot, without so much as a bark.

Lauren called him, but she knew it was

hopeless. Within seconds he'd disappeared around a bend in the drive.

Great. Now I've lost Dalia's dog.

There was no point in chasing him. He had to be making thirty miles an hour. Lauren was a good runner, but not that good.

Well, he'd come back when he came back. No doubt he'd be fine, with his border-collie intellect and his mad sprinting skills.

On the way to the barnyard, she passed a long, low building, overgrown with brush. Jagged shards of glass edged the broken windows, and she thought she saw something moving inside. A varmint, or a ghost? At this point, she was too tired to care.

The barnyard complex offered some protection from the cold. The various outbuildings and enclosures formed an organic cluster that harmonized with the lay of the land. Over in the paddock north of the house, the horses had taken refuge in a little hollow backed by a natural windbreak of dense cedar trees. She couldn't see the cattle, but they'd surely found shelter, as well, somewhere in their pasture. The chickens had wisely gone into their coop; they looked fluffed and surprised, but healthy. She checked their water and gave them some feed. Dulcinea, the Jersey cow, was on a once-a-day milking schedule and wouldn't need any attention until morning, but she was so sweet and pretty with her big black eyes and long eyelashes that Lauren stood a long time scratching the shaggy mop of golden-brown hair on the top of her head.

Last of all, she headed to the enclosure that held the Angora goats.

The Angoras brought in good money for La Escarpa. Their long, silky mohair coats were sheared twice a year and sold to be spun into yarn. Already the cream-colored wool was growing in thick and curly since their fall shearing.

Lauren stopped in her tracks. Just outside the goat pen there was an ancient mesquite, with heavy, sprawling limbs as thick as the trunks of mature trees. One of these had split off at the fork, flattening the fence wire and snapping one of the posts.

Straddling the massive mesquite limb was a man.

And what a man he was.

Her first thought was that he was dressed like a mariachi, but plainer, in his short jacket, ankle boots and dark neckcloth tied in a soft bow. But the suit was a rich butternut color, not black, and the embroidery running along the jackets' wrists and rounded lapels, and down the sides of the tight trousers, was made of plain floss, without any spangly bits. And he didn't have a hat. In an intuitive flash, Lauren knew this must be the sort of clothing that had inspired mariachi costumes to begin with.

Which meant it must be old—*really* old.

But the outfit, striking as it was, was nothing to the man himself.

He was lifting the fallen branch from the fence wire. The broad plains of his thigh and shoulder muscles strained against the butternut-brown fabric. His head was bent deep, chin to chest, and his black hair streamed behind him like a banner.

He was absolutely magnificent.

"Alejandro."

The name came out of her mouth before she knew she was going to say it. She couldn't help it. The name fit him, belonged to him, like a worn pair of leather work gloves.

He raised his head, and his eyes—almond-shaped, amber-colored beneath black crescents of eyebrows—met hers. Sinew stood out in his neck, and his lips were drawn back from strong white teeth.

"Ayudame," he said in a strained voice. *Help me.*

The fallen branch was more or less parallel to the fence. It didn't just cross the wires at a single point; it was lying over them for several feet. The wires were caught on the branch's bark and twigs. The mariachi cowboy, or whatever he was, could handle the weight all right, but he couldn't drag the branch free from its tangle of fencing.

Lauren hurried over and started breaking twigs and pulling the wire loose. A mesquite thorn pricked her finger.

The man didn't say anything. She was close enough to see the actual warp and woof of the cloth he wore. The shoulder seam of his jacket had the slight waviness of hand stitching.

The goats hadn't made a break for freedom. Durango had them huddled together in a corner, curly coats ruffled by the wind. He stood a few yards off, facing them with his ice-blue stare, keeping them in place.

The branch came free. The man released it, sending it crashing to the ground.

He stood to his full height, brushed off his hands and stepped over the branch toward Lauren. She hadn't realized how tall he was. He positively towered over her. His face was broad and well-formed, with high cheekbones and a square cleft chin—a hard, stern, severe face.

"¿Checaste los pollos y la vaca?" Did you check the chickens and the cow?

"Sí, están bien," Lauren said.

He smiled. His lips barely edged up, but somehow the smile reached his cheekbones and eyes right away.

"Bueno," he said.

And then…

Lauren heard music. Classical guitar. Faint, but unmistakable. She had a quick thought—*this ghost has a soundtrack?*—before the apparition spoke again.

"Oh, sorry, I better get this."

He reached inside his jacket and pulled out a cell phone.

"Hey, Tony, I figured you'd call. You been watching the weather, huh?… Yeah, it's pretty gusty, but everything's fine. I'm at your place now and… What?… Yeah, Lauren's fine, too. She's right here… Yeah, the stock is fine. We're all fine. Look, we got it covered, okay? So you and Dalia have a good time on the River Walk and don't worry. All right, then. 'Bye."

He put the phone away and gave Lauren

another smile. "Okay, so maybe that wasn't the whole truth. But he doesn't need to know about the fence just yet. Nothing he can do about it, and Dalia would just worry. Now that we've got that tree branch moved, we can rig a temporary fix with some cattle panels and cinder blocks. Tomorrow morning I'll come back and hitch up the post-hole digger to the tractor, and we'll replace that broken post and fix things up right. Good thing the tractor's running again, huh?"

Lauren found her voice. "I, uh…wait. Who are you?"

His smile faded. "I'm Alex Reyes, Tony's brother. We met at the wedding, remember? I was the best man, you were the photographer?" He paused, then added, "We danced?"

A wave of embarrassment washed over her. *Of course* this was Alex Reyes. She remembered him perfectly now. He even looked like Tony a little.

To be fair, it had been over a year since the wedding, and he sure hadn't been dressed like *that*. But the fact that she was capable of forgetting, even for a little while, a very attractive man, whose picture she'd taken, whom she'd danced with—her best friend's brother-in-law—just went to show what a flake she was.

"Wh-what are you doing here?" she asked.

"I came by to drop off the tractor. I work at the shop. See, there's my truck."

He pointed down the caliche driveway to a truck hitched to a flatbed trailer. Limestone Springs Auto and Tractor Service was printed on the side of the cab, and on the trailer was a Kubota tractor. Lauren remembered now that Tony had said the tractor might be delivered over the weekend. Alex must have driven up and parked while she was in the barnyard.

"Um...what's the story with your clothes?" she asked.

Alex looked down at himself. "What, these? Oh, I belong to a group of historical reenactors. I just picked up my new outfit today and decided to give it a trial run before my next event. I like my reenactor clothes to have some honest wear on them, so they don't look too costumey, you know? Plus the pants have to be broken in. They're made to fit kinda tight."

She let her eyes linger on the long contours of his thighs. They sure were.

The wind picked up. Thunder crashed, and sheet lightning flashed across the sky.

"We'd better get that fence jury-rigged," Lauren said. "I guess Durango will stay put?"

"Oh, yeah. He knows his business, don't you, boy?"

Durango's tail gave a flicker of acknowledgement. He didn't take his eyes off the goats.

In the tool shed, Alex pulled out a sturdy four-wheeled cart and started loading it with cinder blocks and wire fencing.

"Why'd you speak Spanish to me?" Lauren asked.

"Did I? Maybe because you called me Alejandro. Made me feel like I was back on my grandparents' place. Hey, wait a minute. If you didn't recognize me, why'd you say my name?"

Lauren felt her face grow warm. She kept her back turned so Alex wouldn't see. She hated being so quick to blush, so pitifully transparent.

"Did I?" She added some wire tighteners and fencing pliers to the cart. "I guess you just look like an Alejandro."

"Huh. Well, at least Durango remembered me. Came running to meet me as I drove up."

Lauren felt her blush deepening. *So that's why Durango took off down the drive with that weird look in his eyes. He heard the truck engine.*

Durango was still standing in the gap when they returned with the cart. It was getting dark now, but Alex found some battery-powered torchlights in the goat shed.

Lauren shivered. *Why didn't I grab my hoodie before running outside? Oh, yeah, because I was spooked half out of my mind by a book of ghost stories.*

Alex took off his jacket and handed it to her. He was very matter-of-fact about it, with no overblown gallantry or remarks about chivalry not being dead. He had a waistcoat on underneath, in a darker brown with a woven stripe.

Lauren was too cold to politely refuse. "Thanks," she said, slipping her arms into the sleeves. "Wow, this feels like putting on an electric blanket."

"Yeah, I'm like a human furnace. Always have been."

Together they pieced and spliced and rigged the fence back into passable shape.

"You're good at this," Alex said.

"Thanks. So are you. Are you a rancher yourself?"

His mouth tightened. "Trying to be. It's a long story."

And not a very happy one, judging from the look on his face. Probably best not to pry.

"I guess that's it," Alex said at last, giving a final twist to the last of the wire tighteners.

One of the goats let out a bleat like it agreed with him.

Alex laid the wire tighteners in the cart, then straightened and looked down at Lauren. He was a big man, and he had a way of carrying himself that made him look bigger still. Lauren's eyes followed the curve of his waistcoat's shawl lapel as it widened over the broad expanse of chest before tapering to the single row of buttons over the flat abdomen.

"What about tomorrow?" Alex asked. "Shall we say around eleven?"

Her mind went blank. Had he asked her out? Had she accepted?

"To fix the fence," he said. "I'd like to have it done right before Tony and Dalia get back. This patchwork will keep the goats in overnight, but it won't keep coyotes out."

"Oh, right. Yeah, eleven's fine. Other than watching the ranch, I'm free all weekend."

Great, now she sounded like she was hinting. *Please ask me out, handsome vaquero guy. I'm totally free all weekend.*

Alex thought a moment. "I don't know

what the weather's supposed to do tomorrow. Let me give you my number. If it gets bad, we can reschedule."

He felt for the inner breast pocket, where he'd put his phone before, but he wasn't wearing his jacket anymore. Lauren was. He made an instinctive movement toward Lauren and the pocket, then seemed to think better of it and jerked back his hand.

She started to take off the jacket. "Nah, that's okay," he said. "I'll walk you to the house when we're done and give you my card."

By the time they'd put away the tools, the thunder was growling continuously, with lightning flashing like a strobe light. Still no rain.

On the way back to the house, Lauren asked, "Hey, what's the deal with that creepy broken-down building just off the driveway?"

"That's the old bunkhouse, where the vaqueros used to live. Raccoons have taken it over. It's trashed on the inside, but the architecture's still solid. I'd love to fix it up one day."

"Huh. That's not a bad idea."

When they reached the porch, she took off the jacket and handed it to him. He pulled a small ornate metal case out of the pocket, opened it and handed her a card.

"Phone number's on the back," he said.

Printed in a lovely old-fashioned type-face was Alejandro Emilio de Reyes—nothing more. Not a business card, but a genuine nineteenth-century calling card.

She read the name aloud. Both the sight and the sound of it struck her with a strange, half-pleasurable ache.

"Dang, girl, where'd you learn to roll your *R*'s like that?"

"Oh, I lived in Mexico a few months. Long enough to upgrade my high-school Spanish to functional fluency."

The rain fell in a sudden torrent. Alex let out a whoop.

"Finally! I hope it comes down all night. We sure need it. 'Course, it'd be better if it slackened down to a nice soft patter. A down-pour like this is satisfying to hear, but as dry as the ground is, it'll just run off instead of soaking in, and it might flood. Not that I'm complaining!"

"That's what everyone in Texas says about rain. It's like you're afraid to offend the rain gods. You could be getting carried off by a flash flood, and just as it swept you away you'd yell, 'Not that I'm complaining!'"

"Well, I don't know about rain gods. I'm a Baptist. But, yeah, I guess you have a point. We're always scared of drought, haunted by it. Even in a wet year we know there are more droughts to come, waiting."

Lauren understood the feeling. But the things haunting her were empty dreams, lost hope and broken promises.

Alex put on the jacket. One long wavy tendril of hair caught beneath the collar. Lauren felt a sudden urge to tease it free with her fingers.

"Would you like to come inside?" she asked.

The question sounded as doubtful as she felt. This was an exceptionally attractive man, but Lauren knew very well that she had no business getting involved in any way with any man whatsoever. Her life was more than complicated enough just now, and she had someone besides herself to think of.

He looked toward the drive. Rain poured off the edge of the porch roof in a solid gray curtain.

"I don't want to intrude," he said.

"It's no intrusion. Anyway, there's no way

you can unload the tractor in this downpour. You'd be swept away for sure."

He turned those amber eyes on her again. They were tilted downward ever so slightly at the outer corners, giving his face a sad, solemn look.

Then he smiled—just a slight smile, like before, but one that altered the whole character of his face.

"I'll make us some Mexican hot chocolate," he said.

A beautiful man in historical vaquero garb was offering to cook for her—to cook chocolate, no less. Heaven help her.

CHAPTER TWO

ALEX FOLLOWED LAUREN into the house, taking the opportunity to check her out without having to be stealthy about it. She was tiny—dainty, even—with slender wrists and ankles. She wore grayish sweatpants—the clingy kind, not the baggy kind—and a purple T-shirt that somehow managed to hit all her curves in spite of being oversized. Her hair was a sort of bright brown, not quite red and not quite gold, like a chestnut horse. It hung halfway down her back, thick and full, like a mane.

In spite of being so small, she was strong. And capable. She'd worked beside him without complaint in the cold and handled the tools like a pro. They'd worked well together, anticipating each other's movements.

They'd danced well together, too, at the wedding reception two years earlier, but that didn't seem to have made much of an impression on her.

"Power's still out," she said. "But I have a propane camp stove out in Vincent."

"Vincent?"

"That's my van, Vincent Van-Go. He's a Ford Transit."

Right. The van she traveled around in and lived out of. Tony had told him about that. The thought of this tiny woman zipping around North America and camping in remote spots by herself blew his mind. What was she thinking?

Probably not thinking at all. Just looking for thrills. Rootless and shallow. The sort of millennial that gives millennials a bad name.

She picked up a turquoise sweatshirt from the back of a chair. It was a pullover hoodie; she had to stretch up to get her arms in the sleeves and then wriggle her way inside of it. This should have been an awkward process, but she made it look graceful. *Everything* she did was graceful. Fixing fence. Taking pictures at Tony and Dalia's wedding, crouching and twisting and kneeling with her fancy camera, moving around silently without getting in anyone's way. Dancing with him at the reception, her hands light and cool and impossibly small.

"Cars are supposed to be female," Alex said. "Like ships."

She reached both hands inside the hoodie's neck and flipped out her hair. It tumbled over the hood in a glorious shower of color.

"Well, Vincent is a boy."

He swallowed hard.

"We don't need the camp stove," he said. "This range is propane, too, and I can light the burner manually."

He opened the fridge. "Are you a vegan?"

"Why do you ask?"

"Because you kinda look like a vegan, and I can't make my Mexican hot chocolate with almond milk or soy juice or whatever it is that vegans drink. And, anyway, we don't have any of that stuff. Just whole milk and cream from a grass-fed Jersey cow."

"I don't know what you think vegans look like, but I happen to love full-fat dairy products."

He set the milk and cream on the counter. "Good. Now just how authentic an experience would you like? Should I go full-on Aztec or what?"

"I'll take mine without the human sacrifice, thanks."

He chuckled. "Nah, Aztec just means it isn't sweetened."

"Seriously, that's an option? Never mind authentic, then. I want it sweet."

"So do I."

He was unwrapping the baking chocolate when he heard her suck in her breath. He glanced over and saw her staring into the living room.

"What's wrong?" he asked.

She pointed to the cradle. It was rocking.

"Do you see that?" she asked.

Durango let out a low growl. He was staring at the cradle, too.

"Quiet, Durango," Alex said. "Leave the kitty alone."

"Kitty? What kitty?"

"Calypso, the old calico. She loves that cradle. Dalia keeps a pillow in there for her. I guess she's got to move around every few minutes and resettle her old bones to stay comfy. I don't know what Tony and Dalia are going to do when it comes time to put an actual baby in there. I guess they'll have to make another cradle for the cat."

Lauren walked over to the cradle and looked inside.

"I remember now. Dalia did say there was

an old barn cat in the house that had earned herself a cushy retirement. Why does Durango growl at her? He doesn't bother the other cats."

"Oh, those two have history. Calypso once stole a piece of brisket right out of Durango's mouth, and clawed him across the nose. He's never really gotten over it. He won't hurt her, though."

Alex set up the double boiler on the stove, and Lauren straddled a barstool. Suddenly she seemed very close, right there across the range from him, with her forearms resting on the bar and her hair tousled around her face. It was a heart-shaped face, wide in the forehead, pointed at the chin, with dark eyes in creamy clear skin. The nose ring was new since the wedding—not a ring, actually, but a tiny diamond chip, barely visible. He wasn't one for piercings, but she did make it look good.

He took a long match out of the kitchen drawer.

"What, no tinderbox?" Lauren asked.

"Ha ha. I don't really think you're in a position to mock me for being eccentric, Miss Nomadic Van-Dweller. I do own a tinderbox, though. It's very nice."

He lit the match and turned the burner dial.

The burner flame caught with a soft roar. He set the double boiler over the flame and started chopping chocolate.

"The house is getting cold," Lauren said. "We should start a fire."

"I'll get to it as soon as I finish here."

"That's all right. You're already busy. I'll do it."

He wished she'd leave it to him. Starting a fire from scratch was easier than coming along later and fixing someone else's clumsy attempt.

But just as the last chunk melted away in the thick chocolaty mixture in the double boiler, a healthy blaze in the firebox caught his eye. She'd built a respectable kindling tee-pee and was just adding a couple of large sticks.

She came back to the bar and peered into the double boiler. "Is that cinnamon I smell?"

"Yep, two whole tablespoons, and a pinch of chili powder."

"Chili powder!"

"Yep. The Aztecs invented hot chocolate, and they liked it spicy. They called it *xoco-latl*—'bitter water.' It took the Europeans to think of adding sugar, though. One of their better contributions to mestizo culture."

He turned off the burner and poured the chocolate into two mugs. "You want a jigger of rum in yours? That's Día de Muertos style."

"Day of the Dead?"

"Yeah, it's a Mexican holiday. It started out with the Aztecs and eventually got combined with Halloween, which is today."

"Is it? I'd forgotten. How appropriate."

"Why is it appropriate?"

"Oh, you know, the cold front and howling wind and wildly waving tree limbs and all. It's just kind of a spooky night. And I'll pass on the rum."

"That's probably smart, not drinking with a strange man."

"Are you a strange man?"

"So I've been told."

He added rum to his own chocolate, and they took their mugs to the fireplace.

Durango was already lying close to the hearth. As Alex took a seat in the wing chair, Calypso the cat poked her head out of the cradle and gave a hoarse meow. Durango growled a little without opening his eyes.

Lauren set down her mug on the hearth, added a midsize log to the fire and pulled off her boots. Then she curled up in the overstuffed armchair and picked up the mug again.

She held it in both hands and breathed deep, letting the steam warm her face. One leg was drawn up to her chest; the other was draped over the arm of the chair. Her body was one curving line after another: calves and ankles, hips and thighs.

She took a sip and shut her eyes. "Mmm."

Alex realized he was staring, like some sort of creep. He made himself look away.

A book was lying on the floor.

"*Ghost Stories of the Texas Hill Country*! My cousin wrote that. It's good, you should read it."

Lauren gave a choked laugh that turned into a coughing fit. She had to set down her mug until it passed.

"What? What'd I say?"

"Nothing."

"Then why'd you laugh? What are you, some sort of ghost-story hater?"

"No."

"What, then?"

She picked up her mug, took another sip and gave a last cough.

"Tell me," Alex said.

"Only if you promise you won't tell Dalia and Tony. Or anyone else. Ever."

"I can't promise unless I know what it is. You might be a dangerous person. Or a dangerous ghost."

"I'm not! It's nothing bad, just kind of embarrassing. You can safely promise not to tell."

"I don't know that. I don't know you. And I take promises seriously."

She gave him a look like…he didn't know what. Like he'd said something profound and a little sad.

"Okay, fair enough. This afternoon I fell asleep reading about Alejandro Ramirez. You know Alejandro Ramirez?"

"Sure. Me and him go way back."

"And when I woke up the weather had changed and everything was all freaky, and when I saw you in the goat pen in those clothes, lifting that mesquite branch…"

"Whoa. You thought I was him? Alejandro Ramirez?"

"I know how dumb it sounds. But it was such a beautiful story, and I guess my imagination was kind of stoked."

"Are you kidding me? It's not dumb at all.

It's the best compliment any woman has ever paid me in my life."

"Seriously?"

"Heck, yeah. I *love* that story. I was named for Alejandro Ramirez. He was my great-great-great-great-grandfather. He's the character I portray in my reenacting. He's who I'm dressed up as right now."

"I thought he was Dalia's however-many-greats grandfather."

"He's both of ours. Our families used to be related—well, still are, but distantly. Not in a way that makes it weird for her and Tony to be married. Her branch of the family got La Escarpa. Our branch sort of fell off the tree and landed in the septic runoff and got struck by lightning and eaten up by termites. But it's still my heritage, too, and it means just as much to me as it does to Dalia. Maybe more. You don't really know the value of something until you lose it."

"That's true."

He felt a hard-core goofy smile stretching his face. "Wow! Me, mistaken for the actual ghost of Alejandro Ramirez. This is the best thing that's happened to me in a long time. And don't worry, I'll keep it to myself. Your secret is safe with me."

"Thanks. I'm not usually prone to ghost sightings. I just… I guess I was feeling a little down today, and then I fell asleep, and I got mixed up. It's such a sad story, and it hit me hard. A baby without a father. A mother on her own."

"Nothing to be embarrassed about. I mean, what are ghost stories, really? They're all about people who died before their time, or left things undone, or didn't get justice. That's why they hit us so hard. Because we've all got stuff like that. Things that didn't go right, that we wish we could change. Things that haunt us."

She looked into the fire. "You're right."

Suddenly she looked smaller than ever, curled up in the big armchair with her mug cupped in both hands. The firelight made little golden flashes in her hair. She seemed sad and a little lost, and Alex thought about how it would feel to have her in his arms, telling him her troubles.

Instead, he downed the last of his hot chocolate and stood up.

"I'd better go. Rain's slacked off, and I ought to get the tractor unloaded now in case it picks up again. I'll call the power co-op for you and report the outage. They're pretty quick about fixing things. Is your phone charged? Do you have a flashlight?"

She smiled. The smile looked a little put-on, but at least she didn't look like she was about to cry anymore.

"Oh, yeah, I'll be fine. Believe me, I've camped a lot rougher than this. Do you need help unloading the tractor?"

"Nah, you stay inside where it's warm."

The truth was, he needed to get away from this woman, with her gorgeous legs and ridiculously good hair and whatever it was that was making her sad. Alex had his own ghosts to deal with, and they took time and energy enough.

She walked him out as far as the edge of the porch. He took a couple of steps down and reached into the *esperanza* bush. Most of its blossoms were gone or blown to shreds, but he managed to find one intact spray.

He plucked it and turned around to face Lauren. Looking solemnly up at her, he put the yellow flowers in her hands and said, *"Yo prometo volver mañana a tiempo para arreglar la cerca del corral de cabras."*

He could see the wheels turning in her head as she worked out the translation, a variation on Alejandro's parting words to his wife. *I promise to return tomorrow in time to fix the fence of the goat pen.*

Smiling and scowling at the same time, she planted a hand on his chest and pushed. He mock-stumbled down the remaining steps, laughing uproariously.

A few minutes later, heading down the driveway with an empty trailer, he had a feeling of "and not a moment too soon." Something about Lauren made him feel kind of off-kilter. She was an interesting woman, and good to look at. But she wasn't right for him, and he sure wasn't right for her.

CHAPTER THREE

PHOTOGRAPHING A WEDDING was a test of friendship for sure. Even with strangers, wedding work was Lauren's least favorite photography gig. Take a group of stressed, self-conscious people, add some suppressed family tensions and a lifetime of unrealistic and conflicting expectations, bring the whole mess to a rapid simmer with sleep deprivation, financial strain and alcohol, and the result was less than ideal as far as working conditions. She preferred nature photography any day—a coast at morning twilight, a starlit sky, a mossy forest. Trees and rocks and birds didn't talk back, or hide from the camera, or tell Lauren how best to pose them so they wouldn't look fat.

She'd sworn off wedding work repeatedly, only to grudgingly accept a new gig when the money was good, telling herself that maybe this time would be different. She'd come out of retirement yet again at Dalia's request almost two years earlier.

Dalia had promised there would be no such nonsense from her wedding party, and she'd made good on her word, because they'd all complied with Lauren's directions without a peep of protest, and looked gorgeous doing so. Lauren had never encountered a group so photogenic, or so easily managed.

There'd been undercurrents of tension, of course—all of which involved Tony's father, Carlos. Tension between Carlos and his sons, Carlos and his father, Carlos and his ex-wife. He seemed nice enough—charming, in fact, with a sort of shimmery quality that made you notice him. But something wasn't right. Tony and Alex both seemed fine with their mother, Lisa, and Lisa seemed fine with her ex-father-in-law. The trouble, whatever it might be, was with Carlos.

But whatever that trouble might have been, it hadn't affected the pictures. Looking them over on her laptop the morning after the whole haunted-baby-cradle, fallen-tree-limb, mistaken-ghost-sighting scenario, Lauren was amazed all over again. They were *good*.

Dalia, beautiful to begin with, strong and confident, swept along on a giant wave of joy.

Tony, stunned with happiness, pleased with everything and everyone.

She clicked on a thumbnail of Tony and the groomsmen, in their coordinating but nonidentical outfits: dark jeans, brown cowboy boots, mismatched patterned shirts in a muted autumnal palette and waistcoats ranging from ivory to camel. Tony had a brown herringbone jacket, as well.

Alex wore a plaid flannel shirt with a creamy tweed waistcoat. Even in that crowd of fun-loving, good-looking guys, he stood out. There was something special about him—his bright eyes, his quick step. That slight smile that lifted his cheekbones. The full-on smile that dazzled like the sun.

He was an inspired dancer, but Lauren quit after one song. She had pictures to take, she told him; she really didn't have any business dancing at all. And Alex didn't push. He went on to dance with a dozen other girls. He didn't stand still ten seconds once the band started to play, and was as energetic and graceful at night's end as when he'd begun.

Lauren had gotten a lot of candid shots of him. She hadn't realized just how many at the time.

She was sitting on her bed in the back of

her van, propped up with pillows. Alex's calling card stood in one of the windows with the *esperanza* spray lying in front.

Esperanza *means hope.*

The flowers looked like tiny golden trumpets. Lauren touched them, then ran a finger along the line of old-fashioned type on the calling card. *Alejandro Emilio de Reyes.*

The rumble of a truck engine took her by surprise. It couldn't be eleven already; she couldn't possibly have spent the last two hours gazing at wedding pictures.

But it was, and she had.

She'd only meant to spend a few minutes glancing over the pictures. Actually, she hadn't even meant to do that. She'd started her computer with the intention of checking her email and attending to some minor work-related things, but instead she'd opened the album. Now here was the morning nearly gone and Alex ready to mend the busted fence. And what was she doing? Gazing at his pictures, with the card and flowers he'd given her sitting there like some sort of shrine.

Don't be an idiot, Lauren. You can't afford to get all gooey over the first good-looking guy to come along. Remember why you're here.

Last night she'd been entirely too loose and

flirty with him. Today she would be all business. Terse. She would be terse.

She clicked out of the album, shut her laptop and whisked the card and flowers into
the wastebasket.

The truck parked alongside the tractor shed
was not last night's Silverado with the shop's
logo on the door, but a muscular-looking
Dodge crew cab spattered with mud.

Alex stepped out. He wasn't wearing his
vaquero clothes today; he had on jeans, Ropers and a denim jacket. His hair was pulled
back in a ponytail.

"Hey there," Lauren called as she walked
out to meet him. "I almost didn't recognize
you without your clothes."

Wow. Way to start the conversation. And
it wasn't even true. She'd just spent the last
two hours drooling over pictures of him in
his best-man getup, and she was pretty sure
she'd recognize him at a hundred yards in a
tuxedo, or an apron and chef's hat, or a Mon-
golian deel.

"I mean your other clothes," she explained
lamely. "The reenactor ones."

"Yeah, I didn't want to get them messed
up," he said. "We've got fence to mend."

"What about that authentic lived-in look?"

"Lived-in is authentic. Smears of Quikrete, not so much."

"True. I like your ride."

"Thanks."

"What's its name?"

"Rosie." His voice had a defensive, do-you-want-to-make-something-of-it? sound.

Too late, Lauren remembered she was supposed to be terse. Maybe she'd be cordial instead. That would be better, anyway. Terseness would imply that she had something to guard against. Yes, she would be cordial, as cordial as she'd be with any casual acquaintance.

"Nice and warm today," Alex said. "Is the power back on?"

"Yep."

"Goats all right?"

"Yep. Durango's with them. Our fence patch is still holding."

This was good. Weather and livestock: safe topics of conversation.

In the machine shed, Alex filled a one-gallon bucket with work gloves, a level and an iron crowbar, then loaded a bag of Quikrete, a cedar fence post and some two-by-fours onto the tractor's tool rack.

He handed the bucket to Lauren. "Take this

to the goat pen. I'll hook up the post-hole digger to the tractor and meet you there."

The goats were spread out in their paddock, but when Durango saw the tractor coming, he herded them into the shed.

Lauren watched as Alex maneuvered the tractor into place, started the huge auger spinning and lowered it close to the post that had broken. Slowly the auger made its way through the soil.

Once the hole was dug and the tractor was parked, Lauren took the new post off the tool rack and set it in the hole. She and Alex worked together to brace the post with two-by-fours.

"You seem to know your way around a fence," Alex said.

"Oh, yeah, I'm an old hand at ranch work."

"The heck you say."

"It's true. I spent a summer on a ranch in the interior of Mexico."

"What, like a guest ranch? A resort?"

"It wouldn't be much of a resort if they made people mend fence, would it? No, a regular working ranch. I parked my van on the property and worked cattle for three months."

He was quiet a moment as he nailed the last two-by-four in place. Then he said, "Huh."

He cut open the bag of Quikrete and poured the dry powder into the hole while Lauren filled the bucket with water from the pen's hydrant. She poured the water into the hole, where it turned the cement mix to thick sludge. Alex added some large rocks and jammed them in tight with the crowbar. Then they adjusted the bracing, with Alex checking the post repeatedly with the level.

Finally, he nodded in satisfaction. "Perfectly plumb."

They stood together awhile, watching the goats. There was a cool breeze, but the sun was warm on Lauren's shoulders. In Mexico, she'd been pleasantly surprised to learn that a lot of farm work—not most, but more than she would have thought—involved just standing around staring. It wasn't constant drudgery. It had lovely moments of leisure.

"The Angoras are bringing in some pretty respectable money," Alex said. "I got to hand it to Dalia, she has a good head for business. And she sure makes Tony toe the line."

"I think they seem very happy."

"Oh, I know they are. Tony needs someone to manage him. He likes it."

"Yeah? What about you?"

"I toe my own line."

He checked his watch. "Four hours 'til the post is set. Then we can restring the fence."

It was a long time, but she didn't think she'd mind the wait. She'd expected to spend the weekend brooding over Evan, but there was something about Alex, something terribly attractive about his strength and efficiency and attention to detail, that made her ex seem kind of paltry. The effortless way Alex had hefted the Quikrete bag. The way he'd expertly backed the tractor little by little while the auger was running in order to keep the hole exactly vertical.

"What are you looking at?" Alex asked. "Do I have Quikrete on my face?"

"Sorry, no. I guess I'm just surprised by your commitment to the task. Most guys would've thought they'd done more than enough in patching the fence back together last night. No one would blame you for leaving the rest to Tony and Dalia."

"I want the job done right before they get back. Tony and Dalia have been up to their necks in work. Here they've finally taken a weekend off, and with the baby coming who knows when they'll get another chance. I don't want them to come home to a big mess. I'm just so happy they're together, you know?

I mean, you talk about a big mess, that's what Tony was not long ago. The family's thrilled that he got back with Dalia and got his act together. I want to support them all I can."

"You're a good brother," Lauren said. Good brother, nice guy. One who belonged in the platonic category. Cordial. She must be cordial.

"Ah, it's not that big a deal. Couple of generations ago, it was normal for family and neighbors to help each other—in the country, anyway. That's how they survived. Folks today are so insulated from their neighbors, their communities. I like living somewhere that people still look out for each other."

"That's how it is in the van community. I've met a lot of good people in groups and forums online. Everyone is so friendly and helpful and quick to share knowledge. I've met a lot of good people in my travels, too."

He frowned. "That's not really the same thing, though. You can't have the same kind of relationships with people you only know online, or people you're with only a little while as you gallivant along, as you can with people in the same town."

"I don't gallivant along. I'm very purposeful in my travels. And I don't believe friendship has to be limited by geography."

"Maybe friendship isn't, but community is. Neighbors are people you see over and over, day after day, year in and year out, because you have to. You can't just pick up and move, or exit out of the forum or whatever, every time they start to bug you. There's a whole different level of commitment. You can't have a relationship of value without being locked in. You just can't. Being locked in is one of the requirements. Otherwise you're just doing whatever feels good at the moment."

He looked so smug, explaining her own existence to her, lecturing her like some *child*. She could tell him a thing or two about commitment, and about people who did whatever felt good in the moment and then moved on, regardless of who they hurt. *I know about commitment, jerk. I committed—and got my heart run through a meat grinder and tossed back to me like it was garbage.*

What would Alex say, if she told him about Evan? Probably that it was her own fault for falling so fast, for refusing to see what a shallow man-child Evan was.

"You don't know anything about it," she said.

"I don't have to know anything about it. It's

obvious. People who spend all their time traveling around are afraid to put down roots."

"Oh, yeah? Well, maybe people who hide in the past are afraid to let go."

LET GO.

Alex was sick to death of those words. He'd heard them just last night, in his father's latest nasty phone call. *Quit your griping, Alex. You lost—and getting your panties in a wad won't change that. It's time to let go.*

People who only ever saw his dad in charm mode would never believe how vicious he could be. He was as smooth as melted butter as long as everything was going his way and he felt like he was getting his due. But call him on his bull, and out came the poisonous fangs.

And Alex had been calling him on his bull for a long time now.

Let go.

It was the hypocrisy of it that really chapped Alex's hide—as if his father had ever let go of anything. Chasing losses was his entire life, and he didn't care who got hurt in the process.

Lauren was looking up at him with flushed cheeks and her chin tilted and her eyes bright with anger—like she was the one who'd been wronged, like she'd put him in his place. What did she know about him?

He clenched his hands, focusing on the sensation of his nails digging into his palms, letting the pain steady him.

Then he turned and walked away.

"Where are you going?" Lauren called after him.

"To find four hours of work to do until the fence is ready to restring. Go back to your van. I can handle the rest myself."

She followed him. "Who made you foreman? I'm the ranch-sitter. If anyone should be doing the work, it's me."

"I don't need help."

"Really? What about all that stuff you just said about community and helping each other?"

What was wrong with her? Why wouldn't she just go away and leave him alone? It wasn't like she *wanted* to be around someone like him. But he couldn't go on refusing her help without looking like a jerk.

He stopped. "I'm going to drive around the fallow pasture and pick up some of the firewood Tony chain-sawed last year. It ought to be ready to split and stack. If you want to come along, I won't stop you."

CHAPTER FOUR

FIREWOOD WARMS YOU twice. Once when you're cutting it, and again when you're burning it. That's what Lauren's dad had said every single time he'd cut firewood, always with the exact same goofy, self-satisfied smile on his face.

Now Lauren realized that firewood could warm her a third time, when she was watching an exceptionally strong and well-made man do the work, and shed layers of clothing one by one, down to what looked like a many-times-washed, slightly-too-tight, athletic-fit T-shirt.

She and Alex hadn't spoken much since their epic clash of life philosophies. Gathering the firewood had been awkward, to say the least. Lauren almost wished she'd let him stalk off and finish the work himself, instead of forcing her company on someone who clearly didn't want it anymore.

But she had her own reasons for wanting to

make herself useful on La Escarpa, and not all of them were selfless ones.

Alex straightened, stretched and gave her a quick nod.

"Nice job with the stacking," he said.

He was being terse, which was what she'd intended to be with him today before settling on cordial. So far she hadn't succeeded very well with either one, but if things between them were terse now, she could keep them that way.

She'd transformed Tony's haphazard wood-pile into a neat wall of wood, and she'd done it without supports. The wall looked like a bunch of Jenga stacks all pressed together.

"Thanks," she said. "Nice job with the splitting."

His expression thawed a bit. "Thanks. You know, they say firewood warms you twice—once when you're cutting it, and again when you're burning it."

Lauren choked down a laugh that turned into a snort.

"What?" said Alex. "Haven't you ever heard that before?"

"Yeah, a time or two."

Then she pulled out her phone and took a picture of the stacked wood.

"What's that for?" Alex asked.

"Instagram."

She could actually hear him rolling his eyes behind her back, and for a moment she thought he was going to make a snide remark, but all he said was "It's been four hours. Time to restring the fence."

Terse or not, they worked together like old partners. They fastened the fencing back at the previous post, overlapping the last of the old wire, then pulled the new fencing tight with the come-along, attached it at the newly set post and tied it off at the next post. One section of old fencing had some sag in some of the wires. Lauren took the pliers to it, kinking the wire every two inches or so until it was tight again.

Once the job was done, Durango flopped down with a sigh in a patch of sunlight.

"Look at him," Alex said. "He knows we're finished. He looks like he's ready to kick his boots off and open a beer."

The chill was gone from his voice, and he was smiling. Lauren felt her commitment to terseness melting away.

ALEX PUT THE tools back in the bucket, loaded the scrap wood onto the tractor and drove back to the tractor's lean-to. Lauren showed up on foot not long after and started unloading the tools and putting them away. He came over to help, and to make sure she did it right.

"You're a tidy workman," Lauren said.

"Yeah, my grandfather always said you're not done until you've cleaned up and put away all your tools where they belong. He was supermeticulous, way more than me. I'm a backsliding hedonist compared to him."

"I think your grandfather and my dad would get along famously."

Alex hung the come-along from its metal peg. "My grandfather died last year."

"Oh, Alex, I'm so sorry. He was such a sweet old man."

He looked at her, surprised, and then remembered. Of course, she'd met him at the wedding.

"You're right, he was. But not many people saw that. Most folks would call him a real crank."

"Like who?"

She actually sounded indignant, and that made Alex smile.

"My dad, mostly. Used to make my blood boil. All the things my grandfather taught me, all the things I admired about him—stuff he'd say, the hours he worked, the way he reused materials and made do and had a precise spot for every tool. My dad mocked it all, made him sound like a mean old ignorant skinflint, and I had to sit there and listen. Took everything I had to keep from punching him in the mouth."

"That's rough."

"Yeah."

There was an awkward pause, and then Alex asked, "So, uh, are you okay on firewood at the house?"

It was a dumb question; there was no way Lauren could have gone through the big porch stack, or even made much of a dent, in one night.

"I didn't stay in the house. I slept in my van."

"What? Why would you do that when you have a perfectly good house available?"

"I sleep better in Vincent. It's cozy there, and I'm used to it."

"Cozy? It was cold last night. And doesn't that seat kill your back?"

She laughed. "Wow. You think I'm basically a hobo in a freight car, don't you? Come on. You're about to see what van life is really like. I'm giving you the full tour."

He followed her without protest. There were about a million and one things he needed to do out at his grandparents' ranch, but he could afford to spend a few minutes checking out Lauren's van. Truth be told, he was curious.

It looked nondescript enough on the outside. Taller than usual for a van, but not weird.

"So this is your hippie van," he said. "What, no mural spray-painted on the outside?"

"Ha! I wanted to, but my dad said no."

"Because of resale?"

"No, for safety. He said I should keep the outside as low-key as possible so no one would guess this was a van that someone lived in. I could knock myself out on the inside, artistically speaking, but I had to keep the outside plain."

"That's smart."

Lauren slid open the side door and held out her arm in a welcoming flourish.

Alex stepped inside—

And froze in his tracks.

He didn't know what he'd been expecting. Bead curtains, maybe. A reek of marijuana, probably. Terrible disorder, definitely.

He sure hadn't expected this.

It was like a magical gypsy caravan. Color flooded the space: a rich turquoise on the walls, ceiling and cabinetry, red and gold prints on the bed. It was bright, but not jarring, and somehow deeply restful.

The bed took up the back half or so of the van. A red shelf ran along the three walls high above it, about a foot from the ceiling. It held a variety of objects, most of which looked like small pieces of architectural salvage: an old wrought-iron fence finial, a scrap of Victorian millwork. At the opposite end, the driver's and passenger's seats, both wearing slipcovers in a red print fabric, were swiveled around to face into the van's interior. Along both walls in between was a galley kitchen, with a sink and stove on one side and a little retro fridge on the other.

Alex touched the countertop. It had a mottled patina in varying shades of red, green, gold and blue. "Is this copper?"

"Copper foil, wrapped around a plywood base. Beautiful, durable and surprisingly affordable."

Lauren squeezed past him, took a couple of glass bottles out of the little fridge and handed him one. "Take a load off," she said, pointing to the driver's seat. "Best seat in the house. You can even put your feet up, if you take your boots off first."

He pulled off his Ropers and rested his feet on a sort of wooden box with a cushioned top. Then he unscrewed the lid of his bottle and took a swig of the amber-colored liquid. It was fizzy and sweet and a little tart, like hard cider.

"What is this that I'm drinking?"

Lauren had clambered onto the bed and was arranging blankets and cushions into a fluffy nest.

"Kombucha," she said. "Nonalcoholic, probiotic, lacto-fermented. Very good for you."

"That sounds awful." He took another swig. "But it tastes good. And who am I to talk? My ancestors fermented cocoa beans and cactus juice."

He pointed to the kitchen. "Where'd all this cabinetry come from?"

"I salvaged the drawers and door fronts from an old seventies sideboard. It was a truly hideous piece of furniture, all that heavy carving in a fake-looking dark finish, but once I got it painted, it looked gorgeous."

"What is that covering the walls and ceiling?"

"Quarter-inch birch plywood, nice and

bendy for going over contours. There's a layer of insulation underneath. I made cardboard templates, cut out the panels, sanded the edges and painted the pieces before installing them. Then I hid the seams with upholstery trim."

"What's that little fruit-crate-looking-thing mounted to the wall above the sink?"

"A little fruit crate. It holds my supplements."

She sure did take a lot of supplements. He could see labels for folic acid, vitamin D, omega 3 something-or-other and more.

"How do you heat and cool this thing?"

"That's the biggest challenge. The best place to start is with good insulation and window shades. I have custom window covers with magnets to keep them in place. They're not very aesthetically exciting, but I covered the insides with hand-block linen, and ran some curtains along in front to soften the look. Without them I'd broil in summer, and lose heat through the glass in the winter. With them, my climate control has a lot less to do. I have a rooftop air conditioner that works great, and a propane heater for when things really get cold. But most of the time I can get by with my mattress and seat heaters."

"How do you power all that?"

"I have solar panels on the roof, and a battery in one of the upper cabinets, along with a converter for the twelve-volt stuff. But most of the time I'm parked someplace where I can plug into an outlet."

"What about showering?"

"Propane, on-demand. I set it up out back with a curtain that runs between the two open doors. That's just for remote places. When I'm staying in the city, I use my gym membership."

"What about a toilet?"

"Composting."

"No kidding? Where?"

She smiled. "You're using it as a footrest."

"Seriously?"

"Yep. I built that box to house it, plus the little lift-off section that holds the cushion."

Alex looked at the wood-framed box with new respect. "Man, you really thought of everything. Where'd you learn carpentry?"

"My dad. He flipped houses while I was growing up. It was just the two of us, and I learned to help him."

"Must have been nice, learning something useful from your dad. The most useful thing my dad ever taught me was not to chase tequila with beer."

"Really? That's surprising."

"No, seriously. If the tequila is good, then you should drink it straight like a man. And if it's not good, you shouldn't be drinking it to begin with."

"I mean about that being the only useful thing he ever taught you. Obviously you learned a lot of useful skills somewhere down the road."

"All that was from my grandparents. I spent a lot of time with them growing up, on their ranch north of town. Tony, not so much. He had football. I just had the ranch."

The words came out sounding a lot more pitiful than he'd intended, and he didn't want to dwell on the subject, so he asked, "Where do you keep all your stuff?"

"The big drawers under the bed are my pantry. I keep my nonrefrigerated items in there, plus pots and pans and dishes. Then behind that is my garage. There's a sort of sliding sled thing that I can access from the back doors. That's where I keep big items, tools, rock-climbing gear, that sort of thing. But really I don't have a lot of stuff. I consciously keep my belongings pared down. I want to collect experiences, not possessions."

Alex made a scoffing sound.

"What?"

"Nothing."

"Then why'd you go like—" She imitated his scoffing sound.

"No reason."

"Liar."

"Forget it. Let's not fight again."

"Who's fighting? You're the one making sarcastic grunts."

He didn't reply. She imitated the sound again, and again.

"I did not sound like that."

"Yes, you did. Tell me why."

"Okay, okay, but don't get mad."

"What's there to get mad about? Obviously you and I have very different modes of living, but that doesn't mean we can't discuss those differences like civilized human beings."

"Well, it's just that it's easy to say that thing that you said, about collecting experiences and not possessions, when you've always had plenty of possessions."

"Who says I've always had plenty of possessions?"

He shrugged. "You say your dad flipped

houses for a living. I'm guessing he was good at it and made a good living. Solar panels aren't cheap, or composting toilets, or any of this stuff. This is a late-model van. It must have cost a good bit, even before you started ripping stuff out and reupholstering and re-fitting everything."

"My dad and I did the work ourselves."

"But you didn't go into the woods and hew your own birch panels, or make your own battery. There's a limit to what hard work and ingenuity can do. Somebody had to pay for all this stuff. And the whole idea of living this way— I mean, you're not like a person who lives out of a van because they're homeless. This thing is like a miniature apartment." *Nicer than my apartment, by a long shot.* "You have to already be well off to even think of a thing like this, much less pull it off. It's easy to talk about not being bound by possessions, and run around the continent in your van, when you know the bills are all going to be paid no matter what you do."

"I never claimed to be poor or homeless, but that doesn't mean I'm a trust-fund baby. I fixed up Vincent's interior with materials I bought, with money I earned. I change his oil and do routine maintenance myself. And

I pay my way. I make decent money working front-end development, I sell photos and articles and sometimes I hire out as a photographer. I do manual labor, too. I've harvested strawberries in Oregon and done ranch work in Wyoming and Mexico. I work on my own terms, but I still work."

He drank some more of the fermented whatever-it-was. "Yeah, well, I don't know if I believe you did all that."

The thought of her small fragile-looking body changing the oil on her van, or doing field labor, or working cattle, did seem ridiculous, or would have if he hadn't already seen her in action. As it was, he could easily imagine her doing all those things, and he liked imagining it. And he didn't want that. He didn't want to want her. He didn't even want to like her.

Because as beautiful as she was, and as competent as she might be with engines and agriculture, she was still a rootless nomad who would not stay. There was no room in Alex's life for someone who traveled around having "experiences" instead of building something that would last.

She smiled. "Clearly you don't follow me on Instagram."

"Clearly I don't. I don't have time for all that stuff. I live in the real world."

"Says the man who dresses in nineteenth-century clothing."

"Real as in not digital. My historical clothes are real. The past is real, and we shouldn't forget it. If that makes me weird in some people's eyes, so be it."

"So you refuse to live your life kowtowing to other people's false values and arbitrary standards."

"Yeah, that's right."

"Well, so do I. I live according to my own vision. It just happens to be different from yours. And, yes, the past is real. But it can be a snare. The present is all we really have. Life is short, and you never know how much time you have left. I've chosen to make the most of it in my own way, following my own vision. You and I aren't that different. We both question conventions and refuse to be boxed in."

"Huh. I guess you're right."

She chuckled. "But your way is better?"

"I didn't say that."

"You were thinking it, though. It was written all over your face."

He actually had been thinking it, in exactly those words. If she could read him as well as that, he'd have to be more careful. Some of his thoughts would not be so easy to laugh off.

"So your dad sounds cool," he said. "How did he feel about you taking off to travel?"

"Oh, he was incredibly supportive. My mom died young, and I think it was a real wake-up call for him, and a defining thing for me. He taught me to seize the moment and not take anything for granted."

"I didn't know that, about your mom. How old were you?"

"I was four. Old enough to remember, but just barely, and not clearly. Sometimes I don't know whether my memories of her are real, or just imagined from things my dad told me, or things I saw in photos. She always wanted to travel, but she never did. When she and my dad got married, they had big plans for all the places they would visit, but it never happened. There was always something else to spend the money on—a deposit on an apartment, a car repair, a deposit on a bigger apartment after she got pregnant, doctor's and hospital bills, baby stuff, a house with a yard, on and on. Between one thing and another, she never made it outside the Lehigh Valley of Pennsylvania. Then she got sick, and she didn't even leave the bedroom except for doctor's visits. And then it was all over. It happened so fast, you know? She had unfinished paintings when she died, and sewing projects with the pins still in the fabric. My dad kept them all in this box in the closet, and I used to go in there and look at them and feel this sadness that I didn't even have a name for. And when I grew up, I knew what it was—lost opportunities. And I vowed that I wouldn't let that happen to me."

Alex kept silent. He didn't know what to say. He sure couldn't say what he was thinking, because what he was thinking is how secure it sounded—not the illness and death part, but the part about having two financially responsible parents who paid their bills and took care of their kid and didn't do crazy stuff they couldn't afford. He'd never understood what the big deal was about travel, anyway. People in his generation talked about it like it was the be-all and end-all, but all it was, really, was leaving the place you were at to go to another place, and who cared? At the end of the day what you needed was a roof over your head and food in the cupboard and money in the bank, and it was just as easy to have that at home as someplace else. Easier, because you didn't spend your resources going to the other place.

Her mother died, he reminded himself sternly. He forced himself to imagine a little motherless four-year-old Lauren, and the widowed dad, who sounded like a good guy, and tried to ignore the memory of how he used to wish his dad would…not die, exactly, but go away and not cause problems anymore.

"I'm sorry you lost your mother," he said. "I'm sure she'd be proud of you."

That much, he could trust himself to say.

She smiled. "Thank you."

"And your van is amazing. I admit it, I was wrong about the place. I'm blown away by the work you've done, the scale of the planning, how everything is functional and beautiful at the same time. The skill, the artistry, the attention to detail—it's impressive."

"Thank you, again. That's very kind of you to say."

"Yeah, I'm a kind guy."

He finished his drink. "Do you recycle?"

"Yep. The little green bin is recycling, and the white one is trash."

The two bins were standing side by side. Alex got up, dropped his bottle in the green bin...and saw his own name looking up at him from the trash.

Lauren had thrown away his card, along with the *esperanza* spray he'd given her.

He was surprised by the intensity of the pang he felt. Okay, maybe it was silly, but he was proud of those cards, proud of the research he'd done into nineteenth-century typefaces and the appearance of his name on the finished product. It had been a small, inexpensive indulgence, and it made him happy every time he gave one away and saw the person's reaction.

But why should he be hurt, or even surprised? Of course Lauren threw it away. It wasn't like he meant anything to her. Experiences, not possessions—that was her whole value system. No reason why she should make an exception for him.

"Well, I'll be on my way now," he said. "Got to check on the cattle at my grandparents' place. Thanks for the drink and the labor. I don't suppose I'll see you again, so be safe on the road."

"Oh, okay. 'Bye. Thanks for your help last night."

It was good that she'd thrown his card away, he told himself as he walked out to his truck, and good that he saw it when he did. Best thing that could have happened. He was starting to relax too much around her. He needed a reminder, a concrete example of the huge gulf between them.

Let go. That's what people kept telling him. And they were mostly wrong. When something was worth holding on to, he held on. That wasn't being emotionally stunted. That was being a man.

But if something *wasn't* worth holding on to—when it was nothing but a distraction messing with his head and slowing him down—well then, in that case he could let go with the best of them.

CHAPTER FIVE

THE CAT WAS a green-eyed gray tabby with one notched ear and a kink in the end of his tail. The other barn cats were friendly enough when approached, but otherwise held themselves apart. This guy actively sought out Lauren's company, ever since that first afternoon when he'd curled up with her in the porch swing. He'd already gotten into the habit of waiting for her outside Vincent's door, and whenever she came out, he greeted her with his high chirruping meow. He did the Contented Cat Face—sleepy eyes, relaxed whiskers, forward ears—better than any cat Lauren had ever seen. He was doing it now, curled up on her lap with his paws tucked under him, purring with all his might.

She was sitting in the bunkhouse on a camp chair she'd taken from Vincent's garage. Maybe she could stay in this moment forever. It was a good moment, with nothing awful happening. Everything was balanced just right—the late-morning sunshine slanting through the bunkhouse's broken windows, the soft weight of the cat, the velvety roundness of his head against her hand. If she held very still, and kept her mind quiet—

"Knock, knock."

Dalia's voice, and the sound of her knuckles rapping against the empty doorframe, made Lauren jump. The cat scrambled away.

"Sorry," Dalia said. "Didn't mean to startle you."

"It's okay. It's your property. I guess I was a little preoccupied."

"I guess you were." Dalia walked slowly inside, looking as beautiful and radiant as any woman in an advanced state of pregnancy had any right to look, and then some. "What's going on in here?"

Lauren stood, held out her arms and put on a smile. "Wonderful things. I was just about to come get you and have you take a look."

This was a lie. She'd wanted to get as much done on her own as possible before springing her idea on Dalia, but Dalia was here now, and Lauren would have to make as good a case as she could.

Lauren saw her take in the sight. There hadn't been time to do much. Evidently the bunkhouse was being used as a storeroom for out-of-repair equipment and odd items. It was hard to tell what was salvageable and what was not, and, anyway, it wasn't Lauren's stuff, but she'd bagged all the obvious trash and sorted other things into groups: tools, machinery, ancient horse tack, old chains. It looked more organized that way, more under control, like there was a plan. She'd also found a surprising number of houseware-type things: chipped enamel basins, a blue-and-white pitcher and a dozen or so empty bottles, some of them surprisingly beautiful.

"I know what you're thinking," Lauren said. "'Who gave you permission to rear-range my property, Lauren?' But I just kept looking at it, and it had so much potential beyond holding old feed sacks and cultivators and mud-dauber nests. So I thought, why not just dig in? And maybe you don't want this place for any purpose other than deep storage and multifamily housing for raccoons. But it could be so much more! It's structurally sound and good-sized, and close to the main house without being too close. You could turn it into an office, or a guest house, or even an Airbnb for some extra income. It's basically a big long rectangle with wide porches down the sides. Most of the windows are broken, and some of the frames are rotten, and you could replace them with new double-glazed ones if you wanted to go that route, which would certainly be a lot easier, not to mention more energy-efficient, but personally I think the aesthetics of the old ones justify a little fuss. I did find one whole frame that's in decent shape, and it could be used as a template for new ones, since all the window openings are the same size. So! Say we empty the whole house, see what we're really dealing with, figure out which walls are load-bearing, all that. Then we sketch it out, try a few different configurations, see what suggests itself. And we determine what exactly you want from the place, and make a plan."

"Lauren—"

"I know what you're going to say! Renovations don't just happen. They cost money, and they take time. Where is the labor going to come from? Well! You know how I like to winter over in places with mild climates, and concentrate on work for hire, and get maintenance done on Vincent. What if this year, I winter here, at La Escarpa, and do the work on the bunkhouse in exchange for utilities and internet and bathroom privileges and generally taking up space?"

"Lauren—"

Lauren picked up the pace. She had to get it all out before Dalia spoke. The expression on Dalia's face was not encouraging. She didn't look mad, or dismissive exactly, but neither did she look like someone excited about the prospect of a major renovation project.

"Or if you don't want the bunkhouse messed with, I could do other work for you. Clerical stuff. Online stuff. Ranch stuff! You know I can make myself handy. Just tell me what you need done and I'll—"

"Lauren!"

Lauren swallowed. "Yes?"

"Are you pregnant?"

All the air seemed to go out of the room.

"How did you know?"

"I've seen the supplements you're taking. You aren't drinking alcohol. Yesterday you teared up over an insurance commercial. And today you're talking about wintering over and turning my bunkhouse into a habitation fit for humans."

Lauren lowered herself into the camp chair with a sigh. "You always were the smart one."

"I just pay attention."

Dalia turned a five-gallon bucket upside down and sat on it.

"Is it from that weekend when Evan came back?" she asked gently.

"Wow, seriously? You even figured out the date of conception? How could you possibly know that?"

"The timing's right. It was nine weeks ago that you called and told me about him coming back and leaving again. I remember because it was during the Perseids meteor shower. And if you conceived then, you would have started suspecting you might be pregnant around mid-to-late September, but knowing you, you would have put off taking a test another three to four weeks. Right about the time you showed up here."

This was, in fact, exactly what had happened. It was a little unnerving to be seen through so completely.

"Who says it was Evan, though?" Lauren asked. "It could have been just some random guy."

Dalia smiled. "No, it couldn't."

Lauren sighed. No, it couldn't.

"Did you tell Tony?"

Dalia shook her head.

"Please don't tell him. Not yet."

"Why? What are you planning to—"

"I don't know. I mean, I'm going to have it. But I'm not ready to talk about it. It doesn't seem real yet."

"It seemed real enough for you to start taking supplements."

"I'm not a logical person, okay? Not even at my best. I just— I don't know. You're the first person I've told…and I didn't even tell you. You figured it out with your terrifying deductive abilities."

"You didn't even tell your dad?"

"I especially didn't tell my dad. I know how he is. He'll just say to come home."

"Maybe that's not a bad idea."

"I'm not doing it. I've paid my way for this long—I'm not giving up now."

She couldn't go home as a washout and a failure. She wouldn't.

"Have you seen a doctor?"

"Were you listening? I said you're the only person who knows. The only person on the face of the earth."

"You're going to have to get prenatal care sooner or later, and it might as well be sooner. There are good ob-gyns in the area, and mid-wives if you want to go that route."

Lauren pressed her hands to her head. "I

don't know what that means! I don't know what route I should go. It's too much to think about, and I'm not ready for it, and it's just the tip of the iceberg—a whomping big iceberg of things I don't know, and don't even know that I don't know."

"Okay, okay. I'm sorry. I just want you to take care of yourself. But you don't have to do everything at once. Just one thing at a time. And the first thing is, yes, you can stay here for the winter, and as long as you need to. We'll figure out something for internet. I know you need a lot of bandwidth for the work you do. I'll talk to our provider and find out what the next package up is, and what it costs, and we'll go from there."

"Will Tony be okay with that?"

"Yes, we've already talked about it."

"What? I thought you said he didn't know!"

"He doesn't know about you being pregnant. But he knows about Evan, or at least the basics. He thought you might want to crash here awhile and figure out what to do next. He wanted me to tell you to consider this your home."

Lauren's eyes swam. "He's such a good guy."

"Yeah, he is."

"Evan is such a jerk."

It was true, and Lauren had been thinking it for a long time, but she'd never said it out loud before. Now it was like she'd opened a dam. She cried hard—big, messy sobs. Dalia put an arm around her and patted her back softly. The gray cat came back and twined himself around Lauren's ankles.

When the tears started to subside, Dalia pulled a tissue packet out of her pocket. The thoughtfulness and foresight of this made Lauren laugh. Dalia really was the best.

She got all brisk now.

"I'll talk to Tony and we'll…not make a plan, not yet, but brainstorm ideas for the bunkhouse. That Airbnb thing might be good, but I don't know. I don't think I'd like strangers coming and going on the property. A rent house might be fine. Or maybe we'll end up using it as it was originally intended, as a bunkhouse. Not for a whole crew, but for a hired man. We're getting to a point where we need the help."

"Oh, I'm so glad you like the idea! It'll be fun. There are so many different directions we could go with the remodel."

"Yeah, but there are plenty of things that'll have to be done regardless, so we'll start with those. It's surprising how much better it looks already, just being cleaned up a bit. It's not in as bad of shape as I thought it was."

One thing at a time, Dalia had said. And that was one thing done. But how many other things were lined up in the future, crowding each other, clamoring for Lauren's attention? And how would she ever figure out what to do about all of them?

CHAPTER SIX

STRANGE THINGS HAD been happening in Alex's dreams. Only this morning he'd dreamed of being in Lauren's bed in the back of her van, Van-Go, or whatever she called it. He hadn't even realized he'd paid that much attention to the bed while he'd been in the van, but the dream had been awfully detailed. All that red and gold bedding, soft and fluffy and lightly layered, kind of untidy but in a delicate, feminine way.

His alarm had gone off just at the part where a cloud of silky chestnut hair tickled his face and something warm and alive stirred in his arms. It had been a jolt to wake up for real to his barren apartment, which had all the charm of an abandoned storage unit, and an empty bed with threadbare sheets that needed to be changed.

Where was Lauren now? He didn't know and he didn't want to know. He wouldn't ask Dalia and Tony. He would never mention her name again. Another couple of weeks and he'd be in the clear, weaned off the thoughts of her that kept drifting up in his mind, and her surprise appearances in his dreams.

HE RAN HIS hand over the freshly planed wood. Smooth as silk, without a single splinter or rough spot in its tight grain. This was work he loved—it was deeply satisfying, solid, real. His little workshop was like a sanctuary, with its homey smells of wood and lacquer and oil, and walls lined with hand tools as familiar and beloved as old friends. There was no problem here that he couldn't solve. With enough patience and know-how, and the right tools, he could bring back what was worn, broken-down, abandoned, lost. Nothing could disturb him here.

"Alejandro?"

His hand froze in the act of replacing the hand plane in his tool cabinet. The sound of his name—the full, unanglicized version, spoken in *that voice*—flooded him with a strange elation.

No. No! It wasn't possible. She couldn't be here in this most sacred place.

But she was.

She had her hair piled high on her head in a

heap of waves and loops, with some loose ten-drils hanging around her face and neck, and she was wearing black leggings, red hightops and a bright turquoise shirt with asymmetrical ruffles. She looked like she'd tumbled out of bed and put on the first clothes she came across.

Rumpled, disheveled and gorgeous.

"What are you doing here?"

The words came out harsher than he'd meant them to.

Lauren took a step back. "Wow, I can see why they don't have you working the showroom. Your customer service sucks."

"Sorry. I just thought you'd be gone by now, back on the road."

"Nope. I'm planning on staying in the area for a few months. If that's okay with you."

The edge in her voice irritated him. She had no business being snippy. It wasn't like he meant anything to her.

He shrugged. "Sure."

But it wasn't okay. He'd spent a lot of energy convincing himself he would never see her again, and now he was going to have to start all over whenever she left for real. How many months did she mean by "a few"?

Three? More? It was a word that covered a lot of ground.

"So what *are* you doing here?" he asked. "As in, here at Architectural Treasures?"

"Well, Tony and Dalia are letting me stay at La Escarpa over the winter, and in return I'm going to renovate the bunkhouse. I looked online for sources of old building materials and found this place. What are *you* doing here? I thought you worked at the auto-and-tractor shop."

"I do. I have two jobs." *Two paying jobs, anyway.*

But he didn't want to get in to that.

"So you're fixing up the old bunkhouse," he said.

Part of him felt a little sore about that, like she'd stolen his idea. But that was dumb. It was the kind of project he would enjoy, but he sure wasn't in any position to take it on himself. He had more than enough on his plate trying to secure his own property—or what should have been his property.

To do that, he needed money. And to earn money, he needed to keep both his sources of income. And to keep this one, he'd better make his customer service not be so sucky.

He smiled. "You came to the right place."

She smiled, too—a quick, eager smile that almost made him sorry for being abrupt before. "I know! This store is amazing. I've been walking around with my mouth hanging open for the past five minutes."

Alex's workshop was in the back of the main room, a straight shot from the front door. "You've barely scratched the surface, then. Let me tidy up a bit, and I'll show you around."

It was fun seeing the shop through Lauren's eyes. It was a big downtown building, one of the oldest in Limestone Springs, cavernous and drafty, with room after room of merchandise. The main room, where she'd entered, was mostly old furniture and fireplace mantels. Near Alex's workshop, a doorway opened into another space as big as the first.

All along one wall ran a sort of long table—really just glorified sawhorses topped with plywood, with smaller sawhorses on top of that—used as a double-decker display for old windows. Everything from diamond panes, leaded glass and stained glass, to the humblest single-paned sash windows. Some were one-of-a-kind; some were matching sets. Lauren was enthralled by the various finishes on the frames, from raw wood through various colors of peeling paint, and all the old latches. She took a lot of pictures.

Another table held boxes upon boxes of doorknobs, door plates, drawer pulls, latches and hinges in brass and bronze, painted metal and glass. Then underneath the table was an assortment of door grilles in bars and fili- gree of cast and beaten iron, some painted, some not. Old iron gates and fence sections lined the walls.

Alex watched Lauren as they drew near the end of this room, only to come to an open- ing leading to yet another, this one filled with doors. Her face lit up, just as he'd known it would.

"How far does this place go on?" Lauren asked.

"Pretty far. There are two other rooms after this one, and we have a whole warehouse at a different location that has nothing but old flooring—oak, mesquite, even some long- leaf pine."

"Are you kidding me? My dad would lose his mind if he could see that. So would I."

She stopped short, shut her eyes and held up her hands, palms out, like she was prac- ticing great self-restraint. "But first things first. I actually do need a front door. I don't know what happened to the old one, but it's not there now."

There was no real rhyme or reason to the door room. The doors were all pretty much chucked in together, front to back like books on a shelf, separated only by dividers every four to six feet that made it easy to get them in and out. The dimensions and prices were written in chalk on the doors' edges.

Lauren flipped through doors like she was shopping for record albums at some hipster music store. She squealed like a little girl when she came to one arched door made of vertical planks, with a hole in the top for a grille.

"Ooh! I love this one! I wonder if that grille with the ivy filigree would fit in the space. Wouldn't it look great in the bunkhouse?"

Alex put back his head and laughed. "Can you just imagine the vaqueros coming to the door and opening the little thing and looking out to see who's there? No, this door is for an alcalde's mansion, or maybe a mission. The vaqueros would have something more like this."

He showed her a rugged old panel door. "This was salvaged from an old house on a ranch that got bulldozed to make way for a subdivision. It's not flashy, but it's solid."

"I love it! What color should we paint it? I'm thinking a rich, deep red."

Alex put his arms protectively around the door. "Oh, no. No paint. Not when the original finish is in such good shape."

Lauren gave it a doubtful look. "I don't know that it's in *that* good of shape."

"For a door this age it is. Let me give it a light sanding and a coat of tung oil, and then see what you think."

"Well…okay. But the exterior of the house needs some color."

"You have the whole front porch for that. I've always thought it was a shame nobody sits on that porch anymore. It runs the whole length of the house, and overlooks that one pasture with the pond where the two ducks and the egret live. You can just see the spire of the old Baptist church sticking up past the road."

"It is a nice view. Maybe some old wooden chairs and tables arranged in little clusters, with some nasturtiums in window boxes along the rail. I could see that."

"We have some milk paint in stock. Rich, velvety and period-appropriate. Come see."

He took her to the display of sample colors. She grabbed the Barn Red and the Sunflower.

"These would be gorgeous, and really pop against the siding. But is milk paint durable enough for outdoors?"

"It is if you use the outdoor additive."

She put the paint samples back down with that same look of self-restraint. "It's a great idea. But I'm going to wait on it. I've never been in charge of a whole renovation project and I want to do a good job. I mean, if it were just me, I'd putter along and try different things and take forever, but this is for Dalia, and she likes things done in a logical, orderly sequence. I have a budget and a timetable, and I'm sticking with them."

"That's a good plan, especially with the baby on the way. When's it due?"

Lauren looked startled. "What?"

"Tony and Dalia's baby. January, isn't it?"

"Oh, right. Yeah. Early January. Dalia's almost got the baby's room finished."

"As if she didn't have enough going on. But I guess people have to be organized where babies are concerned."

"Yeah, I guess they do. Hey, will you look over my plan? I could use your input for this project. I mean, I know how to do the work, and I know color and design, but I do want to stay true to the period, without spending too much money. You seem to be kind of an expert, and I'd really appreciate it if you could give me some direction."

She could not have said anything more calculated to warm his heart, but he kept his voice cool as he said, "Sure, I'll take a look."

Lauren's graph-paper blueprint was surprisingly easy to follow, with all the pertinent measurements clearly marked. And the layout looked good. Simple as the sketch was, it somehow had a very artistic vibe, like it was going to be printed in a magazine to accompany a renovation feature. All the doors were marked, exterior and interior, with inswing and out-swing, right- and left-handing all specified, and specified correctly. In the margin was a complete breakdown of windows to be replaced or repaired, followed by a list of things to be done, in a sequence that made sense.

"You're restoring the original windows, I see."

"Yes. I have one frame in good shape to use as a template. Do you have someone who can make new frames and do the glazing?"

"That would be me. And you're replacing drywall?"

"Yeah. I'm not looking forward to it, but it has to be done."

"Maybe not. You could install beadboard in some places. And there's this clay stuff you can use that looks like old plaster. The color's mixed in, so you'd do wall repair and paint all at one go. We're an authorized dealer and we have it in stock."

Soon they were zipping around the store like a couple of Ping-Pong balls, talking fast. Two spots of color rose in Lauren's cheeks.

He was leading her past some old fireplace mantels when he got an idea that almost stopped him in his tracks. But he played it cool. Keeping his tone casual, he asked, "Hey, did Tony ever cut up that mesquite that fell on the fence?"

"No, it's still lying there. The goats like to get up on it and play king of the mountain. Ooh! Claw-foot tubs! We've *got* to have one of these for the bathroom. I could paint the exterior some deep, rich color with superglossy paint."

"There's an old cast-iron tub currently serving as a watering trough in the southwest pasture at La Escarpa. If you ask nice, maybe

Dalia will let you use part of your budget to replace it with a new galvanized water trough and put the tub in the bunkhouse."

Her face lit up like he'd said there was Confederate gold hidden in the well. "Oh! I'll bet it came out of the bunkhouse to begin with! There's a set of claw feet on the front porch. They must go together!"

Then she saw an ornate wall sconce and stopped dead.

"This," she said, picking it up and holding it up reverently. "This has to be in the bunkhouse. It's going in if I have to pay for it myself."

"It's too fancy."

"No, it's not. Trust me. I'm not talking about putting in a bunch of gilded, curlicued stuff. Just this one. It's going to go on the living-room wall and it's going to look amazing."

"It is a nice piece. I've always liked it. But it doesn't really work historically. The time period's fine, but it doesn't make sense for it to be in the bunkhouse."

"You don't know that. One of the cowboys could have been really eccentric, or come from a rich background."

"If he's so rich, what's he doing working on someone else's ranch?"

"Maybe he's a younger son and his brother inherited the whole estate. Maybe he got dispossessed because his father didn't approve of the girl he loved, and he defied his father to be with her, but then she died young and he ended up rootless and drifting and alone. Maybe the family fell on hard times and lost their property, but he always remembered his origins and loved fine things, and he started out at La Escarpa as a lowly ranch hand but worked his way up to being foreman. There *has* to be a story to explain it, even if we don't know it, because this thing *belongs* at the bunkhouse. Houses are made by real people with quirks and inconsistencies and backgrounds and personal histories. It makes sense that they would have their odd bits."

Alex thought about this. "Maybe the cowboy isn't even a native Texan. He might have come from some other state or even another country. Texas did attract a whole lot of a certain type of man."

"Like that bumper sticker. I Wasn't Born in Texas, but I Got Here as Quick as I Could."

"Exactly."

Lauren hugged the sconce to her chest. "I'm getting it."

By now she had a substantial order put together—doors and hardware, mostly, and now the sconce. He rang her up; she paid, then walked with him back to his workshop. He brought the doors along on a hand truck.

"You sure do have plenty of hand tools," she said.

"Yeah, I keep a lot of my personal tools here. Some of them were my grandfather's, and quite a few of those were handed down to him from way back. This hand plane that I was using when you came in is about two hundred years old and still works like a dream."

"I guess they don't make them like that anymore."

"No, they do not. Tools used to be made to last. I always find that vintage hand tools are sturdier and hold an edge better than newer ones."

"Is it really worth it to use them, though? Wouldn't it be faster to use a belt sander?"

"It might. I haven't ever done a side-by-side comparison as to time and results. But given a choice, I'll always go with a hand tool if at all feasible. I use power tools when I have to, but I don't like the noise or the feel. It's a barrier between me and the materials. I'm more in tune with the wood when I use the hand plane. I can hear myself think. And there's nothing like the joy of passing a razor-sharp blade that I've honed myself over a piece of wood and hearing that little whisper of sound and seeing that thin slice of wood come out in a big loose curl and feeling that buttery smooth surface left behind. I think the result is better, too. The hand plane leaves the wood brighter and gives it more depth."

She smiled. "You make a good case. You know what you ought to do? Put pictures of your tool wall on the store's website. Really, that website needs a lot of work. I mean it was all right—it got me here—but it did *not* give an adequate idea of the scope or grandness of the place. Who maintains it?"

"I don't know that anyone *maintains* it. Don and Susan set it up—they're the owners—and I remember they grumbled a lot while doing it. I got the impression it was a one-time deal."

Lauren made an indignant sound. "A one-time deal? I'll have to talk to them. This business has potential client written all over it. But you know what would *really* dress up the site, is some pics of you in your workshop wearing your reenactor clothes."

"What good would that do?"

"Are you kidding me? A gorgeous man in nineteenth-century attire, running a hand plane along an old door? That would draw the women in droves. You'd have to beat them off with a stick."

A gorgeous man? Is that what she thought he was?

"Wow," he said. "I think I've just been objectified. Like a bikini-clad woman in a car ad, or a pickle on a sandwich plate."

"Sorry. I guess that was insensitive."

"It's okay. I don't get objectified very often. I kinda like it."

Alex's love life was pretty abysmal. This time with Lauren in Architectural Treasures had actually been better than any date he'd been on in…well, ever. Somehow things hadn't worked out for him that way. It seemed that most women were not interested in a man who worked sixty-plus hours at two blue-collar jobs, busted his rear at an abandoned ranch on his days off, lived in a crappy apartment and never had any time or money to spend on anything but reproduction clothing and old guns. It was for the best; it was easier for a single man to work such hours and sock away money like he did. But it did get lonely.

CHAPTER SEVEN

THE LABEL ON the plastic zipper bag promised that the herbal mixture inside was beneficial for pregnant women and nursing mothers. Among other ingredients, the mixture contained raspberry leaf, stinging nettle and blessed thistle. That didn't sound very promising, but the dried herbs did smell good. Lauren had ordered some in bulk off the internet, officially as a gift for Dalia. The bag had arrived this morning, the same day Tony invited her to the house for a meal to celebrate all the progress she'd made at the bunkhouse.

She already had a gallon of water heating on the stove to make a big batch of the herbal tea, or "tisane," as Dalia said it was rightly called. Once it was brewed, she'd take a quart or so back to Vincent to keep in her fridge.

As she poured the dried mixture into one of Dalia's big vintage canning jars, she heard Durango outside sending up a barrage of what she'd come to recognize as his vehicle-on-the-driveway bark. She set down the bag and went to the living-room window to look out.

"Incoming," she said. "Looks like a Tacoma."

Visitors were always something of an event at La Escarpa. The long driveway meant there was plenty of time to see a vehicle coming and talk about who was in it.

"Oh, yeah, I almost forgot," said Tony. "I told Alex to bring the stuff today from his fancy salvage store."

Lauren's crap detector went off. There was something entirely too casual about his tone.

"Why don't you go meet him, Lauren? Show him where to put the stuff."

"Alex knows where the bunkhouse is, babe," Dalia said.

"Well, yeah, but he'll like seeing everything Lauren's accomplished out there. He's into all that, just like she is."

Lauren went back to her herbs and filled the jar, slowly and carefully, as if she had all the time in the world. She was actually eager to show Alex what she'd done, and would have done it on her own without Tony's suggestion, but now she felt a little funny about it.

By the time she'd finished and cleaned up the stray herbal bits from the counter, Alex was backing the Tacoma close to the bunk-house. She went outside.

The Tacoma had an Architectural Treasures decal on the side.

"You drive a lot of trucks," Lauren told Alex when he got out.

He chuckled. "Yeah, it's hard to keep track of. One day I'm probably going to get confused and drop off a tractor at a home-renovation site."

He lowered the tailgate. There were several blanket-wrapped rectangles lying in the bed of the truck.

He unwrapped the top one. "What do you think?"

It was the front door, the one Lauren had wanted to paint. The roughest of the rough bits had been smoothed out, and the wood's surface glowed with a deep, bright luster.

"You were right," she said. "This was all it needed."

"It did turn out pretty nice, didn't it? Want to go ahead and set it?"

"Sure."

He eased the door out and carried it on his back, the way Lauren's dad had taught her to carry doors. Lauren brought the box that held all the hardware.

When they reached the front porch, he set down the door carefully and looked through the empty doorway into the bunkhouse. "Whoa! You really got the place spiffed up. Looks a hundred times better already."

"I've mostly just cleared out dirt and trash and random stuff."

It was a big job, though, and it had to be done. And Lauren had been glad for the work. She'd needed something to calm her anxiety and help her sleep at night. Now the place was ready for the electricians to come tomorrow, and the plumbers the day after that.

Lauren and Alex got all the doors on their hinges and installed the doorknobs. She'd chosen stamped bronze backplates with keyholes that actually lined up with holes in the old doors. After each door was hung, she stood awhile opening and closing it over and over.

"I see you got that cast-iron tub out of the pasture," Alex said when they walked outside again. The tub was sitting on the porch, ready to be refinished.

"Yeah. Tony drove the tractor out there and I helped him empty the water and weeds and haul it back."

It was kind of hilarious how Tony kept enlisting Lauren's help with all the two-person ranch jobs he normally would have done with Dalia, if Dalia hadn't been pregnant. He'd have been mortified if he'd known Lauren was pregnant, too.

Not that the precaution seemed necessary in either case. Dalia was probably perfectly capable of butchering a hog and tackling a steer, even at seven months; she manhandled livestock and feed bags in a way that would have horrified Tony if he'd seen. And Lauren felt as fit as she ever had in her life. She hadn't had a single day of sickness or even of things tasting funny. She knew false positives were rare—she'd read that much on the internet—but she still couldn't quite believe she was pregnant.

"That hypothetical cowboy who built the bunkhouse loves a hot bath at the end of a long day of ranch work," she said. "He's also very tall. This thing is sixty-eight inches from stem to stern. I measured."

Alex looked longingly at the tub. "Man. The tub at my place is one of those cheap fiberglass things. It's like five feet long, and the part where your back goes is too steep. You can't stretch out and lie back in it, and your legs are all bent."

He stepped into the tub, lay down full-length and shut his eyes with a sigh. "Now that's what I'm talking about. You get in here, you open up the window just a crack, enough so you can hear the frogs out in the pond, and you set your wineglass on the sill."

"Wouldn't have pegged you for a wine drinker."

"Only in the bathtub."

He had his arms resting along the tub's sides and his head tipped back along the rolled top edge. Suddenly Lauren imagined *two* wineglasses on the windowsill. There was room in that tub for both of them.

The gray cat came sauntering by, saw Alex in the tub and jumped in before Lauren could give warning. Alex let out his breath in a strangled yelp, then he laughed a little and shifted the cat without throwing him out.

"Hey there, kitty. Maybe pick a different landing site next time."

"That cat has been my constant companion in the bunkhouse," Lauren said. "He's like a little supervisor, with a paw in everything I do."

"I'm not surprised. He's never really fit in with the other cats. They're all blood kin, but he was just a skinny half-grown vagabond who showed up one day, and he's always been the odd one out. He's probably glad to have a friend."

"I didn't know that." Lauren reached over and rubbed her fingers down the cat's throat, where he liked best to be petted. "You and I are both newcomers, aren't we? We have to stick together, with all these clannish locals around."

"This tub's in good shape," Alex said. "The enamel is discolored some, but not too bad, and the only chips are on the edges."

"I'm going to go after the enamel with some lemon juice and an eraser sponge."

"You might try a pumice stone, too. I've heard of people having good luck with that."

Seeing that Lauren was examining the outside of the tub, the gray cat jumped out and looked at it, too.

"Not sure what to do about all this rust," Lauren said. "It's gritty, and it comes off on my fingertips. Maybe spray paint?"

"You want a grinder with a wire-brush attachment. Wear safety glasses and use a respirator. And be prepared for sparks. Then you can prime it and paint it."

Alex gripped the sides of the tub and heaved himself upright. "Welp. Guess that's it, then. I'll go by the house and say hey to Tony and Dalia and be on my way."

Back in the house, Tony had put on a Texas-flag apron. He greeted his brother with a hard handclasp and two brisk pats to the shoulder. "Hey, bro. Did y'all get the stuff put away?"

"You say 'the stuff' like it's cocaine or something," Alex said.

"It's priced like it," said Dalia.

"Hey, I'll have you know I'm being super-frugal for you guys," said Lauren. "You have no idea. You should see all the things I *don't* buy."

"We got the doors hung," Alex said. "Things are looking good over there."

"Glad to hear it," Tony said. "Stay to dinner? I'm just fixing to fire up the grill."

If Tony was trying to set something up, he must have put a lot of thought and planning into it. Those steaks had been marinating since the night before.

"Nah, I should get going," Alex said. "I got stuff to do."

"I made chimichurri sauce," Tony said.

Lauren didn't know what that was, but it clearly gave Alex pause. While he was pondering the offer, Tony said, "Besides, I need you to make the pico. Nobody does it like you."

He pointed to a tempting-looking heap of produce grouped near a knife and cutting board.

"Pico de gallo is tomatoes, onions, lime juice, cilantro, jalapeños and salt," Alex said. "That's literally all there is to it."

Tony picked up the knife and a tomato. "Okay. So it's cool to chop up the tomatoes real big and chunky, right? And I'll be sure to leave the seeds and juice in there. That way the chips will get nice and soggy."

"Oh, give me that." Alex seized the knife and the tomato and started chopping with precise, practiced motions.

Yep. No doubt about it: Tony was matchmaking. He probably thought he was being subtle. Lauren saw the sly grin he darted at Dalia behind Alex's back.

"Aren't you going to ask about your herbal tisane?" Dalia asked.

"Oh! I forgot all about it." Lauren turned to the stove, but the pot was gone. "Did the water boil?"

"Ages ago. I steeped the herbs and strained the tisane into the pitcher and put it in the fridge."

"Thanks."

Lauren felt uneasy. This was just one more sign of how irresponsible and not ready for motherhood she was, going off and forgetting about a whole gallon of boiling water—water for making motherhood tea, no less.

"What's tisane?" Alex asked.

"It's tea for snobby people," Tony said.

"No," Dalia said patiently. "Tea is the leaf of the *camellia sinensis* plant. A tisane is an infusion of herbs."

"Lauren bought Dalia some expectant-mother tea," Tony said.

"Oh, that was nice," said Alex.

"Hey, Lauren, get the cheese out of the fridge, will you?" said Tony. "We need something to snack on 'til the pico's ready."

Lauren opened the dairy drawer and laughed.

"What's so funny?" Dalia asked.

Still laughing, Lauren held up the plastic-wrapped package of Colby-Jack cheese. It was shaped like the state of Texas.

"What is it with you people and your Texas-shaped things? You are so proud of the shape of your state. So far in my time here I've seen Texas-shaped sunglasses, Texas-shaped waffles and a package of Texas-shaped pasta."

"Oh, there's plenty more where that came from," said Dalia. "My mom has some friends with a Texas-shaped swimming pool."

"We need that," said Tony, pointing at Dalia with his steak tongs. "We need a Texas-shaped swimming pool."

"No, we really don't."

"We don't do that in Pennsylvania," Lauren said. "Nobody puts in a Pennsylvania-shaped swimming pool."

"That's because Pennsylvania is a boring shape," Tony said. "Pennsylvania is just a rectangle with errors. Now if a pool company in Pennsylvania started making swimming pools shaped like Texas, that would sell."

"Hey, check it out," said Alex, gesturing with his knife. "A Texas-shaped cutting board."

"Made of mesquite wood, even better," said Tony.

"And being used to make pico de gallo, for the hat trick!" said Lauren.

"Texas-shaped stuff is all over," said Dalia, "but Tony is the worst I ever saw at it. He would seriously get the Texas-shaped swimming pool if I let him."

"Well, who wouldn't want a Texas-shaped

swimming pool?" Tony demanded. "It's a great shape."

Dalia swatted him on the rear with a kitchen towel. "You're a pretty great shape yourself."

Once the steaks were served, Lauren saw what the big deal was about chimichurri sauce. Over dessert—Dalia's flan—Tony got a crafty look on his face and said in that casual way, "So, Alex, when is your next get-together with your historical-costume friends?"

"Weekend after next."

Tony waited two beats, then said, as if he had just thought of it, "Hey, you should take Lauren with you. She could take pictures, and do one of those journalism things that she does."

It was actually not a bad idea. She could get a lot of mileage out of a piece like that, repackaging it for different markets—travel, local interest, fun things to do in central Texas. Probably a lot of opportunities for nice pics of people and places.

Alex shook his head. "Nah, she wouldn't be interested in that."

"Actually, I am interested," Lauren said. "Is it nearby?"

"Couple hours away. But I don't think you really want to go."

"What do you mean?" Tony asked. "You're always going on about how awesome it is."

"For hard-core Texans and history buffs, sure. Maybe not so much for regular people."

"Well, obviously I'm not on your level as far as Texas history goes," Lauren said. "But I'm not dumb. And I do have some experience absorbing local lore. Where is this thing? I'll go on my own. I won't bother you, and you can pretend not to know me."

"It would be silly for the two of you to both drive all that way separately," Tony said. At the same time he gave Alex a look that clearly said it would also be very rude.

"It's no problem, really," Lauren said. "I can go on my own. I'm used to traveling by myself."

"No, Tony's right," said Alex. "It'd make more sense to go together."

"Good," Tony said. "It's settled, then."

Lauren didn't like the idea of tagging along with Alex when he sounded so far from enthusiastic, but if she insisted on not going at this point, she would be shaming Tony and making things more awkward.

Why was Alex so reluctant to take her?

Admittedly, a few of their conversations had been a bit…spirited, and their views on some subjects were not exactly simpatico, but on the whole he'd seemed to enjoy her company well enough. At any rate, he hadn't seemed repulsed by her.

Besides, he didn't look so much annoyed as…embarrassed. Like he had something to hide.

Then it hit her. Alex had a girlfriend in the reenactor group that Tony didn't know about.

Of course he did. A big handsome guy like Alex, so solid and hardworking and community-oriented—no way could he be single.

Maybe she wasn't quite a girlfriend yet, just a girlfriend-in-the-making. In which case, having Lauren along would cramp his style.

Fine, then. She'd show him he had nothing to worry about from her. She'd give him plenty of space—acres of space. Really, he might have guessed as much. It wasn't like she'd given him any reason to think she was interested in him.

CHAPTER EIGHT

LAUREN TWISTED HER toe into a crack, relishing the familiar grippy sensation as her climbing shoe's sole found purchase in the granite's surface. The rock face loomed overhead, cutting off the sky. Bits of quartz flashed in the sun, brilliant against the black-flecked pink granite. Her shadow fronted her, mirroring her movements like a dark other self.

In rock climbing terminology, a boulder route was called a problem. Lauren loved that. Boulders were big, solid, immovable. They didn't have steps carved into them or ladders affixed to their sides. If she wanted to get to the top of one, she had to work the problem.

First, find a break in the surface—some pocket or crack or crimp—and make a start, however humble. Then find the next hold, and the next, hooking heels and toes over ledges, working her hands into whatever space offered itself. Some holds were pretty straightforward; others called for creative finagling with body tension and counterpressure. Sometimes the next hold could only be reached by a quick burst of momentum—a dyno—and hopefully the right amount in the right direction at the right moment.

No two problems were the same, and no problem was ever a straight route from start to finish, with holds placed just the right distance apart. But unlike so many of the other kind of problems, a boulder was tangible, real. She could see it, touch it, feel the skin-to-rock friction. Every movement of her limbs, every shift in her weight, counted. She was acutely aware of her body—the muscles standing out in her arms and legs, the firm engagement of her core—and confident that it could rise to the challenge.

In almost every problem there came a point where there seemed to be no way forward—usually at the worst, most awkward moment possible, when she was underclinging for dear life, arms shaking, calves screaming. She had nothing left to give, no reserves of strength or reach or ingenuity or anything.

But somehow it came, anyway, like a gift, just enough to pull herself over the top. A warm rush of endorphins flooded her as the sky opened overhead.

Problem solved.

LAUREN STOOD AT the top of the granite dome. All around, for a full 360 degrees, the Texas Hill Country stretched away in gentle rolling slopes of oak, mesquite, prickly pear cactus and low rounded shrubs, interspersed with outcroppings of stone.

She'd started early this morning at Enchanted Rock with an hour-long bouldering session, then explored some of the trails before ending the day with a hike up the main dome. The mountain rose out of the Llano Uplift in a full square mile's worth of mostly bare rock. In some spots the granite was peeling off in big flakes and chunks, with another layer of granite showing underneath, onionlike. Clumps of grass and cactus, and an occasional ambitious tree, grew out of the cracks, and a vernal pool lay at the top of the rock.

The great thing about van life—one of the great things—was how it kept all Lauren's stuff in one place. If she woke in a panic at three in the morning from a freaky dream— say, a dream where Tony was grilling steaks in a Texas-shaped pool, and a shirtless Alex was serving Lauren Mexican hot chocolate, and the hot chocolate was spiked, and Dalia, who was simultaneously nursing a baby and shearing a goat, gave Lauren a disapproving look and said, "Do you really think you should be drinking rum?" and suddenly Lauren remembered that she'd already had the baby, only she couldn't remember where she'd left it, and then she heard the baby's cry and turned and saw her van rolling down a slope with Durango chasing after it, and *the baby was in the van and there was nothing she could do to save it*—and couldn't go back to sleep afterward, she could make the drive to Enchanted Rock before the sun rose and be first at the gate at opening time.

Way before, as it turned out, because the park hadn't opened until eight. She'd spent the hours in between taking pictures of the night sky, then twilight, then dawn.

Now the sun was setting in a spectacular show, setting off all the autumnal tints of russet and gold in the expanse of trees. Lauren took some pictures and started to upload to Instagram before remembering that there was no cell coverage here. She'd gotten some lovely shots today—wild turkeys, a horned lizard, an intricate miniature forest of lichen and tiny translucent fairy shrimp in the vernal pool—but they'd have to wait to be made public.

She took a few more pictures in the dreamy evening twilight before heading home. She was tired now, but in a comfortable, soft-edged way that left no room for anxiety. For as long as she could remember, she'd found her best stress relief in physical activity.

By the time she reached the familiar cattle guard at La Escarpa, she was deliciously sleepy.

But she came alert quickly enough when she saw Rosie parked on the gravel drive behind Tony's truck. The sight of the hulking Dodge sent a quick thrill of pleasure through her.

Calm down. He's not here to see you. He's family, remember? He probably comes over a lot, so you'd better get used to it.

The front door of the house opened, and Alex stepped outside.

She knew it was Alex right away, even though he and Tony looked alike, because Tony was a little taller and had shorter hair. She could tell even now, when he was no more than a silhouette backlit by the living-room light.

He turned and said something to someone behind him, then shut the door and started down the porch steps.

He came down the walkway, through the gate and straight toward her. There was something stiff and purposeful in his stride and the set of his shoulders. By the time she'd pulled into her usual parking spot, he'd reached the driver's-side door and was standing there, waiting.

Then she saw his face.

She felt sick inside. Something had happened—something bad. Was it Dalia? The baby?

She swallowed hard and got out of the van. "What is it, Alex? What's wrong?"

THE SIGHT OF Lauren's headlights coming down the driveway made Alex's knees go weak with relief. He took a deep breath, opened the door and forced himself to keep his steps slow and steady, and his mind calm, as he walked out to meet her. There could very well be a perfectly reasonable explanation. He prepared himself for stories of family emergencies, flat tires, a shattered phone, sudden amnesia—basically anything short of a claim of alien abduction.

And then she asked him, "What is it, Alex? What's wrong?"

For a moment he couldn't speak. She wasn't

playing dumb. He could see that from her face. She was serious.

She honestly had no idea.

"Where the heck have you been?" he asked.

She took a step back.

"Me? I've been at Enchanted Rock."

She was all sincerity and wide-eyed baffled innocence. Alex actually felt his blood pressure rise.

For the first time he noticed that she was dressed in outdoor gear—not the bulky, shape-shrouding kind, but the thin, clingy, ultra-insulating kind. It showed off her form to great effect, and the fact that he noticed that just made him angrier than ever.

"You *what*? What on earth made you go there?"

"I just decided to go. You and Tony and Dalia were talking about it last night and it sounded cool. So this morning I got up and went."

"You got up and went. And you couldn't be bothered to tell anyone?"

"It was early. If I'd called, I would have woken people up."

"Dalia gets up at five a.m."

"Well, I drove off at three thirty."

"You *what*? You hit the road at *three thirty*

in the morning? What on earth possessed you to do something so reckless?"

Now she actually looked mad. "I really don't think it's any of your business if I happen to decide to get an early start."

"Early start? It was the middle of the night!"

"What does it matter? I've driven through the night lots of times. If anything, it's safer then, because there are fewer drivers on the road."

"But the drivers that *are* on the road are all drunk or high or sleep-deprived."

"That's ridiculous. People don't get drunk or high only at night. And most late-night and early-morning drivers are probably just shift workers."

"Why didn't you leave a note?"

"Why would I? I don't have to check in or get permission every time I decide to go somewhere. I'm a grown woman."

"A responsible adult would have given some consideration to other people. Do you have any idea how worried Dalia's been? You could've been dead for all she knew. She's been trying to get in touch with you all day."

"There's no cell coverage at Enchanted Rock! And I have my phone set to not give me notifications while I'm driving, because I'm *responsible* that way."

"You should've realized she'd be worried without her having to call you and tell you so. If you'd been in an accident, or gotten kidnapped or something, nobody would have even known where to begin to look for you or what hospitals to call."

"What business is it of yours what I do? Why are you even here?"

"Tony texted me. He thought maybe I knew where you were, or maybe you were with me—which there wasn't any reason for him to think, obviously, but by that time he and Dalia were just grasping at straws."

"So you came over, what, to organize a search party? Or did you just want first shot at jumping all over my case the instant I got back?"

"I came to support my family. For your information, Dalia's so worried she made herself sick. She's been in bed all day. That kind of stress can't be good for someone in her condition."

For the first time, Lauren looked a little unsure of herself. "I didn't mean to make her worry."

"'Cause you didn't think at all. You just

took off in the middle of the night on some random whim, with no warning and no word to anyone."

She gave a short, incredulous laugh. "Alex, have you been listening? *I do that all the time.* I travel at all hours by myself, across the country and *out* of the country."

"I know you do, and it's dangerous and irresponsible. A woman traveling alone, living out of a van? It's a miracle you've survived as long as you have."

"I've survived because I know what I'm doing."

"Bull. You've survived because nothing catastrophic has happened to you so far."

"Now you're just being dumb. Catastrophic things happen in lots of places at lots of times. Why should I be any less safe at Enchanted Rock, or on the road, than any other place I might be, alone or with other people? I could get T-boned at the four-way stop in Limestone Springs, or slip and fall on Dalia's front porch steps. Or I could get acute lymphocytic leukemia and be dead in three months, like my mother."

He swept a hand up, brushing away the words. "I can't even reason with you if you're going to be like this. I'm going home. But will you just do this one thing, please? The next time you take off from La Escarpa on some spur-of-the-moment adventure, have the decency to at least leave a note taped to the front door."

LAUREN SWALLOWED OVER a painful lump in her throat as she watched Alex drive away. The good feeling from her day of rock climbing and exploring was gone.

She couldn't think, couldn't breathe. She felt like she'd been hit in the solar plexus. She sat on the gravel driveway with her head on her knees.

Dangerous. Irresponsible. Reckless.

That's what he'd called her. And he didn't know the half of it. He'd reamed her for being inconsiderate of Dalia, because of Dalia's "condition." What would he say if he knew Lauren was pregnant, too?

He'd probably add *criminally negligent* to the list.

But that was silly. Wasn't it? People didn't miscarry just because they went rock climbing. Any accident that was bad enough to endanger the baby had to be something pretty severe, to the point of endangering the mother, as well. Hadn't she heard that once?

And she was fine. Better than fine. Strong, fit. It was good for the baby for her to work out, to keep herself in top physical condition.

But she could have fallen. She hadn't, but she could have. Rock climbing during pregnancy was an unnecessary risk, the kind of thing other people knew instinctively not to do. Other people were cautious; they stayed on the safe side. They weren't like Lauren. They didn't go off and leave things on the stove. They didn't marry guys like Evan. They knew better.

Her heart pounded, and she felt sick to her stomach. She could hear her own ragged breathing and see it fogging in the cool night air.

She made herself get up and go to the house.

This was going to be rough, but it had to be done, and the sooner, the better.

Before she reached the door, Tony opened it.

"Hey there, stranger! Where'd you disappear to all day?"

"I went to Enchanted Rock. Tony, I'm really sorry. I guess I've gotten used to not having to answer to anyone but myself. It honestly didn't occur to me that you and Dalia might worry."

"That's all right. Come in! How was E-Rock? Did you love it? You want a beer?"

The TV blared with what looked like preparatory football stuff, and the coffee table was covered with snacks. If Tony was putting on a brave front, he was doing an awfully good job.

Dalia came stumbling into the living room in a bathrobe, looking more helpless and weak than Lauren had ever seen her.

"Hey, babe," said Tony. "Feeling any better?"

"Not really. Hey, Lauren."

"Hey, Dalia. I'm sorry I didn't tell you where I was going today. I left early, and I didn't want to wake you, and then I got to Enchanted Rock and there was no cell service."

"Oh, is that where you went? I should have guessed, after the way we were all going on about it last night. I know you like to do things on the spur of the moment. But just FYI, it's fine to send me a text whenever. I keep text noises off at night so they won't wake me."

This was so sensible and Dalia-like, and so much better than what she'd been expecting, that Lauren hugged her.

"Careful," Dalia said crossly. "You don't

want to catch whatever I've got." But she did return the hug.

"She's been sick as a dog all day," Tony told Lauren. "Hey, where'd Alex go?"

Lauren looked out the window and saw Rosie's headlights rounding the bend in the driveway. "Um, Alex left."

"What?" Tony followed her gaze, then hurried to the window. "Oh, man. Why'd he go? I thought he was going to watch the game with me."

Something wasn't adding up here.

"Hold on a minute," Lauren said. "I thought you guys were superworried about me."

"Sorry to disappoint you," Dalia said.

"Believe me, I'm not disappointed. I never even thought about it until Alex told me."

"Told you what?" asked Tony.

"That the whole household was in an uproar over my disappearance. He said Dalia was bedridden with worry."

"What?" Dalia looked annoyed. "I've never been bedridden with worry in my life. I've just got a nasty cold. Worry had nothing to do with it."

"Huh," said Tony. "I wonder why Alex said all that."

"He said you told him," said Lauren.

"Wha-a-at? That's not right. That's not what I said at all."

"What did you say, exactly?" asked Dalia.

"I just invited him over to watch the game. But I didn't want to, you know, interrupt anything." Quick glance at Lauren. "So I asked if he had anything else going on."

"You mean you asked if Lauren was with him?"

"Well, yeah. I mean, it was possible, right? They'd made plans last night to go to Alex's thing together, and it's not like she knows a lot of other people around here."

"Did you call or text?" Dalia asked.

"Text."

"Let me see your phone."

Tony handed it to her, and she scrolled through the conversation.

"Ooh, yeah. This would definitely wind him up."

"How could it? I never said we were worried sick or you'd collapsed with nerves or whatever."

"No, but you did say we didn't know where Lauren was and I was sick in bed. He filled in the rest himself. You know what a nervous old woman he can be."

"Come to think of it, he did seem kinda

jumpy. He wouldn't settle down and watch the pregame show with me."

"Babe, Alex doesn't even like football. He never would have come over just for that."

Tony groaned. "You're right. I messed up. I'm such an idiot."

Dalia smiled and put her arms around him. "You are *not* an idiot. You just don't have a suspicious mind, and you don't expect other people to, either."

He kissed the top of her head, then put a hand to her forehead. "Baby, you're burning up with fever. What are you even doing out of bed?"

"I just came out to make a cup of tea."

"Go back to bed. I'll make it for you."

"You don't know how to do it right."

"Sure I do. I've got that whole step-by-step instruction guide that you made me. Seriously, babe, you look awful."

"Thanks."

"You really do," Lauren said. "Go to bed. I'll help Tony with the tea. Between the two of us, we ought to be able to get it right."

"Okay. Make sure he doesn't forget to put the tea leaves in. Or set the timer. G'night."

Dalia shuffled back down the hall.

In the kitchen, Tony opened a cabinet door

and studied the printed sheet that was taped there. "'Step one. Fill the electric kettle with fifteen ounces of distilled water.'"

He took the jug down from the cabinet while Lauren found the measuring pitcher. Then he poured the water precisely into the pitcher, stopping and starting several times, and bending down to check the level. Finally satisfied, he emptied the cup into the kettle.

"'Step two,'" Lauren said, reading. "'Turn on the kettle.'"

Tony made a scoffing sound as he pushed the little tab down. "I think I would know to turn on the kettle without being told. This whole multistep instruction list is pretty insulting. I know how to make a cup of tea."

"'Step three. Take a Fiesta latte mug from the cabinet.'"

"I know, I know."

He glanced at Lauren. "So…did Alex go off on you?"

"Like a load of bricks. He was so mad I could see him shaking."

"He wasn't just mad, he was scared."

"Why should he be scared? What was there to be scared about? I'm perfectly capable of taking care of myself."

"I know that. But you have to understand,

the way me and Alex grew up…well, let's just say there are good reasons why he freaks out when people aren't where he expects them to be."

Lauren swung herself onto the counter. "What reasons?"

Tony set a tea infuser inside the mug. "How much do you know about my father?"

"Not much. I know he and your mother are divorced. I met him at the wedding. He seemed like a charming man."

"Yeah, that's the word, all right. Do you know what people call him around here? El Jugador."

Lauren mentally translated. "A player. Like a risk-taker? Manipulator? Swindler?"

"All of that, plus a real live, crap-shooting, poker-playing, clean-out-all-your-bank-accounts-and-drive-to-Louisiana gambler."

"Oh! Oh, I didn't know that. Did he really clean out bank accounts?"

"He sure did, lots of times. Over the years he won and lost some mind-boggling amounts of money. It was a giant emotional roller coaster for the family. When things were good, they were awesome. Nice cars, expensive presents. Pricey football camps for me. But he never quit while he was ahead, and when he was losing he wouldn't cut his losses and walk away. He always thought he could turn it around. And he did, sometimes, for a while. But it never lasted."

"When did it start?"

"I don't even remember. Gambling was always part of our lives, but me and Alex only gradually figured out what it all meant. I actually have a lot of fun memories of going to fancy casino resorts with those kid play areas and big pools, staying in nice rooms, eating at buffets. That was when our parents were still together. Dad was always so happy when he was winning, and when he was happy, everyone was happy. He'd talk about all the nice stuff he was gonna get us. And then he'd start to lose, and keep on losing. The whole atmosphere of the house would change and I wouldn't know why. I used to think it was my fault, like I'd done something to make my parents mad. Cars got repossessed, bills went unpaid, utilities got turned off. I tell you what, that's an experience you never forget, having your electricity cut off in the dead of winter by some poor dude from the power co-op who looks like he'd rather cut off his own arm."

Lauren thought of her own father, toiling away patiently on his construction projects, managing expenses, plugging numbers into spreadsheets to determine whether a house was priced low enough to realize a good profit after remodeling. He'd been the most reliable thing in her childhood. What would it be like to grow up without that, with the opposite of that?

The electric kettle went off with a click. Tony picked it up and poured the boiling water through the infuser into the mug.

"Did you remember the tea leaves?" Lauren asked.

Tony froze, then put the electric kettle back on its stand and opened the tea canister.

"It says to use a heaping teaspoon," Lauren said, handing him a measuring spoon.

He spooned the leaves onto the top of the hot water. Some of them spilled over the edge of the infuser.

"Timer," Lauren reminded him.

"I know," he said huffily. He set the timer for five minutes.

"So did your dad have a regular job?" she asked.

"Sure, lots of them. It's amazing anyone would hire him, with his work history, but he was a good talker, and smart, and really pretty capable when he put his mind to something. He always managed to burn his bridges eventually, though. Most workplaces are not real tolerant of employees who skip work to drive to Louisiana for the day. He could always justify it to himself, because he thought of gambling as like a thousand-dollar-an-hour job. But it never worked out that way. My mom worked crazy hours just trying to keep me and Alex fed and clothed with some semblance of normalcy, but there was only so much she could do. Sometimes we'd come home to find the house cleared out—cars, furniture, TVs—and Dad would be gone, too, and we didn't know if he was at work, or out hocking our stuff, or at a casino, or dead. We just never knew what we were going to find coming home from school."

"That's awful."

"Yeah. So you can see how Alex's mind kinda got wired to automatically go to high alert whenever people are missing."

"Yeah. Yeah, I can see that."

"Really, I think the whole thing was harder on Alex. I was older, and I had football. I should have taken better care of him."

"You were just a kid yourself. Besides, Alex had the ranch to go to, right?"

"Yeah, but that was no picnic, either. The

worry and stress over my dad really wore my grandparents down. They were getting old, and there was so much work to be done on the place just to keep up, and no one else to do it. My dad's an only child, and my grandfather was pretty invested in the idea of having his son take over the ranch. It must have been hard to admit to himself that my dad was never going to step up and be a rancher, or even a responsible landowner. In fact, he never really did admit it."

Tony sighed. "He should've disinherited my father and left the land to Alex, is what he should've done. Alex was the one who cared about it. I mean, seriously, you don't leave a thousand-plus acres of family legacy to a man who's blown through literally hundreds of thousands of dollars during his adult life on gaming, and who would trade the family dog for a buy-in at a poker game. But that's what my grandfather did. When he died, my father inherited the whole thing."

"Oh, no. And is your father selling it?"

"Not yet. Alex contested the will, so the estate's tied up in probate."

"That sounds hopeful."

"It's not, really. It's just a stalling tactic. Alex doesn't stand a chance in hell of getting the will thrown out. Even his attorney thinks it's a waste of time and money. It's a shame, you know? He ought to be a well-off landowner right now, instead of working two jobs and living in a crappy apartment. But that's Alex. When he thinks he's right, he won't let go."

It explained a lot about Alex—his fierce love of the ranch, his obsessive dedication to hard work and doing things the right way, his deep suspicion of anything that hinted at irresponsible behavior, his reverence for the past.

He was like the anti-Evan. Evan believed that once something got at all difficult, it was a sign from the universe that you shouldn't be doing it, that it wasn't meant to be. But what about perseverance? Dedication? Did true love—or true anything—really mean there wasn't supposed to be any effort involved?

When the timer finally went off, Lauren slid down from the counter.

"I'll let you get back to tea-making and football. Thanks for filling me in."

"Sure, no problem. I'm sorry for what happened. I didn't mean to cause any hard feelings."

"It's not your fault. And to be fair, Alex had a point. I should have let you and Dalia know where I was going. But he didn't have to go off on me the way he did."

"I know. But he really is a good guy, Lauren."

There was something almost pleading in his tone. Lauren suppressed a smile. Tony sure was a heavy-handed matchmaker. No wonder Alex was keeping his love life under wraps.

She trudged slowly down the porch steps. She needed a shower, but she didn't have the energy to get her clean clothes together and go back to the house. All she wanted was to crawl into bed and sleep for eighteen hours or so.

Just as she was shutting the yard gate, her phone went off.

It was Alex.

She'd had his number in her contacts since the night they'd met, but he'd never called or texted her before.

She steeled herself. "Hello?"

"Hey. It's Alex."

He paused, as if giving her a chance to hang up.

"I know."

"Listen, I'm sorry for being such a jerk just now. I was out of line. I'm not your father or your brother, and it's not my place to tell you how to live your life. I was really worried about you, but that didn't give me any right to talk to you the way I did."

His voice sounded rich and soft, with no hint of a grudge.

"I appreciate that," she said. "The truth is, you weren't wrong. I should have left word with Dalia about where I was going. While I'm staying here, it's only right that I give her a heads-up before I take off for the day."

"Thank you for saying that."

Silence. There didn't seem to be anything more to talk about, but she didn't want to hang up. She wanted to hear Alex say something in that velvety dark voice again.

But what was the point? Much as she enjoyed his voice, and his company, and his presence, it was silly to seek them out. They both had other things they'd be better off paying attention to.

"Look," Lauren said, "let's just forget about the two of us going to your festival or whatever it is together."

More silence. Lauren could hear weed stalks rustling in the wind, and the goats in their pen making chuckling sounds to each other.

"Okay," Alex said. "I mean, if you really…

Do you not want to go? Or do you just not want to go with me?"

"I don't want you to have to take me. I know it wasn't your idea, and I don't want to cramp your style."

"Cramp my…?" He laughed softly. "But do you want to go? You said last night that you did. Was that true?"

"Well…yes. But—"

"But nothing. We're going."

"No. I don't want my company to be forced on you just because I'm your sister-in-law's friend. I mean, I think it's pretty clear that left to ourselves, the two of us never would have chosen each other as friends."

"You're probably right. But that doesn't mean we can't *be* friends. Don't overthink this. We'll go, we'll have a good time and you'll write your article or whatever, and learn lots about Texas history."

And I'll see the girlfriend that Tony doesn't know about yet.

CHAPTER NINE

"HOLD ON A MINUTE," Lauren said. "Are you telling me that the defenders of the Alamo weren't wearing any underwear?"

"I'm saying it's impossible to know," said Alex. "Information on historical underwear is pretty sparse. People didn't leave written accounts of their underwear, or hand it down in families like old military uniforms and ball gowns. We know that by the nineteenth century, some people wore little linen drawers, but it took a while for that to become the standard thing. Before then, it's safe to guess that for the most part, women just wore their shifts as the bottom layer, with nothing underneath. And the men had really long shirts that they tucked down into the legs of their breeches or trousers."

"Huh. All those old-timey people running around commando. Who'd have guessed?"

"Well, like I said, we can't know for sure."

"So what's the historically accurate thing to do?"

"Your guess is as good as mine."

"Well, what *is* your guess? What do *you* do? Are you even wearing any underwear at this moment?"

He gave her a sideways glance. "Why do you want to know?"

"I'm curious. Come on, you can tell me. Which is it? Modern underwear? Reproduction linen drawers? Or a long-tailed shirt doing double duty?"

"Will this make it into your article?"

"Yes. I'm absolutely captioning a picture of you with a description of your underwear. Or lack thereof."

"Ha ha. In that case you'll just have to wonder."

"Wow, your face is so smug right now. I can just feel the smugness coming off you in waves. You're really not going to tell me?"

Alex's face got smugger still. "Let's just say I like to err on the side of authenticity."

Lauren let out a shriek. "I knew it! I knew it!"

She wasn't sure where all this hilarity was coming from. Maybe she needed to be flippant to counteract the sudden and vivid image in her mind of Alex, sans jacket, waistcoat and trousers, sans modern underwear or reproduction linen drawers, wearing just the pale linen shirt, with the hem hanging almost to his knees, and the outline of his bare legs showing through. To remind herself that this was just a friend, someone she could joke around with.

Who just happened to be a devastatingly handsome man.

Yes. She could be flippant and fun with him, both now and later today, when she met his girlfriend. She'd even give him some good-natured ribbing about the girl. There wouldn't be any change in her attitude or behavior. No one would have any reason to think she was jealous.

"What about bathing?" she asked.

"What about it?"

"How did people handle it back in the day? How did they stay clean?"

"They changed their linen as often as they could—their shifts and shirts and such. And they bathed. Not every day, maybe, but more than most folks think. They didn't have hot running water, and full-length bathtubs weren't a thing until the late nineteenth century, but they had washbasins and little hip tubs. They did their best. Men sometimes bathed in streams and rivers."

Now Lauren was imagining Alex bathing in a stream. Their first time driving anywhere together, and she couldn't stop imagining him in various states of undress.

Though why should she think of it as the first time? It wasn't like this was some sort of *relationship*, with milestones.

She was working on a story, and Alex was the friend who was helping her.

It didn't mean anything more than that.

ALEX BACKED THE truck into the unloading area. The tension he'd felt in his stomach that night at La Escarpa, when Tony had first made his ham-fisted suggestion for Alex to take Lauren to his festival, came back with a vengeance.

The drive had been great fun, with Lauren in uproariously high spirits. He'd almost thought she was flirting with him, but that couldn't be right. But now it was over. She was here, about to lay eyes on something precious to him.

This group was like family. These were people who shared his passion for Texas history, who weren't content to just read about it in books, but loved it so much they had to do something about it. Restore old artillery. Cook in an iron pot over an open fire. Reproduce old clothing in exquisite detail.

Alex loved that. But Lauren loved immediacy, the moment. Things as they were right now. And then the next thing, and the next. Just parking her van in the same spot for longer than a few weeks was stifling to her. What would she think of a whole group of people fixated on the same period of history in the same small geographical area? Enacting the same battles over and over every year?

"I'm going to get my booth set up," he said. "We've got about twenty minutes before opening time."

"Okay. I'll help you."

"That's all right. I'm used to setting up on my own. Why don't you walk around and check things out? Some people are mostly set up already."

He didn't want to be there when she saw the scene for the first time: the old chairs and trunks and chests, kneading troughs and spinning wheels, quilts and sunbonnets, muskets and cartridge boxes, quill pens and stacks of parchment.

Would she mock? Or act polite while letting him see how silly she thought the whole thing was?

Tony teased him about his reenacting all the time, and Alex didn't mind. But he would mind very much if Lauren looked at this thing that meant so much to him, and belittled it. Her opinion shouldn't matter to him, but it did.

"Okay," Lauren said.

She took the clip out of her hair, stuck it in her mouth and shook her hair loose, running her hands through the whole thick wavy mass. She did that a lot—took her hair down and rearranged it and put it up again. He loved watching the whole graceful, business-like process. Every time she put it up, the configuration was a little different—sometimes an upside-down ponytail with the ends cascading over the top of the clip, sometimes a tight aggressive twist. This time it was a high loose knot with a few wavy tendrils at the neck.

She picked up her camera case and got out of the truck. "I'll catch up with you later."

LAUREN SAT DOWN on a granite slab and scrolled through the pictures in her camera. She'd been exploring the festival and taking pictures for two hours now, and she had yet to figure out the identity of Alex's girlfriend.

Not that that had been her exclusive aim, of course. She'd gotten lots of great shots and interviewed some reenactors. But she kept finding herself looking at attractive young women, trying to figure out which ones looked like actual or potential love interests for Alex.

She'd spent a long time with a reenactor named Tamara, who seemed a likely candidate. Tamara had a spinning wheel and baskets of wool and other fibers in her tent, she lived on a farm where she raised her own sheep and llamas for their fiber, she was superknowledgeable about the Texas frontier and she looked a lot like Jenna Coleman. When Tamara asked how Lauren had found out about the festival, and Lauren told her she was a friend of Alex's sister-in-law's and that Alex's brother had suggested that she go and do a story on it, Tamara smiled warmly and said, "Oh, Alex!" in such a sweet, affectionate tone that Lauren felt sure she had a winner. But then a tall man with serious gray eyes, dressed in sober black, showed up and gave Tamara a kiss. The tall man turned out to be Jay, Tamara's husband, who portrayed a circuit-riding frontier minister and acted as the group's chaplain. Tamara told Jay that Lauren was a friend of Alex's, and Jay beamed at Lauren in an approving sort of way. So maybe Alex was just very popular among the reenactor crowd.

Then Lauren visited Jay's booth and took pictures of his bookbinding equipment and reproduction early edition Bibles and other books. After that she talked to a blacksmith and an herbalist and a Mexican cavalry officer and a retired college professor from South Carolina who traveled around the country doing reenactments.

Come to think of it, there was no reason to suppose that Alex's girlfriend was a fellow re-enactor. She might just as easily be a visitor.

She stood and looked around. There were plenty of booths left to visit; she'd barely scratched the surface.

Then she saw Alex.

The day was warm for November, and as usual, he'd been shedding layers. She could see his jacket hanging from a peg in his tent, with the waistcoat over it, and the black neck-cloth over that. He had his linen shirt open at the neck and the sleeves rolled up. He was doing something-or-other to a piece of wood—carving, probably—and leaning into the motion with practiced skill.

But it was the look on his face that made her stop and stare—absorbed, content, tranquil.

She looped her camera strap over her head. Time to get back to work.

ALEX WAS INTENT on a tricky bit of carving when he heard a *click-whir* and looked up to see Lauren's camera focused on him.

"What are you making, sir?" she asked.

"A cradle."

"What kind of wood are you using? It looks like oak."

"It is. White oak."

"That's a hard wood. Isn't it difficult to carve?"

"Not for those who have the patience and skill to work it."

She glanced up from the viewfinder and smiled at him. "Do you have patience and skill?"

He smiled back. "I think my work speaks for itself."

"I see you have an array of tools."

"Yes. These are my gouges. And here are my chisels, and the wooden mallet I use to move them along and control the angle of the carving."

He picked up a piece of wood.

"The cradle has a symmetrical sleigh shape, so I cut out four of these curving side pieces. I have them all in different stages so you can see the progression. This one just has the design drawn on. I'm going to secure it in my vise…and now I'll start roughing in the cuts. It's easy to be timid at this stage. One slip of the gouge can ruin a whole piece of wood. You can ooch along, all careful and cautious, but that'll take forever. I like to cut boldly in the beginning. I know what I'm doing, and I'm not afraid to go deep. That way I conserve my time and energy for the detail work."

He sounded good, he thought—knowledgeable and confident. Lauren asked intelligent questions, and they were the right questions to take him to exactly what he would want to say next. Sometimes she came close to get a shot of his hands.

"Here I'm making a running cut, creating a long channel in the wood. Then for this curved part, I'll make a sweep cut. That's tricky because part of the cut goes across the grain, which could make splinters if I'm not careful. But I have a good edge on my gouge so it should be fine. I keep my sharpening stone handy so I can sharpen my blades whenever they start to get dull. There's just no point in slogging along with a dull blade at any stage of the process."

He made the sweep cut, holding the gouge's shaft steady and controlling the direction with his wrist. Then he made some stabbing cuts, deep and dark for hard, crisp shadows.

"How do you decide on a design?" Lauren asked.

"It's basically just imagination plus common sense. I usually start with an actual historical piece as a model—this cradle is based on a family heirloom—and from there I make some changes, whatever I think will look good. I don't fuss too much. If you're a nineteenth-century woodworker and you're making a cradle, there's probably a baby already on the way. There's a built-in deadline. But still, you want it to look beautiful. This is where your children will sleep, and you're going to be looking at it for years. And I do find that people in past centuries put a surprising amount of beauty into functional things. It was a more elegant age."

He went on for a while, answering Lauren's

questions, demonstrating techniques and talking about woodworking on the Texas frontier.

Finally Lauren shut off the camera and said, "Thank you."

"You're very welcome. Are you having a good time?"

"Oh, yes, lovely. Everyone is so friendly and knowledgeable, and so dedicated. I like being around people who are passionate about what they do."

"I'm glad. I'm glad you like it."

"Now I'm ready for a break. I'm going to go get something to eat."

"I'll come with you."

"Can you leave your booth?"

"Sure. Hey, Kevin," he called to the leatherworker across the aisle, "keep an eye on my place, will you?"

Kevin nodded. "Sure thing, *teniente.*"

Alex followed the rich aroma of roasted meat toward the food area, Lauren at his side.

"What did that guy call you?" Lauren asked.

"Teniente," Alex said. "Because Alejandro Ramirez was a lieutenant in Juan Seguin's company, and that's the character I play."

He braced himself. If she was going to mock, this would be the time. A grown man parading around in costume, pretending to be a nineteenth-century soldier, complete with rank and backstory.

He waited for a laugh, a smirk, a snide remark.

Instead, she stopped in her tracks and laid a hand on his arm.

Her touch sent a shiver through him.

She was staring straight ahead, eyes wide, mouth open a little.

"Hold on," she said in a hushed tone.

He followed her gaze to a man who could have stepped right out of the Texas frontier. His hair was long and grizzled, and he had a lean, stringy, weather-beaten look. Silently, invisibly, Lauren approached him and got his picture.

She'd been about as stealthy as a photographer could be, but the man turned as if on instinct and looked at her. He had narrow, knowing eyes in a creased face.

Lauren smiled and nodded as if saying "thank you"—as if he'd given her permission to take his picture. It was disarming, and it worked. The man smiled and nodded back as if to say "you're welcome."

They exchanged a few words. Alex couldn't hear, but he could see that the man was charmed. Lauren got some more shots of him, focusing on details of his clothing and gear. The traps hanging at his belt. The firing mechanism of his musket, with his hand resting on the stock. The worn leather folds of his boots. The fringe on his jacket. His bowie knife. A scarred wooden canteen.

Alex watched, feet rooted to the ground, utterly captivated. Not by the sight of James, the reenactor—he was used to James—but by Lauren's reaction. She was doing her in-the-moment thing, and it wasn't flaky at all.

It was wonderful.

She was wonderful.

She wasn't mocking his world. She was embracing it.

This moved him deeply with a strange stirring. He hadn't hoped for this. The highest he'd aspired to was that she wouldn't make fun. He'd hardly dared hope she would appreciate it on some minimal level.

He hadn't dreamed that she would enter into it, boldly, joyfully.

As Lauren returned to Alex, James gave him a meaningful glance, a hey-your-girl-is-hot kind of glance.

Lauren looked at Alex, and smiled.
"Let's go, *teniente*."
From that moment, he was a lost man.

CHAPTER TEN

LAUREN LOOKED UP from her third taco to see Alex smiling at her.

"What?" she said suspiciously, hoping he wasn't about to comment on her appetite. She'd been ravenously hungry of late, which didn't seem right, because at this point how big could the baby even be?

"You like *barbacoa*?"

"Is that what this is? If so, then yes, I thoroughly approve of *barbacoa*."

"Good for you! I like to see a woman enjoying good food. Hello there, how are you?"

The last bit was addressed to a man in a fringed frontier shirt who'd greeted Alex as he walked by. Lauren was getting used to Alex's conversation being punctuated with greetings to other people. Their walk from his carpenter's shop to the food area had been a constant stream of smiles, nods, greetings and waves. Everyone seemed to know and like Alex.

The funny thing was how he went on talking to Lauren after these greetings, without losing his train of thought, as if there had been no interruption at all.

Lauren wiped her fingers and wadded up her paper napkin. "So what's going on the rest of the day?"

"Well, in a little while Jorge's gonna do a presentation on Tejanos in the Texas Revolution, and people will go on doing their demonstrations at their own booths. What all have you seen so far?"

"A blacksmith, an herbalist, Tamara and Jay, and a guy from South Carolina."

"Yeah, I know that South Carolina guy. He'll be at Béxar next month, playing a New Orleans Grey. There's a Comanche warrior running around, have you seen him? His name is Ted. You ought to get some pics of him for sure. Leon's a farrier, and he's going to shoe a horse at some point—you don't want to miss that. Hey there, Tom, Annie, good to see you! Oh, and you should see the writing guy, with his papers and quills and wax seals and iron gall ink and things. Then late in the afternoon we'll have some black-powder shooting. It's best we do that all at one time and place—hello!—because of the noise and smoke, and the fact that we're, you know, discharging weapons. I've got my Escopeta and my pistols, and that South Carolina guy has a nice Kentucky rifle, and Steve brought his cannon. Then in the evening we'll have a dance. The Chicharrones are gonna play—mostly traditional pieces, but some modern stuff, too. And I know you want to take lots of pictures, but maybe this time you'll dance with me for more than one song."

"In my fleece hoodie and running shoes, with all these nineteenth-century people? I'd look like some kind of freak."

"Like you really care about being different from other people. But if you want some nineteenth-century threads, you ought to go see Claudia. She makes reproduction clothing on spec and sells it ready-made at events. You ought to meet her, anyway, because she's so awesome."

Lauren's ears perked up. Maybe she had a name at last for Alex's love interest.

"Let's go see her now," she said.

Claudia was strikingly attractive, in a strong-boned, dark-browed style, with a spectacular figure, shown to advantage in a deep red, corseted dress. She was also around fifty years old. Was this a cougar-type situation? No wonder Alex didn't want Tony to know.

"Alex! Good to see you, *mijo*. I see you brought a friend."

"Yes, I did. Claudia, this is Lauren."

"Hello, Lauren, and welcome. I hope you're enjoying our festival."

No, not a cougar after all. An honorary aunt.

"Thank you, I am."

"Lauren needs an outfit for the dance," Alex said. "I told her you're the one to see."

"You're right. Now you run along, *mijo*, and leave it to us. I'll let you know when she's ready."

She spoke like someone who was used to being obeyed, and she wasn't wrong. Alex simply said, "Yes, ma'am," and left.

Claudia had a larger, more elaborate setup than most of the reenactors—a long tent with room for multiple rows of clothing hanging from strung-out twine, and a curtained-off area that looked like a dressing room.

Lauren started sifting through some dresses. "Your work is beautiful. Are you a seamstress full-time?"

"Oh, no. I'm a property attorney. Sewing is what I do for fun."

"Did you make what Alex is wearing?"

"I did. That was a custom job. I don't go for that level of authenticity for my off-the-rack things."

Lauren thought of all the hand-stitched seams in Alex's jacket, trousers, waistcoat and shirt. "You must be a very busy person."

"Yes, I like to stay busy. Come over here and let me look at you."

Claudia took Lauren by the shoulders, held her at arm's length and looked her over with a piercing gaze. She would be a powerful force in the courtroom. Then she went straight to a rack and pulled out a dress.

"Try this on."

It was a scoop-necked, long-skirted dress in a pale floral print. Unlike the dress Claudia was wearing, this one had a high waist—very high, just below the bust.

Lauren felt a stab of panic. Just how much had been laid bare to that piercing gaze? Was she beginning to show already?

"This style predates the Texas Revolution by a good bit," Claudia said. "But it's still appropriate for the Texas colonial period. For a while, around the turn of the nineteenth century, women stopped wearing stays, and the Empire waist was all the rage. Skirts were

narrower, too. The whole style was very columnar and simple. It didn't last long—cor-
sets came back big-time just a few decades
later—but it happened. I like to keep these
dresses on hand, because the Empire waist is
easier to manage for an off-the-rack garment.
If you wanted to go full-on Victorian you'd
need a corset and petticoats, and that gets
complicated. You'd look great in it—you're so
tiny—but this style is a lot less of an invest-
ment for a newcomer, and a lot more comfortable for walking around. And even though
you don't get to show off your waistline, you
can make up for it with cleavage. Try it on
and see what you think."

"Yes, ma'am."

Claudia led her to the changing area and
held back the hanging panel door. There was
a full-length mirror inside, and a small stool
in one corner.

Lauren was pulling off her fleece hoodie
when Claudia said from just outside, "So, you
came to the festival with Alex."

She didn't ask questions; she made state-
ments.

"Um, yes," Lauren said. "It's a mutual-
friends kind of thing. I'm staying with my

friend Dalia, and her husband is Alex's brother. You know Tony and Dalia?"

"All their lives."

"Dalia and I met in college. I'm spending the winter at her ranch in my live-in van. I'm a photographer, and I write for some travel blogs, and Tony thought the festival would be a good opportunity for me."

"I remember you now. You were the photographer at the wedding. So you and Dalia met at that fancy Yankee school?"

Lauren smiled at the description of the small Pennsylvania liberal arts college as a "fancy Yankee school." She'd already noticed that the word *Yankee* was used a lot more broadly around here than in the north, signifying not only New England, but also the Middle Atlantic states, as well as the Midwest, the Northwest and any state north of the person who was speaking, including Oklahoma.

"That's right. We weren't together for the whole four years, though. She stuck it out and got her degree, and I took off partway through a semester and drove to Tennessee."

"Tennessee! What for?"

"Oh, the college discontinued the degree program I was pursuing, and that made me mad. So I decided to go to the Smoky Mountains, and see if they were really smoky."

"Were they?"

"Yes."

Claudia chuckled. "And now you're staying at La Escarpa. Beautiful place. Wonderful how a big working ranch like that has kept running all those generations, and stayed in the same family—all the way back to Alejandro Ramirez and the Texas Revolution."

"Alex told me his family and Dalia's family are both descended from Alejandro Ramirez. How did the land get divided up?"

"Oh, the Reyes place was always a separate rancho, separately run. Gabriel Ramirez— that's Alejandro and Romelia's son, the one born during the Revolution—had two surviving sons by two different wives. The firstborn got La Escarpa, and the younger boy got the Reyes place. La Escarpa was always the better property, but the disparity wasn't so wide back then."

"What made that change?"

"Lots of things. Political unrest, market fluctuations, weather, sickness. Pieces of the Reyes land got parceled off and sold little by little over the years. By the time Alex's grandfather inherited there was barely enough left to make a viable living with ranching. But Miguel dug in and refused to sell more. Said he was going to make a success of ranching if it killed him. He was smart and hardworking and relentless, and he managed to turn things around to a surprising degree. Even managed to buy back some of the land that had been sold off."

How sad for Alex's grandfather, to spend his life working to get the land in shape, only to come to realize that his son wasn't fit to take it over.

Except that the grandfather apparently hadn't realized that at all, or hadn't wanted to admit it.

Lauren threw out a line. "Do you know Alex's father?"

"Oh, yes. I went to high school with him. He was popular, but those bad-boy types always bored me. That particular apple fell pretty far from the tree. It's a shame."

Lauren wondered what Claudia thought of Alex's chances with the will. Tony had said Alex's legal battle was a lost cause, that even his attorney said he was wasting his...

"Wait, you said you're a property attorney? Are you *Alex's* attorney?"

"Yes, I'm representing him."

Lauren was silent as she finished undressing, trying to phrase her next question in a way that would respect attorney-client privilege, and good taste.

"Hypothetically speaking, what are the chances of success for someone contesting a will?"

"Hypothetically speaking, it would depend on a lot of things. Is there something fishy about the existing will? Is there any reason to think the testator was incompetent at the time he made it, or coerced? If so, then the contestant might have a chance. If not, then the best he can realistically hope for is to create a delay, which might motivate the heir to make some sort of concession—like sharing the estate with the contestant, or selling it to him."

Lauren pulled the dress over her head. What were the odds of a heavily indebted Carlos voluntarily choosing to do right by his sons? Or of a working-class man in his twenties raking up enough cash to buy a large rural property?

Probably not good.

"How are you coming along?" Claudia asked. "Can I help you with the fastenings?"

"Yes, please."

She looked at herself in the full-length mirror while Claudia buttoned her up. Claudia was right about the cleavage. The neckline was wide and low, edged with a narrow ruffle. And the high waist didn't look frumpy at all, but stately and dignified. The color was good, a pale coral with a small print.

"I like it," she said.

"I do, too. It suits you. I knew that warm, light color would work well with your skin and hair. And speaking of hair, let's see if we can contrive some sort of Federalist-era hairstyle for you. The period-appropriate thing is up in the back, with ringlets in the front. The way you're wearing it now is actually not far off. Switch out your hair clip with a pearl bandeau and you'll be all set. Here, sit down. I'll be right back."

Claudia pulled the stool closer to the mirror and left the dressing room. She returned soon with a basket of hair accessories.

"I guess you know Alex's family pretty well," Lauren said.

"Oh, yes. My father made Miguel's will, decades ago, and our families have always been close. But the whole town knows about the situation with the land, and pretty much every other aspect of the Reyes family drama."

"That can't be easy for Alex."

"No. But he soldiers on, working his two jobs and going out to his grandfather's ranch on his days off. Someone's got to feed cattle and make sure the fences are holding while the estate is in probate, and do you suppose Carlos does that? No, he does not. He'd just as soon sell off all the livestock and the equipment for whatever he can get. And will he reimburse Alex for his time and labor once the property is awarded to him? I don't think so. But that's Alex. Faithful to the death."

Claudia finished fastening the bandeau and locked eyes with Lauren's reflection in the mirror. Beneath all the praise Lauren sensed a strong don't-hurt-my-boy vibe.

"He seems like a great guy," she said. "But we're just friends."

Claudia smiled. "Okay."

She gave Lauren a hand mirror. "Here, see what you think."

Lauren turned around and used the hand mirror to view the back of her hair. She tilted her head, pleased with the cascading fall of curls and the pearl bandeau.

"I love it. The dress, too. I'll take them both."

"Great! I'll give you a bag for your other

clothes. You can leave them here and pick them up later."

Lauren gave Claudia her card and took the bag into the dressing room. When she came out, Alex was just returning.

He halted in midstep, with his eyebrows slightly lifted, his mouth open and his gaze fixed on her.

"What do you think?" she asked.

He shut his mouth, cleared his throat and nodded. "Very authentic."

"Wow, you sure know how to talk to the ladies, *mijo*," Claudia said. "How are you still single?"

Lauren handed the bag to Claudia and signed the card reader. She could feel Alex watching her. His gaze was like a caress, the soft, light kind that raises a shiver.

Claudia smiled at them. "Have a good time!"

Lauren and Alex answered together, "Yes, ma'am."

"Isn't she great?" Alex asked once they were out of earshot.

"Oh, yes! And a little terrifying. I wouldn't want to be on her bad side, but she seems like a good person to have in your corner."

She hoped that meant Claudia could help

Alex get the land—but how likely was that, when Claudia herself seemed to have little hope? It wasn't fair.

In a little while she was learning about something else that wasn't fair, when Jorge gave his presentation on Tejanos in the Revolution. The Texas Republic had not been kind to the Mexican-born, even to those who'd fought for independence. Texas was their home; they'd settled it, and defended it against their own former countrymen. And then they were cast out, treated like strangers, aliens, enemies. Many were forced off their land by greedy opportunists—just like what was happening to Alex.

It wasn't right. Alex loved the land and its history; he wanted nothing more than to live and make his living there. He would care for it, cherish it, respect the old ways. But it didn't look like he was going to get the chance.

"STAND THE WEAPON UP, stock on the ground, barrel to the sky. Put the powder down the muzzle. Now the ball. Now take the ramrod and push the ball down the barrel. Lift the frizzen and put the hammer on half-cock… that's it. Pour more powder in the pan. Close the frizzen back again, nice and tight against the flint…there you go. Good."

Lauren's mind swam with all the new terminology. Everything was so precise and intricate and *old*. The flint was an actual little wedge-shaped stone held in the jaws of the cock with a small piece of leather, and Alex said it was only good for twenty to thirty shots before it would have to be replaced. A tiny brush to clean the pan, and a tiny pick to clear burned powder from the touch hole, both hung from the cartridge box on little chains. A slender pipe under the barrel held the ramrod, which had to be put back there after sending the ball home. It was amazing anyone ever kept track of all the steps.

Alex locked eyes with her over the Escopeta's muzzle. "Now, at this point the weapon is ready to fire. Do not fire, or even put your finger on the trigger, until I say."

He showed her how to hold the Escopeta, with the butt snugged between her shoulder and rib cage, and how to line the center post between the rear sites to take aim.

"Pull the hammer back with your thumb. Now you're on full cock. Once you squeeze the trigger, you're gonna set off this whole chain reaction. The flint sparks against the frizzen, and the powder ignites in the pan, and that ignites the main charge in the barrel. All this means you're about to experience a small explosion right near your face. It happens fast, but not instantaneously. You have to keep still, and not flinch, or you'll mess up your aim. Hold still, keep steady and follow through. Ready?"

"Ready."

"Okay. Fire."

Lauren squeezed the trigger.

The discharge *was* loud. The butt kicked into her shoulder, but she held as steady as she could.

"Did I hit the target?"

"Nope, missed it by a good yard," Alex said cheerfully. "It takes a lot of practice to get even somewhat accurate with a smooth-bore weapon."

"That's why rifles are better."

The guy who'd spoken was a young man Lauren hadn't met yet. He smiled at her and said, "Aren't you going to introduce me to your friend, *teniente*?"

"Lauren, that's Zander. He's new to reenacting. That's why he makes sweeping generalizations. Rifles aren't 'better.' They're more accurate, but the old ones take longer to reload—not that loading is fast for any sort of muzzle-loading firearm. It's a trade-off."

Zander made a gesture that seemed to say "maybe, maybe-not." "Debatable," he said.

"Exactly," said Alex.

"What kind of gun do you have?" Lauren asked.

She felt a little sorry for Zander because his gun looked so shabby compared to Alex's. The stock had some sort of brass decorative thing on it, but the brass was tarnished and the wood looked dry. All the metal parts were pretty corroded.

"It's a Jacob Dickert rifle. Very rare, and a lot bigger than that sawed-off little carbine. Come over here if you want to fire a *real* gun."

"What did you say?"

There was an edge in Alex's voice—little more than a warning, but unmistakable.

Zander chuckled. "Come on, I'm just messing with you, man. Don't get all bent out of shape."

He aimed and fired, but instead of a loud discharge there was a small click, followed by a flash of light and a puff of smoke from the lock mechanism, right by the trigger.

"And there you see the origin of the expression *flash in the pan*," Alex told Lauren.

Zander looked annoyed, but there wasn't much he could say. He'd kind of set himself up.

"The Dickert is a nice rifle," Alex told him. "Have you met Ron, the gunsmith? You should take it to him. I don't know if your stock can be saved, but he can make you a new one if necessary, and probably get the barrel and the lock in good shape. I've seen him do some excellent work on weapons that were pretty far gone."

"Actually, this rifle was in near perfect condition when I bought it off eBay," Zander said.

"What happened? Did you leave it outside overnight in the rain or something?"

"That's exactly what I did."

Zander seemed strangely proud of this.

Alex looked dumbfounded. "On purpose?"

"You bet. I didn't want it to look all slick and shiny and new-minted. Now it has a nice, weathered, authentic vibe."

Lauren could feel Alex's shock and outrage. "It's weathered, all right, but it's not authentic," he said. "No Revolutionary soldier would have dreamed of treating his weapon that way. They cleaned them, oiled them, kept them dry, babied them. Their lives depended on keeping their weapons functional and ready to fire."

Zander smiled a smile so superior that even Lauren wanted to punch him. "You overestimate the intelligence of the common soldier."

"Oh, yeah?" Alex held out his own weapon. "This Escopeta belonged to my great-great-great-great-grandfather. It's never been restored, just maintained. It's as clean and functional now as the day he carried it to the Siege of Béxar."

Zander's smile got even more odious. "Oh, is that what your daddy told you?"

Lauren saw the change that came over Alex's face as he realized Zander was calling him stupid, or a liar—the dusky flush, the tightening of the jaw. He was fighting to keep control.

"Hey, Alex, let's go see Steve and his cannon crew," she said. "I want to get some pictures of them."

Alex went willingly enough. He was not just angry, but visibly shaken.

"I'm sorry I encouraged him," Lauren said. "I didn't realize he was such a jerk."

"What a little *punk*," Alex said. He said the

word like it was the ultimate put-down, and Lauren supposed that for him, it was. A shallow, flimsy person who didn't take things seriously. What would he think of Evan?

"He's a poser," she said. "He probably won't last long as a reenactor."

"I hope not. Do you know how rare those Jacob Dickert rifles are? And to think he actually found one in pristine condition, and spent money on it, and ruined it—something old and valuable and functional and beautiful. I just... I can't be around people like that."

People like your dad, Lauren thought.

"So," Alex said, "what did you think of your first experience with black-powder shooting?"

"I liked it. I'm impressed by the thought of soldiers going through all those steps, all those minute little motions, over and over in the right order, with nothing left out."

"It is impressive, isn't it? Fifteen seconds was the goal for loading and firing, but it took a lot of drilling to get that fast. And that's under the best of conditions. Imagine doing it with lead balls whizzing past your head, and your friends dropping all around you, and artillery fire knocking the fortifications to pieces. Fire and load, fire and load, until you die or run out of ammo. Then you're down to a brace of pistols and a bowie knife, if you have them. And then—that's it."

"Unless you win."

"But you might not. And sometimes you know you won't, like at the Alamo. And still you have to keep on. It takes muscle memory and physical strength. Discipline. Nerve."

He could have been talking about himself. His fight for the family land sounded like as much of a lost cause as the Alamo, but he seemed determined to go down fighting.

ALEX WAS HAVING a hard time keeping his mind on his dancing. Fortunately he was a good enough dancer that he didn't really need to think about what he was doing. He was free to let his thoughts wander to other things...like how jaw-droppingly gorgeous Lauren looked in her new dress.

He'd seen Federalist-style dresses before, and he'd be the first to admit that by modern standards they were not all that exciting. On any given day, unless he stayed in his apartment without going online, watching TV or looking at any images designed to sell pretty much anything, he was almost guaranteed to see plenty of female flesh casually displayed, with little left to the imagination. If anyone had asked him, he'd have said that those neoclassical dresses with their long skirts and high waists were nothing to write home about.

And then he'd seen Lauren.

The light, filmy fabric wasn't tight anywhere, but as she moved the skirt kept showing hints of the shape within. And the bodice—well, he suddenly realized he had never payed proper attention to the Federalist-style bodice before. So many little folds of fabric gathered at the neckline, widening as they curved down, and then gathered again.

The overall effect was understated, simple, restrained…

And spectacular.

The Chicharrones were playing traditional dances from the early nineteenth century, when mestizo culture was just beginning to emerge. Lauren was a quick study, with almost an intuitive grasp of the essentials. Alex could see other men looking at her.

He was used to this warm feeling of shared vision and like-mindedness from other reenactors. But for Lauren to enter into his world that way was an entirely different sensation.

She was an international traveler. He was

a small-town boy—the worst kind of small-town boy, the kind who didn't leave. Who stayed, with a vengeance. He might hear or read about some interesting place in one of those parts of the country with its weird Yankee accents and fancy weather, and he might go so far as to say it sounded cool. But then he went on with his life, in the same twelve hundred or so square miles where he was born and grew up. Lauren got up and went to the place, and saw the thing, and when she was done, she went someplace else.

What would it mean for someone like that to choose him? It couldn't happen.

Could it?

No. It was too fantastic to even think about. And even if it did happen, he didn't have room in his life for that kind of complication.

And yet he suddenly found that he wanted it.

He wanted it bad.

CHAPTER ELEVEN

LAUREN WAS SUPPOSED to be selecting edited photos from the festival to use in the various articles and pieces she hoped to sell, but what she was really doing was looking at the same photos over and over, the ones of Alex. There was something luxurious about this. In person she couldn't stare at him constantly, but here, in the privacy of her van, under her soft bedcovers with her mattress heater on, there was no one to see and judge her. It was like eating a whole box of chocolate truffles in private.

Alex, talking and laughing, amber eyes crinkled at the corners, smiling his full-on, all-out smile, the wind teasing a few black strands loose from his ponytail.

Alex at his carpenter's bench, planing a board, stretched out, body leaning deep into the cut. Big loose curls of pale wood spilling through the little opening in the plane. A look of absorbed contentment on his face.

Alex standing, backlit by the afternoon sun, jacket off, waistcoat and collar open, sleeves rolled up. One leg straight, the other slightly bent at hip and knee, both of them sharp and clear against the western sky. Carbine held low across the tops of his thighs. Face in almost a full profile, with that sad, sober expression. Every line of him radiating confidence and strength, from the set of his head to the curve of his spine.

A knock at her door made her jump. "Hey, you in there?"

It was Alex's voice. Just like before, he'd shown up at her place while she was gazing at his image on her computer screen, and just like before, she closed the window and folded down the screen.

"I'm here. Come in."

He slid open the door, and the gray cat came darting inside and leaped onto Lauren's lap.

"Oh, sorry," Alex said. "I didn't even see him. You want me to pitch him out?"

"No, he's fine." Lauren ran her hand along the cat's spine and down his kinked tail. "It's cold out there, isn't it, Chester? Of course, you want to be in the nice warm van."

Alex followed the cat inside. "Chester, huh?

How 'bout that, buddy? You got a name now. You're moving up in the world."

"Yeah, he looks like a Chester. And he's just so darned friendly, I had to call him something. Look at him doing the Contented Cat Face."

"Yep, that's the Contented Cat Face, all right. It's a good look for him."

"You want a drink?"

"Sure. Got any of that kalucha?"

"Kombucha. In the fridge."

He handed her a plastic grocery bag. "Got something for you. I stopped by the house, and Dalia gave me your mail."

"Anything good?"

"Maybe. There's a big hand-addressed manila envelope from a Peter Longwood. Dalia said that's your dad. It looked promising. I wasn't rooting through your mail or anything. I just saw it lying there before Dalia put it in the bag."

"No worries."

She found the big envelope and tore it open. Then her stomach dropped away.

"Oh. My divorce is final."

Alex froze in the act of sitting in the driver's seat. "Your what is what?"

"My divorce is final. This is the final decree."

"I didn't know you were married."

"Well, I'm not, now. And I wasn't for long. I wonder why my dad sent me this. He usually keeps all my important mail at his house, so it doesn't get lost. Oh, here's a sticky note. 'Sweetie, Mike just received this and sent it on to me. Be sure to read it through carefully and make sure everything is correct. Then mail it back to me for safekeeping. Love you. Dad.' Wow. Is he considerate or what? Look, he even sent a self-addressed stamped envelope."

"Who's Mike?"

"His attorney. They've been friends since college."

The thought of her dad going to his old friend and asking him to handle his daughter's divorce was faintly nauseating. He was probably still getting congratulated on her marriage.

"I'm sorry. I had no idea. I saw the big envelope and thought it might be a nice surprise."

"It actually is a surprise—well, sort of. I mean, it isn't exactly a bolt from the blue, but I am a little surprised that Evan actually followed through."

"Why? He didn't want the divorce?"

"No, he's just lazy. He wanted the divorce, more or less, but he doesn't have a whole lot of perseverance for anything in the nature of a process. Married, divorced—to him it wouldn't make much difference either way. It sure didn't stop him from shacking up with someone else. In fact, I'm going to go out on a limb and say his new girlfriend was the driving force here. Well, that won't last. He'll get tired of her, too, and slither out somehow like the snake that he is."

Alex looked distressed. "That's awful. How did you ever end up with this guy in the first place?"

"Oh, I was stupid, I admit it. But he was charming enough in the beginning. Like out-of-this-world charming. He couldn't get enough of me. Completely swept me off my feet. I thought something amazing was happening. I didn't know then that that's just how he is. Whatever he's into at the moment, he's into it with his whole being. It just doesn't ever last. And I didn't know him well enough to realize it. And that's on me, marrying someone I didn't really know."

Alex twisted the lid off his kombucha bottle. "How long ago was all this?"

"Well, let's see. I was staying in Venice

Beach back in July—the one in Florida, not the one in California. There was this music festival going on, and Evan's band was playing. He really is an excellent musician. I guess that's the exception to the rule, the one thing he's actually been able to stick with long-term. We met at the festival, and then we had this incredible whirlwind courtship. I wasn't imagining it. He really did pursue me, like, hard. I'd never had a guy that into me before. It was…exhilarating. Intoxicating."

For some reason it was important to her that Alex understand this. She'd been a fool, yes, but not a complete fool. A woman would have to be a pretty hardened cynic to resist the treatment Evan had given her.

"Next thing I know, we're getting married on the beach with his bass player officiating. I wore this terrific dress I found in a little boutique, and we were both barefoot, and the weather was perfect, and the gulf was this pure clear aquamarine, and my dad flew in from Pennsylvania, and about a dozen strangers showed up, and someone had made an enormous sandcastle that we ended up having in the background. It was like everything came together to make a perfect day for us, and I was going to spend the rest of my life with this beautiful, brilliant, spectacular man who made me feel like a queen."

She looked out the window at the overcast sky. "And then the moment passed. Evan's band split up, or he split from the band, or something—I never did get a straight story on what happened there. The way he told it, they were completely in the wrong, envious of him, trying to keep him down and practically forcing him out of the band out of petty malice. But in hindsight, I wonder if it was just Evan being a diva. So he left the band, and we left Venice Beach, and for a while things were still good. It was kind of nice having him to myself, without random women hitting on him all the time. There was another music festival at Clearwater Beach, and so we went there. Evan made a lot of new friends right away, and I was happy for him at first because he was doing what he loved and people were finally recognizing his talent the way he deserved. But then he started staying out later and later, and one night he didn't come home at all. And even then I was willing to make excuses for him—he'd lost track of time, spent all night composing new songs, whatever. I thought he'd come back and talk to me for hours, like he used to, about what he'd been doing. But when he did come back, it was only for a change of clothes, and he barely spoke to me and didn't give a straight answer about where he'd been. And he didn't come back the next night, either. And finally he came, and looked at me with this hollow-eyed tragic expression like some haunted poet, and I just felt sick inside."

She felt sick now, talking about it, but less so than when she'd broken the news to her dad. Even in the beginning, even in those rosy days of their early courtship, she'd had a feeling, a darkness in the back of her mind, that it couldn't last, wasn't real. She could acknowledge that now, and there was a kind of relief in it.

Alex didn't say anything, but his face was wrung with sympathy.

"He tried to give it a good spin," Lauren said, "like this was all about who he was as a musician and who he was destined to become and all that, but I knew there was someone else at the back of it, and I said so. He denied it at first—well, kind of. He wasn't self-aware enough to even lie about it in a convincing way—this woman just kept coming up in all his talk about the music, and it didn't take a genius to figure out the rest. And once I pointed it out, he acted all surprised, like he hadn't realized it until right then when he was talking to me, but now he knew and he had to follow his destiny."

She didn't tell him how she'd groveled, begging Evan to stay, basically offering to do anything he wanted, be anything he wanted, to make their marriage work. It made her ashamed now to think how desperate she'd been, how little self-respect she'd shown— and this in spite of her absolute certainty that Evan had already slept with the other woman.

"Wow," Alex said. "And how long was this after the wedding?"

"Two weeks, I kid you not. Two lousy weeks. So he left. Took his guitars and his clothes and his toothbrush and walked out of my life. And for a long time that was it. No contact. For weeks it was like he just dropped into a void. It was…rough."

She couldn't possibly express—didn't want to express—the utter misery of that time. It was like a physical illness, or poison, or something heavy pressing on her constantly. Every few days she'd generate fresh content for Instagram or her travel blog—nature and local-interest stuff that didn't have Evan in it. She felt like a fraud—a transparent, pathetic fraud—trying to carry on like nothing was wrong. But acknowledging what had happened would have been worse.

She took a deep breath. "And then, about a month later...he came back."

"No way!"

"Yep. It was August. I was camped at a Dark Sky Park at Kissimmee Prairie for the Perseids meteor shower. Evan saw a post I made about it on Instagram and just showed up unannounced. And the sight of him framed in the door of my van with his guitar slung on his back just hit a giant reset button in me. I forgot what a self-centered jerk he was, forgot all the pain and suffering he'd put me through. I just saw him with that look in his eyes and fell as hard as ever. Harder."

"How long did he come back for?"

"One weekend." One glorious, blissful weekend, in which they'd scarcely gotten out of bed. "And then...he left again. He got a call, and he went outside to take it, and I couldn't make out the words but I could understand the tone. Near as I can guess, he'd had a falling out with his band or his girlfriend or both, and came running back to me to get his ego stroked. And then whoever it was made up with him...and he left again, after giving me a whole new set of speeches to justify his actions. It was the same sort of high-flown language he'd used when he was pursuing me, and when he'd left before. And for the first time I saw how empty it all was, how shallow he was and always had been. Only difference was, this time he actually filed for a no-fault divorce, which in Florida apparently takes four to five weeks to go through if uncontested. No-fault! There was plenty of fault, all on his end. Adultery for sure, and lack of good faith. Dalia said I should get an annulment for fraud."

"Dalia knew?"

"Oh, yeah. Not when he left the first time—I was still in denial at that point—but after he left the second time I called and told her everything. You can imagine how mad she was. If she'd been in the same room with him I'm pretty sure she'd have throttled him with her bare hands. It was comforting. I needed someone to say, 'you're right, he's a terrible person.' I kind of liked the idea of the annulment—compared to the divorce, anyway. Seemed like the closest I could come to just undoing the whole thing. But it turns out that proving fraud is a lot more complicated than you might suppose. And in the end, I signed the divorce papers. What else could I do?"

"Then what?"

"Then I came here. Dalia told me right away that I should come, but it took me a while to actually pack up and make the drive." Eight weeks, to be exact. Long enough for her to finally feel silly pretending not to notice how late her period was and take a pregnancy test. She'd been in denial in more ways than one.

"I'm sorry," Alex said. "I'm so sorry all that happened. I know how painful it is to deal with a narcissist."

"You mean your dad?"

The words slipped out before she could stop them.

"Sorry. Tony told me about him, and Claudia, a little. I hope that's okay."

He shrugged. "It's not like it's a secret. Whole town knows what he's done, and half of them have been burned by him themselves. He's just one of those toxic human beings who trample your heart and then show no remorse whatsoever, no awareness of what they've done."

"That's the worst of it. You feel so angry, and you know you're right, but they twist things around until you can't see straight. They somehow make it sound like *they're* the ones you should feel sorry for."

"Yes! Exactly! That's just how it was with what happened with my truck."

"Rosie?"

"No, Amelia. Rosie is my grandfather's truck—or she was."

"I didn't know that."

"Yeah. See, I used to drive this 1960 Chevy stepside—that's Amelia. I got her for a song because she was just sitting in this dude's garage for decades, collecting dust. I spent years restoring her. Did all the work myself."

"I can totally see you driving a vintage Chevy stepside."

"Yeah, she was a great vehicle. Still is, but—well, you'll see. So one night last October, I was working late at the garage. Manny lets me come in odd hours to work around my other job. So I lock up and go out to my truck, and these two guys are waiting for me, and one of them is holding a baby sledgehammer. And I'm thinking they're gonna rob the garage. And then the one with the sledgehammer says, 'Hello, Alex.'"

"Ooh. That's ominous."

"Yeah, no kidding. So then he proceeds to

smash my headlights, my taillights, the windshield, the door windows including the vent glass and the little back glass. Knocks the side mirrors clean off. One after another, all calm and slow and methodical. And I'm just standing there in shock. And when he's done the guy turns to me and says, 'I don't like doing this, because it's bad for business. But if I need to do it and I don't do it, then that's bad for business, too. You tell your daddy I want my money. And if he's late again, next time it'll be your fingers and kneecaps.' And then they both just walk away."

"Whoa! Oh, Alex, how awful."

"Yeah. I didn't even know we had loan sharks in Limestone Springs—though I guess they weren't local, because I didn't recognize them, and they didn't seem concerned about me seeing their faces."

"Wow. *Wow.* What did you do then?"

"Swept up the broken glass, taped some clear plastic over the openings and drove home."

"You didn't call the cops?"

"Nah. What was the point? What could the cops do other than file a report so I could make an insurance claim? And if I did make a claim and the insurance company paid out, that would mean higher premiums, which I couldn't afford. In the long run it was better to bite the bullet and do the work myself."

"Yeah, but still. Those thugs vandalized your vehicle, and threatened you with physical harm. Technically that's assault."

"I guess so. But the only reason it happened was because my father is an irresponsible jackass who doesn't care. It's just... It's humiliating."

Pride and self-sufficiency. Lauren could admire that, though she wasn't sure he was right.

"Did you tell your dad what happened?"

"Oh, yeah. And you know what he said to me? That it was all my grandfather's fault for not lending him the money to begin with. He was *forced* to go to a loan shark, see, because his own father was such a mean old skinflint. And then he said for me to tell my grandfather what happened with my truck, because if *I* asked, if *I* was the one being pressured and threatened, he'd pay the loan shark back. He's making out like he's the victim, and I'm the favorite child who gets preferential treatment for no reason."

Lauren shook her head. "Classic narcissist."

"Yeah. Everything is about him."

"So what did you say to him?"

"I said heck no. You're the one who borrowed the money, you're the one who created this mess, so handle your own business and leave my grandfather out of it. But he must have gone to my grandfather, anyway, and told him all about it, because the next morning my grandfather went to town and made a big withdrawal from his bank account. I know, because I was on the account, too, and I could see its history. And the day after that is when he died. I came out to the ranch early to help with the haying, and I found him. Massive stroke while he was making morning coffee. And on the passenger seat of his truck, he'd left the paperwork for a gift deed, turning the truck over to me. I think maybe he knew he didn't have much longer, and he wanted to do something for me."

Privately, Lauren thought it would have been a lot more useful if the grandfather had left Alex the ranch. Yes, it was his own property, and it was his right to dispose of it as he saw fit, even if that meant giving it to his wastrel of a son. But it was a mistake. Anyone could see that.

"And you've been driving Rosie ever since?"

"Yep."

"What happened to Amelia?"

"For now she's sitting at the ranch under a tarp, waiting. Replacing the windshield and back glass wasn't too bad, but door glass is a major pain. You've got to open the interior-door panel and get every last bit of broken glass out, and reassemble the new glass just so, with the seals and the felt and everything. A lot of people opt to replace the entire door rather than deal with the hassle of installing new glass. But Amelia still has her original paint, so I can't just stick a couple of different-colored doors on there. And whatever I end up doing about it is gonna take a hefty chunk of time and money, neither of which I have a lot of right at the moment."

They went on trading stories about his father and her ex-husband. It was weirdly comforting, talking to someone who really understood.

"You want to go get a beer?" Alex asked suddenly. "I'm actually off work today, so I have time. We could go to Tito's and drown our sorrows over the narcissists who've done us wrong. Or you could drown your sorrows, and I could stay sober and drive you home after. Wait, that doesn't sound right. Maybe we could just get a twelve-pack and bring it back to your place. Wait, that doesn't sound right, either."

I would love to go on talking with you. But not over alcohol, because I'm pregnant.

The words were right there in her mouth, ready to be said, but she held them back, and switched them out with completely different ones.

"As appealing as that sounds, I'd better get back to work. It was fun commiserating with you, though."

"You, too. Be strong, okay? You'll get through this."

"Thanks."

She stared at the door a long time after he left. Why hadn't she told him? At some point she would *have* to tell him, because it would be weird not to. She couldn't expect her stomach to stay flat for much longer. Sooner or later, he'd know.

But she was just here for the winter. Not even the whole winter, necessarily. Just long enough to regroup and get her head on straight and figure out where to go next.

She signed the divorce decree and stuck it in its envelope.

CHAPTER TWELVE

WHEN ALEX GOT HOME, the first thing he did was to Google music festivals in Venice Beach, Florida, over the past summer. He found one that fit the bill, then started going through the featured bands one by one until he found one with a front man named Evan.

He knew instantly that he'd found the right Evan. He knew it by the breezy confidence, the pretty-boy face. The skinny jeans. The man bun.

Evan. What a punk name. Alex had never known anyone named Evan before, never thought about the name one way or another. Now he hated it.

It didn't take long to find confirmation in the form of another picture of Evan, this time with his arm around Lauren.

She had her hair twisted up high on her head, with lots of loose tendrils curling around her face and neck. A hint of sunburn glowed on her cheekbones and the bridge of her nose. The straps of an emerald-green swimsuit showed around the wide, off-the-shoulder neckline of a thin, see-through T-shirt. She was holding on to Evan and looking straight at the camera with an open, happy, beautiful smile.

The sight hit Alex like a gut punch. He actually couldn't breathe for a moment, and he felt like he might throw up. All that love and trust and joy, and Evan had treated her like last week's trash.

He went through all the band's pictures from the festival, then googled the band and found its official site. Plenty more pictures here, from before and after Lauren, of Evan looking infuriating in a dozen other cities, always with a beautiful woman or two at his side.

Why on earth had he married her to begin with? What had he been thinking? Why go to the trouble of marriage if you didn't mean it, if you weren't ready to follow through? Maybe he knew Lauren wouldn't go for a casual hookup, so he tailored his approach. And maybe he got drawn in by the challenge of the thing.

Come to think of it, for someone who had

so little regard for marriage to begin with, there wasn't any reason *not* to marry her.

It was even possible that on some level, he thought he wanted to do it. Maybe he'd convinced himself with all his emotional talk. People like that were just as capable of fooling themselves as they were of fooling other people. But they didn't have the substance to back up their promises.

He went back to the picture of Evan and Lauren together. Lauren was tagged in it, and Alex saw a hashtag for Vincent Van-Go. He clicked the link.

It took him to Lauren's Instagram. The pics at the top of the feed, the most recent ones, were of Enchanted Rock. He worked his way down to a shot of a night sky, all purple and blue, slashed with white lines in different directions—the Perseids meteor shower, captured with some kind of fancy camera with time-lapse capabilities. Evan would have been with her then; that was their stolen weekend of lovemaking and stargazing, when he'd made his brief return. Alex imagined Lauren lying on her back on a blanket on the ground, with Evan beside her. Had she suspected how fragile her happiness was?

He skipped the next few pics, all nature

shots, and clicked on a thumbnail of a view through the open back doors of the van, with two sets of legs stretched out side by side, crossed at the ankles—one set obviously hers, the other just as obviously Evan's—and the rolling surf beyond. There was a time gap of a few weeks between that one and the Perseids one, filled by the nature shots.

Before the legs pic came a shot of Evan, shirtless, lying on Lauren's bed in the van, with a coffee mug resting on his abs, facing the camera with a daydreamy smile on his face, like he was gazing at the most important and fascinating thing in the world. Alex wanted to punch him in the mouth.

More pics of Evan, and the beach, and the band. Selfies of Lauren and Evan together.

The wedding.

Alex shut his eyes, forced himself to take some slow, deep breaths. His heart was pounding with hot rage. He felt genuine physical distress, like an actual fight-or-flight response.

He opened his eyes and looked at every last picture of the wedding. It was all there, just like Lauren said. The bare feet, the sandcastle. Lauren in her wedding dress.

The pic just before the wedding was a

shot of Evan wading in the surf. The caption said something about "this amazing man just asked me to marry him," followed by a bunch of hashtags.

Until now he hadn't been looking at the captions, just the images. Now he went through a second time and read the words. All the Evan-related captions, from the beginning of the romance to what had to be the last one before he left, had a kind of giddy vibe—Evan this and Evan that, how blessed she was to have this wonderful man and blah, blah, blah. The post-Evan ones, between his leaving and the Perseids, didn't mention him at all. No doubt she'd felt too bruised then to deal with explaining his absence on a public forum, and was still holding out hope that he'd come back. He'd come back, all right, the jerk—just long enough to get laid.

Alex went back further, to what must have been Lauren and Evan's first meeting. It was the same pic he'd seen on the band's site.

He went back further still, to places Lauren had stayed in the van earlier in the year. It looked like she'd spent a few months on the southeast coast. Georgia. Some beaches in South and North Carolina—Little River, Myrtle Beach, the Outer Banks. Assateague

Island, with wild ponies. She'd wintered there.

Then suddenly, she was in Oregon, at a place called the Willamette Valley, working as a harvest hand at a winery in the fall, and at a berry farm before that. The pictures were truly breathtaking—berry bushes thick and heavy with ripe fruit, grape clusters hanging beneath leaves in vivid fall colors, red and green and gold. Moody shots of rain falling outside the van windows.

On and on he went, back in time through Lauren's travels. Big Sur in California. The ranch in Mexico. Everything started getting jumbled in Alex's mind—pictures of landscapes, close-ups of plants, leaves, moss, animals, people. The occasional selfie.

Then suddenly he was looking at a picture of himself, wearing a plaid shirt and vest and a boutonniere made of sunflower and Texas sage. He'd reached Tony and Dalia's wedding.

He'd never bothered to check out the wedding pics before; he'd been there, he didn't need to see pictures of it. Now he was amazed by how excellent a job Lauren had done. She'd captured not just the images, but the whole spirit of the event, and Tony and Dalia's personalities. She was good, really good.

There he was, dancing with his cousin Annalisa. And there he was alone, with a hashtag of "handsome cowboy." He actually felt himself blush.

Another candid shot of him, and another, and another. He'd never realized she'd taken these. She'd made him look good, too.

The wedding pics ended, and he kept going back. Rapid-riding in Colorado, rock climbing in Utah. Months turned into years. He saw a pic of Lauren about to set out on Vincent Van-Go's maiden voyage. Then further still, to pics of her fixing up the van, looking amazing in a worn leather tool belt. A man was in some of these, a tall, bearded, fifty-ish guy with a friendly, open face, and Alex knew right away it must be Lauren's dad. He looked like the kind of calm, quiet, easygoing, capable, likable, reliable guy that everyone was happy to have around.

One more shot, of the exterior of the newly purchased van. And that was it. He'd come to the end…actually, the beginning. He'd gone through the whole dang thing, Lauren's entire Instagram.

His eyes were burning, and his back ached. He looked at the clock. Had he really wasted that much time on the internet? It didn't seem possible, but in a way it felt like he'd been gone a lot longer.

He got up, stretched, yawned, blinked. Compared to Lauren's van, his apartment looked cramped and dingy and pathetic. 'Course, those Instagram shots were all carefully staged and curated and whatnot, but still. His place wasn't even close to Instagram-able. It was barely livable.

Admittedly, he didn't have much to work with. An efficiency apartment. Micro kitchen, bar for eating, twin bed, narrow closet with accordion-style doors. Dirty laundry all over the floor.

Okay, maybe the dirty laundry wasn't an actual feature of the apartment, or the dirty dishes all over the counters. But the mess was a natural result of living in a small cheap place while working two jobs and maintaining a ranch *and* keeping up with a complex legal tangle. Better to save his money, and use his time and energy to work and earn more, and let the discomfort of his living conditions drive him to work harder.

At least, that's what he'd been telling himself. But in all honesty, it wasn't like having a dirty kitchen was helping him achieve his goals. If anything, it held him back, wasted his time by forcing him to scrounge for clean dishes, or wash a few at a time.

He cleaned the kitchen. Changed the sheets, made the bed. Picked up his laundry, sorted it, started three loads in the apartment complex's laundry room.

A paneled cupboard—Spanish, seventeenth century—stood in the corner. One door was completely off the hinges, and the bottom drawer was in pieces. He'd gotten the piece at Architectural Treasures—gotten it for a song, because it needed work, work he could do. He could see it in his mind, tenderly restored, standing in the dining room of his grandparents' house, once the house belonged to him.

But it had been sitting there in ruins for months now, ever since he'd brought it home. He'd told himself there was no hurry; it wasn't like he was very close to moving to the ranch. Just like there was no point in paying for a nicer apartment now, or exerting much effort in making it look good.

The dovetail joints of the large drawer needed repair, and the drawer and cabinet pulls were all loose, but the wood was sound. Not much more to it than some wood glue and band clamps, wood filler and new screws. No need to refinish; the old patina was gorgeous just the way it was.

He went to work. And while he worked, he thought of Lauren. He was coming to understand her better, had been ever since the reenactment festival. That whole in-the-moment thing wasn't just an excuse for a short attention span. It was the opposite. She focused her attention on what was right before her, appreciated it, experienced it to the full. It was kind of beautiful. He understood the appeal of van life better now, too. He still wouldn't want to do it, but he got it, a little.

And another thing. He had just spent an embarrassing amount of time online. Why had he gotten so drawn in? Because he was mad in an impersonal way that a woman had been so mistreated? No. That didn't explain three hours online stalking—yes, stalking— a woman and her ex, or the roller coaster of emotions he'd experienced with the different pictures. Everything from dizzy pleasure to deep-down rage that felt an awful lot like jealousy. Or how he'd kept going back chronologically, hungry to get more of her, even on an electronic level—to understand her, to know her.

All of which raised some disturbing questions. Was he actually falling for her? And if so, what was he going to do about it?

CHAPTER THIRTEEN

LAUREN HEARD ROSIE'S engine a microsecond before Durango started barking, which didn't even seem possible for a human being to do. But then, she was listening pretty hard. Alex had texted last night, Be at bunkhouse tomorrow a.m. Special delivery. He'd refused to say more.

What could it be? They'd already installed the refurbished doors with their hardware, and the new windows Alex had built. The ornate sconce and other light fixtures wouldn't go up until Lauren had made a decision on walls. What else was there, at least that Alex would be involved in? And why the secrecy?

He backed the truck close to the bunkhouse. Tony had cleared the area just that morning with the brush hog; the old chopped-up weed stalks were still lying on the ground.

When Alex stepped out of the truck, she was waiting for him. "Well? What is it?"

He smiled loftily. "You'll see."

He went around to the back and lowered the tailgate. Something was lying in the bed of the truck, covered with a blanket. Alex pulled back the blanket to reveal...

A pile of lumber.

A big sort of beam, maybe ten inches in width and depth, and five or six feet long. Two plank sections with wavy edges. Several smaller pieces roughly the size of floorboards, already cut in tongue and groove.

But it was the color that caught her attention: deep reddish-brown heartwood, dark and rich against pale yellow sapwood.

Lauren touched the beam. Its grain was wildly irregular, with several sworling knots; the surface felt silky smooth beneath her hand. "Is this...mesquite?"

Alex's face shone, and his words came out in a rush. "It's the mesquite that fell on the fence. I took it to this guy I know that runs a sawmill. He specializes in this kind of thing—milling lumber out of trees that have fallen down or have to be taken out. I couldn't be sure what we'd end up with until he took a look, but I thought we could probably count on a nice character piece, at least. So I just lopped off the branches, loaded it up, took it to the mill and told him to use his own judgment. He cut it up, and then he put all the pieces in the dryer for two weeks to kill bugs. I just picked it all up this morning. Do you like it?"

"I love it! Alex, you're a genius!"

He made a sort of modest face, not very convincing. "It's a little punky in spots, and it has some bug holes," he said, putting his finger into one small hole. "But I thought it turned out pretty nice, overall."

"The punky spots are part of what makes it great. It's perfect for the bunkhouse. This beam looks just the right size for the mantel. And we can use these plank sections for counters."

"That's just what I was thinking. I don't know about the flooring, though. There's not a lot of it, but it might do for an entry."

"Or even a small wall space, like at the back of the hallway. I think there might be just enough. Let's get it all inside."

"Hold on. There's one more thing. And this one isn't for the bunkhouse. It's for you."

He picked up a small piece wrapped separately in a towel and handed it to her.

"You'll have to excuse my gift-wrapping," he said. "I was in a hurry."

It was a little end-grain section, eight

inches or so in diameter, organically round-ish. The surface was glassy smooth, and the underside had little rubber feet.

"This is the only piece I requested special," Alex said. "It's a cutting board. The guy removed the sap wood and filled in all the checks in the surface with bar-top epoxy. The sides and bottom are coated with ure-thane, and the top is finished with butcher-block mineral oil. I thought it'd be a nice size for the kitchen in your van. I know you're not big on possessions, but I wanted you to have something from the bunkhouse renovation, to remember it by."

Tears welled up in her eyes. Pregnancy hor-mones again, no doubt.

"It's beautiful. Thank you."

"Are you *crying*?" Alex asked. He sounded alarmed.

"Just a little bit. I love it so much. Look at these growth rings. They're like a little cross section of time. One of them might be from the year Alejandro Ramirez went off to fight in the Texas Revolution."

"It's old enough. And did you know you can actually track years of drought and such in tree rings, if you know how? The rings from low-growth years are smaller."

"Are they really? I love that."

Alex smiled. "Tony would say I should have made it Texas-shaped, but I figured this was more your style."

They carried the wood to the bunkhouse, their voices and footsteps echoing in the empty, clean-smelling space. Chester the cat took the opportunity to slip inside with them.

"The place begins to look habitable," Alex said.

"I know, isn't it great? Doors and windows are all up, so varmints can't get in anymore, and the plumbers and electricians have come and gone. From this point on it'll all be pretty much play—at least until it's time to refinish the floors, but that'll have to wait for last."

"Good thing there's no central air, otherwise you would have raccoon-infested air ducts to deal with."

"True. I think Dalia would like to install central heat and air down the line, but that'll be a big expense. For now we have the fireplace, and we can set up window units."

They took the beam to the fireplace and hefted it into place above the brick facade.

It fit the space perfectly.

"Did you give the dimensions to the wood-milling guy?" Lauren asked.

"No! I didn't even measure."

They both stared a moment.

"That's almost spooky," Alex said.

"It's destiny. This beam was meant to go here. I'm going to have to figure out what to do about this brick before it goes up, though."

The brick was unbelievably ugly—bland in color, with harsh, razor-sharp edges that looked out of character with the rest of the house. They set down the beam, and Chester immediately hopped on top of it.

"It's pretty hideous, all right," Alex said. "Probably added in the sixties."

"I wonder what it's even *doing* here," said Lauren. "Whose idea was it? Why didn't they use the same stone they used on the exterior of the house?"

Alex got a dreamy look on his face. "Oh, Lauren, you should see the fireplace at my grandparents' house. It's faced in limestone taken from the property. The limestone has fossils in it. I used to just sit and stare at it when I was a kid."

"Oh, I love that. I wish we could do something like that in here. But I'm already cutting things close budget-wise. I can't afford to hire a mason. I'll just have to work with what's on hand. I guess I could paint the brick, but that might look too modern. Whitewash would be better, but it wouldn't solve the problem of those sharp lines and corners."

Alex rubbed his chin. "What if you did a German smear?"

"What's that?"

"It's a little like whitewash, but instead of dilute paint, you cover the bricks with a layer of wet mortar. You smear it on to get an irregular look and let some of the brick show through. It would give a nice rough texture and soften those harsh lines."

"Is it hard to do? Expensive?"

"Nah, total DIY job, very affordable. A little labor-intensive, but doesn't take much skill. All you need is a bag of premixed mortar, a five-gallon bucket, a grout sponge and a trowel."

"Is it a one-day job?"

"For a surface this size? Not even half a day."

Lauren stared at the ugly fireplace. She imagined it coated with the German smear, with the mantel installed.

She looked at Alex. He was looking at her.

"You want to?" he asked. "We could go to the hardware store right now, get it done today."

"Do you have any place you have to be?"

"Not 'til this evening, when I go to the garage."

"You sure you want to spend your day this way?"

"What am I gonna do, sit around sipping mimosas? I like doing stuff like this."

"Then let's get going."

"I DO HAVE one concern," Lauren said on the way into town.

They had Rosie's windows down. It was a clear, sunny November day—the sort of Texas day, Alex said, that made up for the harsh summers.

"Oh, yeah? What's that?"

"Would a German smear be appropriate period- and place-wise?"

Usually Alex was the one who raised questions about historical correctness, and Lauren who tried to come up with a justification. But this time Alex had a comeback ready.

"Oh, that's easy. There were lots of German settlers in Texas. There are whole communities where you can see a strong German influence even today in the culture and architecture. Our cowboy could have a German mother, or he might have known some Germans growing up. Or maybe he just saw features of German architecture out and about, and always admired them. Or he might have hired a German mason."

The shopping trip felt like other trips she'd made over the years with her father. The whole process was familiar: puzzling together over how to solve some house problem, brainstorming solutions, weighing pros and cons. The eureka moment of the idea they both instinctively knew was right.

Walking with Alex in the hardware store was a lot like walking with Alex at the festival, a constant stream of greetings and pleasantries.

"Do you know *everyone* in this town?" Lauren asked.

"Pretty much."

Back at the bunkhouse, they mixed the mortar slurry in a bucket, then smeared the slurry over the brick with grout sponges. Almost as soon as they'd covered the whole area, it was time to start removing the excess with the trowel.

Sooner than seemed possible, they were done, standing side by side with their hands on their hips, gloating.

"Oh, yeah," Alex said. "This was the right choice."

It really was.

Alex fetched another camp chair out of Vincent's garage while Lauren grabbed two bottles of kombucha. Back at the bunkhouse, Chester was waiting at the front door. They'd shut him out during the actual work, lest he dip a paw in the slurry. Now he bounded confidently inside, then stopped short with a surprised chirrup when he saw the refurbished hearth.

They set the camp chairs in front of the fireplace and drank their kombucha. Chester alternated between laps, purring and rubbing with all his might.

"This place is gonna be really special," Alex said. "You've put a lot of yourself into it."

He had his legs stretched out toward the hearth and crossed at the ankles, and he was smiling his half smile at Lauren with his head tilted back lazily in his chair and his eyes half-shut.

"So have you," Lauren said. "You did all the windows and the front door. And the German smear was your idea. I never would have thought of it without you."

"True. It's a pretty good feeling, isn't it?"

"It is. There are a whole lot of houses where I grew up that my dad and I left our mark on."

"I would think it'd be hard to walk away from that. A house is so personal. Once you put so much of yourself into it, how do you leave it?"

"It was hard, especially with our first house. I was still pretty little when we left it. That was the house where my mother had lived, and leaving it felt like giving *her* up, not just the work we'd done on the place. But it was the right thing to do. We'd increased the value substantially, and we needed the money. The whole point of flipping houses was that it was something my dad could do at home, staying close to me. So when we left that first house, he gave me one of the original corner blocks from the window casement in the master bedroom. It was too cracked and chipped to reuse, but still beautiful. And it's tied to the only clear memory I have of my mother. After she got sick, she ended up confined to bed, and I had my little Playskool desk set up in the corner of the room, right by that window. I'd sit there and color while she rested and watched me. I still have that corner block now, and whenever I see it I remember the feeling of being in that room with her. And ever since then, with every house my dad and I have lived in and fixed up, we took something along when we left. So now I can look at those things, and remember."

"I've seen that corner-block thing. It's in your van, isn't it? Up on the shelf above the bed?"

"It is. That's where I keep all my old house keepsakes. Oh, I can't wait until Tony and Dalia get to see this place! But I *will* wait. I'm not giving them any peeks. They won't see a thing until the whole project is finished. They're gonna freak."

"Dalia doesn't freak very often. She's pretty chill."

"Well, I would defy even Dalia's chill to hold out against the awesomeness that will be the finished bunkhouse."

Alex looked at his watch. "I'd better head to the garage. Someone brought in a tractor that needs its carburetor overhauled."

"Sounds like a fun evening for you."

They put Chester out of the bunkhouse and locked the door.

"Hey, listen," Alex said. "There's going to be a reenactment of the Battle of Béxar in downtown San Antonio in December. Would you like to go with me?"

This wasn't much like how they'd ended up going to the other event together. Tony had set that up, and Alex had agreed with great reluctance. It also wasn't like how she would have imagined Alex asking her to another one. That whole would-you-like-to-go-with-me thing sounded...well, almost like a date.

And before she could stop herself, she felt a bright flare of hope and pleasure at the prospect.

Oh, get over yourself, Lauren. Not every guy is into you. Alex is just being a good friend—and that's all you want him to be.

"All right," she said. "That sounds like a good time."

"It is. I really think you'll enjoy it."

"What is Béxar? You say it's in San Antonio?"

"Yeah, near the Alamo. But this isn't the actual Battle of the Alamo, where all the defenders died—Travis and Bowie and Crockett and those guys. This is the battle where the Texians first took the Alamo, and the town, San Antonio de Béxar. Before that, the Mexicans had it. What a lot of people don't know is that after the Texians won, Sam Houston ordered them to take the artillery and blow up the Alamo and get out of there. San Antonio de Béxar was strategically insignificant, and too close to Mexico to be defensible. Trying to hold on to it was a waste of resources."

"I never knew that. Why didn't they do it?"

"Because they were a bunch of stubborn daredevils who didn't like being told what to do. That's the kind of man who went to Texas—brave, determined, ornery and arrogant. It's a good personality type for settling a wild and dangerous country, but it doesn't make for a very cohesive army. They fought together when and where they wanted to, and left when they got bored or disagreed with the plan. They basically took orders as suggestions. They did have some impressive victories with that fighting style, but they also wasted a lot of effort and life. It's amazing the army held together as well as it did."

"So you're saying the whole Alamo disaster never should have happened?"

"That's right. But at the same time, it ended up being a rallying cry for the revolution. It unified Houston's army like nothing else could have done. In the long run, it was more powerful as a symbol than as a stronghold."

"That's…sad, but cool."

He drove off, and Lauren went back to Vincent. Over a cup of motherhood tea, she started browsing the internet for travel destinations. December was creeping up fast, and she had no idea where she wanted to go after leaving La Escarpa. The whole point of being here was to regroup and figure out where to go next, but for almost the first time since she'd started traveling, there really wasn't anyplace she had a burning desire to see. Where should she go? East coast, west coast? North, south? Midwest? Canada? Mountains? Desert? Ocean? Forest? Nothing sounded appealing, and she was having trouble concentrating.

Maybe she was trying too hard. Maybe she should give the subject a rest and wait for inspiration to strike. It had never failed her yet.

In the meantime, she'd allow herself to daydream about what color of plaster to use in the bunkhouse, and whether the wavy-edged mesquite planks would work better as counters or kitchen shelves.

CHAPTER FOURTEEN

LAUREN HURRIED OVER the bridge, head down against the driving wind. Dead leaves scudded along the sidewalk. Underfoot, below street level, she caught a quick glimpse of big trees hung with Christmas lights, and more lights along the eaves of buildings, and bright flashes of water, but it was too cold to stop and drink in the sight.

She checked her phone's screen. Alex's blip had been in Alamo Plaza since midafternoon, when he'd joined other reenactors to set up camp for the night. Now it was moving her way.

And there was Alex himself, glancing back and forth between his phone's screen and the crowd.

He saw her, and his face lit up. "You made it!"

"I made it. What are you wearing? That's not your usual outfit."

The jacket had the same shape as the other

one, but it was red, and he had on high black boots instead of the ankle boots he usually wore.

"I've had this one for a while. I've worn it every year I've reenacted at Béxar. Come on. It's not much farther to the plaza."

They walked fast. It was too cold not to.

"Did you find the parking garage okay?" he asked.

"Easy peasy. I parked Vincent between a couple of tough-looking trucks. I've got plenty of juice in my battery, so I should sleep warm tonight."

Alex had been careful to make the accommodation situation perfectly clear ahead of time.

"Some of us, the hard-core people, like to camp out in our tents in the plaza the night before," he'd told her. "You're welcome to try that if you want, but it's supposed to get down to the thirties that night, and the canvas isn't much defense against the wind."

"You make it sound superappealing, but I think I'll just park Vincent downtown and sleep in my own bed. That'll be no rougher than I'm used to."

"That's what I figured. In that case, there's a good parking garage that ought to be safe."

So that was a relief. He hadn't invited her to sleep in his tent, or assumed that she'd want to. There would be no awkwardness or weird expectations. Clearly this was another just-friends situation.

In the plaza, the tents were circled around a dozen or so reenactors sitting by a camp-fire. Behind them, the Alamo's unmistakable stone facade, bright with floodlights, loomed up crisp against the night sky. Someone was playing "What Child Is This?" on guitar.

The reenactors saw Lauren and Alex com-ing and let out a cheer. Lauren recognized Tamara and Jay, and Ron the gunsmith, and a few others. They looked like such a brave, plucky, game little group, all huddled together under their blankets, that Lauren laughed.

"You guys sure are dedicated," she said when she reached them. "It's *cold*. Wicked cold. I think it's dropped twenty degrees since I drove away this afternoon. How can it be this cold this far south?"

"It's 'cause there aren't any east-to-west mountain ranges," Alex said. "When a north wind blows, there's nothing to break it up. My grandfather used to say the only thing stand-ing between Texas and the Arctic Circle is a barbed-wire fence."

"Just as well," said Ron. "It's more historically accurate this way. It was cold at the Siege of Béxar, but that didn't stop the Texians, and it won't stop us."

"Yeah, and we've got something the Texians didn't have," said Alex.

He stirred a dark liquid that was steaming nicely in a kettle hung over the fire. "My Mexican hot chocolate. Almost ready."

"Ooh, lovely," Lauren said. "But is there time for an interview first?"

"If it's a short one."

She started the video camera on her phone and framed Alex in it.

"Sir! Can you tell me about what's going on here tonight at the Alamo Plaza?"

"Yes, I can! We're a historical society, and we've gathered here for a reenactment of the Siege of Béxar, an important event in the Texas Revolution. Back in the fall of 1835, following the Come and Take It battle on October the second, forces continued to gather in Gonzales, and they eventually combined to more or less form the Texian army. Stephen Austin was elected commander, because that's how commanders were chosen back then. Meanwhile, Santa Anna sent his brother-in-law, General Cos, to Béxar with reinforcements. Then in mid-October, Austin led his men to Béxar and settled in for a siege. There were several minor engagements associated with this siege, but what we're going to reenact tomorrow is the final battle, when the Texians stormed the town and took the Alamo."

Alex was terrific in front of a camera—a good talker, and unbelievably photogenic. He looked up at the camera now with his half smile and said, "And just like the real Texian army, we reenactors have our own issues with deserters, because it can get really cold out here overnight in a period-correct canvas tent. Only in our case, the deserters go to a hotel."

"I can't say I'm surprised. Just how period-correct are you inside those tents? Do you sleep on bedrolls, or are you hiding air mattresses and catalytic heaters in there?"

Alex looked smug. "Well, I can't speak for everyone, but you won't find anything like that in *my* tent. I pride myself on being a strict historical interpreter. The most I might do is heat up some stones in the fire and put them under my blanket."

The guitar player spoke up. "Dude! There are better ways of staying warm in a tent. Skin-on-skin contact is the way to go."

It was Zander, the guy who'd left a valuable antique gun out in the rain to make it look more "authentic."

Alex scowled. "Wow, Zander. Real mature."

"You're the one who's cuddling with rocks, *teniente*."

"Punk, shut up! She's filming this."

"All right, all right. You don't have to be so sensitive."

"It's okay," Lauren told Alex. "I can edit that part out. So what time is the event tomorrow?"

"We'll be doing two battle reenactments, at ten and two. In between, there'll be reenactors set up at La Villita, ready to give presentations to visitors. A tour guide will lead groups through the various stops. The wind's supposed to die down by morning, so show up early and spend the day on the beautiful San Antonio River Walk for one-stop Christmas shopping and Texas history."

Lauren stopped recording. "Nice! I'll edit it back in my van and post it tonight. Now give me some hot chocolate."

"Yes, ma'am."

Alex poured the hot chocolate into an assortment of mismatched mugs and handed

them around. Even Zander got one. He was
playing "O Holy Night" now. He was good,
but Lauren was feeling pretty soured on guitar players.

She wrapped her hands around her mug
and felt the warmth seeping into her fingers.
She wished she'd dressed warmer. Maybe she
should walk back to Vincent and add some
layers.

Everyone was sitting around the fire on
cushions and blankets and low camp chairs.
Alex had a cozy-looking nest with a big cushion and a striped blanket draped over his
shoulders.

He looked at Lauren and lifted an arm,
opening his blanket like a wing, in wordless
invitation.

Lauren didn't hesitate and crawled in beside him. It would be silly to sit there and
freeze when a human furnace was ready and
willing to provide heat.

She settled her back against his chest. He
closed the blanket over her, and his arms went
around her in a deliciously warm cocoon of
security and comfort and—and something
more, something she didn't want to put a
word to just yet. It felt so good, so safe and
right, that she just relaxed into the embrace

and didn't think about the consequences anymore. Alex's solid warmth behind and around
her, the smell of wood smoke and chocolate,
the beauty of the town and plaza, Christmas
music and firelight, all came together in the
loveliest sense of contentment.

The rest of the evening passed like a dream.
She could hear Alex's voice behind her and
feel it resonate in his chest as they sang one
carol after another. None of this seemed real.
It was too perfect and too improbable. She let
it carry her along in a tide of happiness.

When at last the fire burned down and
Zander put away his guitar, she felt like she
was coming back after a long time away.

She started to get up. Alex slipped out of
the blanket and wrapped it around her like
she was a small child. She stood there, clutch-
ing the blanket, as he gathered the hot chocolate mugs and put them inside the kettle.

She could see inside Alex's tent a little. She
knew it was his because she recognized the
rip in the canvas, mended with big stitches. A
thin slice of bedroll, neatly laid out, showed
through the opening at the flap.

Then she saw him, looking at her looking
inside his tent. He smiled awkwardly, and she
felt her face grow warm in spite of the cold.

Zander stood up and slung his gig bag over his shoulder. "I'm deserting to the Hyatt," he announced to no one in particular. "Who's joining me?"

"Traitor," someone said.

"Tenderfoot," said someone else.

He smiled a superior smile and looked at Lauren. "What about you? Are you going back to civilization, or will you stay here and keep warm with rocks?"

"I'm sleeping in my van," she said.

The words came out a lot more forcibly than she'd intended. She wanted there to be no doubt about it, in spite of what might have appeared to be longing looks inside Alex's tent, but she wasn't sure who she thought needed convincing.

"Ooh," said Zander. "How edgy of you."

"Come on, Lauren," said Alex. "I'll walk you."

The streets were almost empty now, and the wind had lessened, but it was still cold. They walked in silence. Sooner than seemed possible, they reached the parking garage.

"I'll be making breakfast for everyone around eight," Alex said. "Coffee, eggs, chorizo. You're welcome to join us. Then you'll be all set to start the tour around nine."

"Okay."

She unlocked Vincent and slid the big side door open.

"Sure is dark in there," Alex said.

"Yeah, I put up my magnetized window shades after I parked."

"They really are perfectly fitted to the windows, aren't they? They don't let in so much as a sliver of the outside. You've got a whole little world of your own in here, and nobody passing by has a clue."

"That's one of the things I love about it. Feeling all snug and secret and safe, like a chipmunk in a burrow."

Alex chuckled. "A chipmunk with a hot plate and an electric kettle."

His smile faded, and his gaze sharpened. For one heart-flipping moment Lauren thought he was going to kiss her.

Then he was walking away, saying goodnight over his shoulder.

"Good night," she called after him. "Thanks for the hot chocolate."

She shut the door and let out her breath. Her hands were shaking, and not with cold.

ALEX HAD BEEN doing his Alejandro Ramirez spiel for so many years now that he didn't even have to think about it. He never got self-conscious or experienced anything like stage fright. He knew what he was saying and felt perfectly at ease saying it.

But when he saw Lauren in the crowd around the porch of the adobe building where he'd stationed himself, something changed.

It wasn't like he was surprised to see her. He'd known she would be here; he'd seen her not two hours earlier at the campsite, eating chorizo and scrambled eggs that he'd made with his own hands. But the sight of her, right here and now, in her mango-colored coat, with her camera slung over her shoulder and her cheeks flushed in the cold morning air, stunned and amazed him. And when he said the familiar words for the umpteenth time that day, he didn't just tell Alejandro's story. He stepped into his skin, took on his hopes, his fears, his resolve.

"My name is Alejandro Ramirez. I am a ranchero with land near Béxar. Six weeks ago I left my rancho and my young bride to join the siege of Béxar under my captain, Juan Seguín. For Tejanos like myself, it was difficult to decide which side to take in the conflict. Texas is our home, but we are Mexicans by birth and language and culture, and the flood of Anglo settlers troubles us. We hardly recognize our home anymore. We fear that in time these new Anglo colonists will crowd us out. But I love my country, and when Santa Anna suspended the Mexican Constitution, my own course was plain. I am a republican, not a monarchist. I believe that man was made for liberty, not to cower under tyrants. I may be cast off, I may be dispossessed, I may be exiled from my home, but I will not flinch from my duty. I will keep faith. I will fight to the death for Texas independence."

And Lauren listened, her eyes dark and shining and fixed on him, like he mattered more than anything else in the world—like there wasn't anything else in the world, just the two of them.

Then he finished, and the group moved on, and the spell was broken. He was being idiotic, reading so much into a facial expression.

She's just paying attention, that's all. In the moment. It's no different than how she looks at a piece of moss she's taking a picture of, or a fireplace brick she's smearing with mortar slurry. It doesn't mean anything.

Unless it did.

The groups kept cycling through the different reenactors' stations until about a quarter to ten. Lauren came back to Alex then.

"Having a good time?" he asked.

"Oh, yes. I've met Ben Milam and Juan Seguín, and some New Orleans Greys, and even General Cos—a very sassy General Cos, who threatened to have us taken away for interrogation when he found out we had been talking to people on the Texian side. But we gave him the slip."

"Good for you."

He shouldered his Escopeta. "This siege has gone on long enough. Time to storm the fortress and take back the town."

BLACK SMOKE CLOUDED the plaza, and the air rang with the cracking shots of muskets and rifles and the louder booms of cannons. Lauren watched from a spot that gave her a good view of Alex—information that Tamara had kindly volunteered.

La Villita was a historical district, one block square, with architecture ranging from adobe to Texas vernacular limestone to early Victorian. She'd learned that much from the internet. A fountain stood in the center, and big live oak trees shaded the plaza.

Her visits to the various reenactors had

been interspersed with skirmishes all along, with Mexican soldiers and Texians taking shots at each other from porches, around buildings and behind iron fencing and stone walls. But now they were fighting in earnest in the open plaza—Mexican soldiers on one side, Texians on the other.

The Mexican soldiers wore white trousers and dark blue uniform coats with red cuffs and sashes and gold trim. There weren't many uniforms on the Texian side other than the New Orleans Greys; the freedom fighters were a ragtag bunch, with their fringed frontier shirts in linen and leather, and wool coats in various colors.

And then there was Alex, in his red jacket and knee breeches, high black boots, black sash and black hat with the brim rolled up in the back. Leather straps crossed his back and chest, holding his cartridge box, canteen and powder horn.

He made his way forward now, advancing on the fortifications, with a quick glance over his shoulder and a follow-me gesture to his men. Fire and load, fire and load, over and over. Grim and determined, businesslike and cool.

Then he jerked back like something had

hit him, and dropped like a stone to the brick pavement.

He's been shot. Some moron actually loaded a ball into a Mexican musket and shot him.

Lauren stood frozen in shock, waiting for one of the reenactors to yell for a cease-fire and do something for him. But the battle went on as if nothing unexpected had happened.

And then Lauren remembered. This was the battle where Alejandro Ramirez was killed.

Alex lay perfectly still with arms outstretched, eyes shut, and the Escopeta at his side. But no blood spread across his waistcoat or pooled on the paving tiles beneath him, and she could see his chest rising and falling slowly.

Lauren's own breath was coming fast and shallow, and her knees suddenly felt weak with relief. She gripped a nearby stone pillar for support.

This is who he is. That's why he's so good at it—because he knows that if he were in Alejandro Ramirez's place, he'd do the same thing. He'd risk everything for what he loves and believes in, and die fighting.

COLD WATER RAN down Alex's parched throat. The cedar canteen gave it a sharp flavor, like some kind of nineteenth-century sports drink. Sitting on a stone ledge that circled a live oak tree, he downed the whole canteen in one go. All that firing and loading, the noise and smoke, hour after hour, coming on the tail of a none-too-restful night in a tent, really wore on a guy.

"Tired?"

Lauren smiled down at him, looking as fresh and flawless as a just-opened blossom.

"A little. But I've still got to break camp, so I can't get too comfortable."

"I'll help. After a full day of freedom fighting, you deserve a break."

He was used to packing and loading his gear alone, and Lauren was an experienced camp packer herself. Within minutes they had everything stowed under Rosie's camper shell.

"Have you ever been to the River Walk before?" Alex asked.

"No."

"It's beautiful, especially at Christmastime. As a Texan I feel obliged to make sure you experience it."

"All right. But first, let's get you cleaned

up. You've still got some black powder on your face."

She got a paper towel from Tamara and dampened it with water from a wooden bucket. She started to reach up to his face, then said, "You're too tall. Sit down on this crate."

Alex obediently sat, and let her wipe his face clean like a child. Her eyebrows were drawn down a bit in concentration, which was cute, but what mostly held his attention was the fact that her chest was at a much-closer-than-usual level to his eyes. Her coat was unbuttoned now, revealing an emerald-colored sweater that ran smoothly over the contours of her form. Before long he was practically in a trance.

She lifted his chin, took a last searching look and smiled. "There. All done. You ready?"

Alex was in fact suddenly ready for a lot of things, and a stroll on the River Walk was pretty far down on the list.

THE RIVER WALK.

Big trees—oaks, palms, cypress. Flower beds crowded with lush tropical plants, impossibly green and bursting with bloom. A complex system of masonry—arches, alcoves, bridges, benches, ledges, stairways. Patio eating spaces sheltered with colorful umbrellas. Swags of Christmas lights.

Alex still had his reenactor clothes on. People stared and smiled as he walked past. One guy in a Spurs sweatshirt laid a hand on his arm to stop him.

"Hey, you were one of the reenactors at the thing today. You were the one that got shot, right?"

"That's right."

"Man, you're a good actor, you know that? I thought for a minute you'd been shot for real. You didn't ham it up or fall all awkward or anything. You nailed it."

"Thank you, I appreciate that. I was playing my great-great-great-great-grandfather, who died at Béxar, and it's important to me to represent him well."

"That's so cool. Thank you for doing all that with the reenactment, for giving to the community that way. I know it must be a lot of work."

"It is. But people like you make it all worthwhile."

The guy turned to Lauren. "What about you? Do you ever dress up with him?"

Lauren's mind went blank. "Um…"

Alex rescued her. "She's still pretty new to the whole scene."

"Ah, I gotcha. Well, I'm sure it's only a matter of time before she gets sucked in."

Then he nodded goodbye to them both. "Merry Christmas to you."

"Merry Christmas," they said.

"Does that happen a lot?" Lauren asked as they walked on. "Accolades from your adoring public?"

"Oh, yeah, all the time. I'm a major celebrity in the greater San Antonio area."

"It's true, though, what he said. You are serving the community, keeping Texas history alive in people's hearts and minds."

"Yeah, and that's important. But it's not just the history, you know? I want to remind people that things like courage and honor are real."

"What do you mean?"

"I mean people used to believe in good things more than they do today. Nowadays you just mention words like *patriotism* and *faithfulness*, and everyone's guard goes up. If something looks really solid and good, people think there must be something wrong with it that they can't see yet. And they don't want to get fooled, so they act all snide. They make fun. And if you're the one who's talking about the very good thing, you have to throw some irony in there to show that you're not taking it too seriously. And I think that's sad. I mean, I get that people don't want to be taken in, but this is more than that. It's like people don't even believe in the possibility of virtue anymore, the whole idea of it. I'm not gullible, but I would rather believe in things and be wrong once in a while than be cynical about every single thing just so I can say I saw it coming when something does fail. I don't want to be that guy."

"Well, you're succeeding. You're probably the most unironic person I know. *Oh!* Oh, my gosh. *Look* at that. Is that the most amazing thing you've ever seen?"

They'd reached a restaurant, and a server was walking past with a cast-iron platter filled with sizzling fajitas. The aroma made Lauren's mouth water.

"I am *so* hungry. Are you hungry? You have to be—you haven't had anything since breakfast, and neither have I. I want that exact fajita platter *right now.*"

"I can't let you take those people's food, but I can do the next best thing."

He stepped over to a little outdoor hostess station.

"Two, please."

They were seated at a round table close to the river's edge. When the chips and salsa came, Lauren dug in, but the salsa burned her mouth and made her nose run. She watched in disbelief as Alex went on calmly eating chips mounded high with the stuff.

"How can you do that?" she asked him. "How is your mouth not on fire?"

"I don't know. It's in my blood, I guess."

"It's not in mine. The Delaware Valley was not settled by spice-loving cultures."

Their fajitas arrived, just as sizzling and fragrant as the ones that had lured Lauren in—long strips of juicy meat mingled with browned slices of onion and red and green bell pepper.

"What a gorgeous sight," Lauren said. "And look, they're even Christmas-colored."

That was the end of the talking for a while. They ate and ate of the tender, flavorful meat and vegetables. It was restful, Lauren thought, eating with someone you didn't have to keep up a conversation with all the time.

Alex leaned back in his chair with a contented sigh and laid a hand on his perfectly flat abdomen. "Got to let my belt out a notch or two," he said.

Lauren laughed. "As if."

She leaned back, too. A riverboat passed by, filled with people. More people drank glasses of dark beer at a bar across the river. Someone, somewhere, was playing "O Christmas Tree" on a trumpet.

"What a lovely place. Do you come here every year at Christmastime?"

"I do now, because of the reenactment. It wasn't a tradition when I was growing up, though."

"My dad was heavy on tradition. I think he wanted to make sure I didn't miss out. We always spent holidays away from home so there would be lots of cousins for me to play with. My grandmother would make orange cheese at Christmas—it's this custard thing, an old Quaker recipe, very good—and lots of pies. We had pretty, sparkly, storybook Christmases—lots of lights, decorations, music. It was fun."

"That sounds amazing. Our Christmases weren't all that great. Dinner at my grandparents' was always good, and my mom did her best, but it was such a stressful time overall that it was hard to relax and enjoy the good parts."

"Why was it so stressful?"

"Well, we always had money troubles, and holidays just made it worse. And my dad would not let up on the gambling for one minute. He used to give me and Tony those scratch-off cards in our Christmas stockings—which I guess could be fine for some families, in moderation, but my dad was never moderate, and he made way too big a deal out of the whole thing. He'd get us everything from the little ones where you win a few dollars to the pricier ones that can bring in four figures. Mostly we wouldn't win anything—because that's, you know, how lotteries work—but sometimes we'd win a little. Usually not enough to break even on the cost of the cards themselves, though, and eventually I figured this out. I said to my dad, why not just take the money you would have spent on the scratch-offs, and put *that* in our stockings?"

"What did he say to that?"

"He said I was an uptight killjoy who needed to lighten up. I was eleven at the time."

"Wow. That's harsh."

"Yeah. And then the very next year, I actually won a thousand dollars on one of my Christmas stocking scratch-offs."

"No way!"

"Yep. And my dad was all like, 'See? What'd I tell you? I knew your ship was going to come in.' He was as happy and excited as I was—like how he'd get with Tony over football, like I'd done something that made him proud."

"What did you spend the money on?"

"Well, I *wanted* to get a horse of my own and keep it at the ranch. I could have gotten a pretty decent older horse for a thousand dollars. But a few days later, the card disappeared."

"Oh, no!"

"Yeah. I freaked when I couldn't find it, ransacked my room. Turned out my dad had redeemed the winnings himself and then 'invested' them at the blackjack table. And now the money was gone, all of it, and then some. He didn't apologize. Didn't even admit he'd done anything wrong. He talked about it like it was some kind of *account* he'd set up for me, and sooner or later it was gonna make money, and when it did the money would be all mine, and way more than the original thousand. 'Course, none of that ever happened. But if I were to ask him about it today, I *guarantee* he'd just say the account was currently in the red but that he expected it to turn around any day now."

"Gosh, Alex. What do you even do after something like that?"

He gave a dry chuckle. "I'll tell you what I did. The next Christmas, when I pulled the scratch-offs out of my stocking—yes, he did it again—I threw them straight into the fireplace. Man, the look on his face! He busted my butt, but it was worth it. I never got another scratch-off in my Christmas stocking again. Tony did, but I didn't."

"Did you get the equivalent amount of money instead?"

"Are you kidding? Of course not."

Lauren thought of cozy Christmases with her extended family. She was the youngest grandchild; her cousins were always extra nice to her and her aunts all seemed to be trying to load her up with enough mothering to last the rest of the year. She felt wrung with pity for eleven-year-old Alex, with his modest, never-to-be-realized dream of owning a horse. But there was something valiant about twelve-year-old Alex, defying his father by refusing to take part in a system he despised.

"Sorry," said Alex. "Didn't mean to be such a Debbie Downer."

Something about the way he said this struck Lauren as hilarious. She let out a strangled squeal of laughter, started coughing and had to take a drink of water to clear her throat. When she had her voice under control, she said, "Well, you're grown up now, so your holidays are what you make them. Have you come up with any Christmas traditions of your own?"

"Oh, yeah, you bet. Working all the hours I possibly can, and stocking up on marked-down grocery items afterward. Last year I got a dope party platter for pennies on the dollar, and enough butter to last me 'til spring."

"That can't be all you do. What about your mom? Do you see her?"

"She lives in Longview now with her husband. I like the guy, he's good to her, but it's too far to visit very often, especially with my work schedule, and taking care of the ranch."

"That's not right. You need some holiday traditions—*fun* holiday traditions."

He thought a moment. "Well, how 'bout

this right now? This is pretty nice, don't you think?"

Did he mean the Siege of Béxar reenactment and the River Walk afterward, or the reenactment and the River Walk with her? He couldn't possibly be hinting at a future for the two of them together...could he?

Of course not. It was just the sort of thing people said. "Let's get together and do this every year," they'd say, but no one ever did.

Well, most people never did. But Alex? Was anything ever just talk with him?

Careful, she told herself. *Be sensible.*

Then sensible got swallowed up in a great swelling wave of joy, made up of stonework and trees, stately old architecture, festive music, happy people, good food...and Alex. He was a sensory experience in himself, with his amber eyes and his glossy black hair and his clothing from two centuries ago. He still gave off a faint whiff of sulfur from the blackpowder shooting once in a while, and he had a tiny black smudge in the corner of his eye. He was so easy to be with, so strangely familiar, and yet he kept surprising her with unexpected depths.

"Yes," she said. "Yes, it is."

They sat there a moment, smiling awkwardly at each other and not saying anything, until a duck came sauntering up and gave Alex an expectant look.

"Give me a fajita," Lauren said in a cranky and entitled duck voice.

Alex didn't miss a beat. "Sorry, bro," he said to the duck. "No fajitas for you. It's bad for you to eat people food."

"Don't care," said Lauren-as-duck. "Want a fajita. Give it to me."

"Listen, you hungry? You go catch a bug out of the river. That's your natural food."

"No. Beef skirt steak is my natural food. With bell peppers and onions."

"You mean to tell me you take down domestic cattle in the wild? Let's see you do it."

Alex deadpanned his part perfectly, and the duck cocked its head like it had been caught in a lie.

"Give me a tortilla chip, then," Lauren said. By now she could barely keep her duck voice steady.

"No can do. Feeding the ducks at the River Walk is prohibited."

In perfect comedic timing, the duck suddenly lifted its wings at Alex in a mildly aggressive gesture.

Alex held his hands up peaceably. "Whoa!

Whoa! I don't want trouble here, man. You got a problem, take it up with the San Antonio River Authority."

The duck stared at him a second more, then abruptly turned and ambled back toward the water.

"'Kay then," Lauren said in the duck voice. "'Bye."

"All right then," Alex said. "Peace out."

"Yeah. Keep it real."

The server brought their check. Alex took it before it had a chance to touch the table, and paid in a low-key but masterful way.

The sun had gone down, and the Christmas lights glowed in the twilight. Lauren and Alex walked slowly, without any destination in mind. Sometimes Lauren stopped to take a picture. One small curved nook of a stone railing offered a terrific view of some old architecture across the river. She got several shots from there, then set her camera on the railing to review them.

Suddenly she felt a presence just behind her, a big, warm presence that smelled of black powder and woodsmoke.

"You get some good pics?"

His voice was so near. He wasn't touching her, but she felt his breath on the top of her head.

"Mmm-hmm. Want to see?"

"Yeah."

She scrolled through some of the shots. He made comments, and she supposed she replied, but she hardly heard what either of them said. She couldn't think about anything, feel anything, other than the solid six-plus feet and hundred-and-eighty-some-odd pounds of man standing bare inches away.

Something brushed along the nape of her neck. Her hair was down, and he'd just drawn it all sideways, off the collar of her coat. She shivered, though her body temperature had definitely just gone up. Her heart hammered in her chest; she could actually hear the frantic *swoosh-swoosh* of her own pulse in her head.

He waited, like he was giving her a chance to draw away. She turned her head and saw him looking down at her with a question in his face.

Then he leaned in and kissed her.

He kissed her.

He'd waited so long to do this. Agonized

over it. Doubted himself. Was the timing right? Did she even want it?

But he'd seen the answer seconds ago in her eyes, and now he felt her mouth against his, kissing him back. She turned and faced him, and as he circled her with his arms he had just enough rational ability left to think *Careful, don't knock over the camera*. Then her smooth, cool little hand was on his face, his neck. He pulled her close.

A loud cheer broke out, which didn't exactly make sense, but seemed kind of fitting, really. Lauren broke away enough to see where it was coming from. A crowd of college-age kids across the river was applauding them.

"Time-travel romance!"

"I love that trope."

"Hope the dude isn't fated to die at the Alamo."

Lauren chuckled and looked back up at Alex. She was more beautiful than ever.

They waved at the appreciative crowd, who cheered them even louder.

"I've been wanting to do that a long time," he said. His voice sounded strange to him, sort of young. "I almost did it last night, but

I stopped myself just in time because I didn't want our first kiss to be in a parking garage."

Man, that sounded dumb. Talking about "our first kiss," like he was fifteen or something.

"I wondered why you ran away all of a sudden," Lauren said. Her voice sounded funny, too.

"Yeah, it was touch-and-go for a minute there. I had to, like, spin myself around and propel myself away."

She slid her hand down his chest. "You chose your moment well."

They made up for lost time now. They kissed under a mountain laurel tree, under a bridge, on top of the same bridge, in front of a Starbucks. They walked, held hands, joined a group of carolers for a few songs. Alex felt like he'd just woken up after being asleep for months, full of energy and life. Everything he saw was brilliant and spectacular—every sparkling wave on the river, every star in the sky, every leaf and stone. It was as if he'd never really lived until now—as if everything up until now had been a prelude to this night.

He wanted it to go on forever, but well before midnight he walked her to her van. Some precipitation was supposedly on its way, and he wanted her safely home before the roads got wet.

"I'll be over Monday with the plaster samples for the bunkhouse," he said. "Text me when you get home so I'll know you made it, okay?"

She smiled up at him. "Okay."

She clicked the key fob, and he opened the driver's door for her.

"Good night," she said. "Thank you for a lovely day."

"Good night."

He kissed her again.

THEIR PREVIOUS KISSES had all been in more-or-less public view. This one was private, and lingering and long. Lauren ran her thumb along that concave leanness between Alex's cheekbone and chin. His hands were pressed tight against her back.

There wasn't much space here between her van and the car in the next spot. But there was plenty of room *inside* the van. She felt a sudden urge to pull Alex inside with her and kiss him senseless.

And then...

She felt something else.
A tiny fluttering in her abdomen.
The baby's first movement.

CHAPTER FIFTEEN

LAUREN LEANED AGAINST the fence post and stared at the ultrasound printout on the slick little paper. She'd managed to get in right away with Dalia's ob-gyn after they'd had a last-minute cancellation for a Monday-morning appointment. She'd expected to see no more than a blurry little bean-type thing. She'd been completely unprepared for the reality: the rounded head, the sturdy abdomen, the arms and legs moving and kicking. The technician had even been able to tell the sex.

It was a girl.

A girl. An actual person. Not Lauren herself, and not Evan. Not even half of each, but a unique person with a genetic package all her own—a personality, an eye color, a future.

Lauren's daughter.

And why had she been surprised by how much the ultrasound would show? Because she hadn't bothered to do a simple Google search to find out. Oh, she'd known enough about pregnancy to knock off the alcohol, and she'd looked up what supplements to take. But that had been the full extent of her research.

Dalia knew every stage of fetal development, and every milestone of the baby's first year of life. She could recite the symptoms of gestational diabetes and roseola, and she knew what to do for febrile convulsions. Lauren, meanwhile, had learned the exact angle of Alex's jaw and the contour of his hairline. How many hours had she spent ogling pictures of him on her laptop—hours she could and should have spent researching babies and maternal health? At this point she knew more about the Siege of Béxar than about the first trimester of pregnancy.

And she wasn't even *in* the first trimester anymore. She'd missed the whole thing.

The shameful truth was that there'd been lots of times when she'd straight-up forgotten she was even pregnant. That day in San Antonio with Alex, she hadn't thought about the baby a single time—until that tiny flutter kick had brought her back to reality.

On the other side of the fence, the Angora goats browsed for food. Besides their hay, they still had plenty of grasses and roughage to nibble. They were fluffier now than when

Lauren had first seen them, with thick coats of corkscrew curls. Occasionally one of the babies would get lost from its mother and let out a little bleat, and wherever the mother was, she would bleat right back and find her baby. None of the other mothers would so much as raise their heads. Each mother knew her own baby's voice perfectly.

The goats were better mothers than Lauren. They didn't forget their babies. They couldn't.

But Lauren had been so caught up in her new romance—a romance that she'd started when she *hadn't even had the previous guy's baby yet*—that nothing else mattered to her. Even now, memories of her time on the River Walk with Alex kept rising up like champagne bubbles. The things he'd said, the way he looked. How it felt to be with him—talking, eating, doing duck dialogues, walking hand in hand. The solid strength and warmth of his body, the feel of his mouth against hers. She was half-drunk already on the mere thought of him.

All of which meant that she was a terrible mother.

But terrible or not, she was this baby's mother, the only mother this little girl would ever have. So she'd better rise to the occasion and do the job.

And it wasn't just a job, not anymore. The moment she'd felt that first kick, she'd felt something else besides: a powerful sense of possession and belonging, an overwhelming love for this person she'd never met but would do anything for. Anything.

"I won't forget again, baby," she whispered. "I won't let you down."

She remembered so little of her own mother—just a few fragments, bright as dewdrops, and a lingering impression of peace and longing that made her throat ache. Just like Lauren, this baby would grow up with only one parent. And just like her dad, Lauren would have to supply everything that was needed. She couldn't let herself fall apart over failed romantic relationships. She couldn't keep making the same mistakes, getting involved with random men.

Okay, so maybe it wasn't fair to put Evan and Alex in the same category. Alex was light-years out of Evan's league. But that's exactly what she *would* think now, in the heady days of infatuation. She'd thought Evan was rarefied perfection, until she'd found out he wasn't. She couldn't go through that again—not now, not ever. She couldn't do that to the baby.

No. She had to stop being distracted by her own feelings and plan for the future, make a stable environment for her child. She had to break this cycle of heartbreak.

It was time to make some changes, no matter how painful.

It was time to grow up.

Rain had fallen overnight, sharpening the fall colors of the Texas Hill Country—the russets and bleached yellows of summer grasses, the dark brown of weed stalks and leafless trees, the patches of bright green. Lauren swallowed over a lump of soreness in her throat. She loved this place, this hard country with its thorns and stones and big skies, its harshness and its beauty, its history and its people. Of all the places she'd lived in over her years of travel, this was going to be the hardest to leave behind.

"There you are."

Alex's voice made her heart leap into her throat. She put the ultrasound picture in the kangaroo pocket of her hoodie and turned around.

He was standing there in his jeans and work boots, and the familiar denim jacket, and a plaid shirt she'd never seen before, looking even more gorgeous in person than in her imagination.

"Hey!" she said. "What are you doing here?"

Her voice sounded unnatural in her own ears.

He blinked. "What do you mean, 'what am I doing here?' It's Monday, isn't it? I told you I'd come out today with the sample tiles for the American Clay. We're gonna put them against the walls and decide on colors. Remember?"

Oh, right. He had told her that—but she'd forgotten, because she was an airhead. And now, in the midst of all her emotional turmoil, she had to cope with Alex's actual physical presence, without any preparation whatsoever.

She'd texted him after she made it home from San Antonio, like he'd asked—just the word home, no more. He'd replied with a thumbs-up and a sleep well. All pretty neutral stuff. And that was it. No hearts, no kissy faces, no "I had a wonderful time" or "can't wait to see you again"—nothing.

Which could mean absolutely anything.

Act natural, she thought. It was a pretty

flimsy straw, but it was all she had, so she grasped it.

They walked to the bunkhouse, side by side. She kept her hands in her hoodie pocket, and he didn't try to take her hand or touch her in any way.

So far, so good.

In the living room, he pulled out some colored tiles and lined them up across the fireplace bricks.

"Okay, so you got your Tuscan Gold, your Bryce Canyon, your French Quarter and your Sugarloaf White. I brought the Chesapeake Bay on my own. I know you didn't ask for it, but I thought it might work well with the German smear."

He took a step back. "Dang, that fireplace looks good! We did an amazing job. I can't get over what a difference it makes. Our imaginary cowboy should be proud."

"It's gorgeous, all right. And I do like the Chesapeake Bay. But I don't know. I'm leaning toward the Bryce Canyon for this room."

"We should look at both of them against the mantel wood, too. I can't wait until we get the walls done so we can get the mantel installed."

They went through all the rooms with the

samples, keeping up a steady stream of brisk, businesslike talk. Nothing the least bit romantic passed between them. Maybe Alex was as eager to forget what had happened on the River Walk as she was. Of course he was. No doubt he was relieved to find Lauren so matter-of-fact and unclingy.

Reality always set in sooner or later. If Lauren hadn't already decided to end things with Alex, she'd be getting a stiff dose of disappointment right about now. As it was, all she felt was a sort of dull sensation in her stomach, and the cold, hard satisfaction of having things under control.

Well. This must be what growing up was like.

When they came full circle to the living room, Alex turned and faced her.

"So I was thinking. I want to take you someplace other than a historical reenactment or the hardware store. So how about if we go to my grandparents' place, and then out to eat? I'd really like for you to see it. Assuming the weather is good, we can check out some of the main pastures and walk down to the creek. Strictly speaking, with the estate in probate, we might be trespassing, but I think it's a pretty low-risk activity as far as actually getting arrested goes. It's not like anyone stops me from going out there to feed cattle. Then afterward, dinner. We may not have high-class cuisine in Limestone Springs, but we do have access to some good plain food. What do you think? I've got my work schedule for two weeks out, and I've been looking at the ten-day weather forecast, and I have some days that ought to work."

He was standing there all braced, with his head high and his chest out and his smile fixed, and Lauren understood. He hadn't been trying to pretend like the River Walk had never happened, hadn't been trying to weasel out of anything.

He was just nervous.

"I don't want you to think I'm never going to take you on a real date," he went on. "So far it's been mostly construction work and historical reenactments and hanging out with family. Which is cool that you like that kind of thing. I like it, too. But I want you to know I'm not cheap. I'm frugal but I'm not cheap. And for sure it's going to be challenging with my jobs, finding days when we can spend time together, but we've made it work so far, haven't we? I think we have. Not that it's enough! It's not enough at all. It's killing me that I can't spend more time with you. I want to see you every day. But we have to work with what we have, and this is just the reality right now. But there are ways we could be more creative about it. Like you could maybe drive into town sometimes when I'm working and meet me for lunch. That's just half an hour, but it's better than nothing. But we can talk about all that over dinner. So what do you think?"

His smile was almost brittle now. She didn't know what kind of signals she was giving off, but clearly they weren't encouraging.

"I can't," she said. "I'm not going to be available."

The words sounded brusque and flat, like she was turning down a carpet-cleaning demonstration rather than a date. Her desperate hope was that if she played it that way, he'd catch on and match her tone, and they could get through this without a meltdown, and without the explanations that she was completely unprepared to give.

A little crease started between his eyebrows. "What do you mean? I haven't even told you which days yet."

"I know. But the thing is, I'm leaving."

"Leaving? For where?"

"Arkansas. There's a festival in the Ozarks I want to hit up."

His smile faltered but didn't go away. He looked like he was waiting for things to make sense.

"What, like a weekend trip, something for your blog?"

"No, it's a long festival, it'll go on for weeks." And it was completely imaginary.

"So when are you coming back?"

"I don't know," she said brightly. "Someday, maybe."

The smile died. "But—but I thought... I thought you were spending the winter here."

"Yeah, I considered it. But I changed my mind."

"Oh."

She saw him swallow hard. He looked like he'd been gut-punched.

"When are you leaving?" he asked.

"Tomorrow, probably. It won't take me long to pack. It never does."

He stood there a moment like he didn't know what to do.

"Well," he said at last. "I guess I'd better go."

He started to reach for her, like maybe a friendly goodbye hug was in order, but changed his mind, and rather than turn the hug into a handshake or even a wave, he made a few awkward movements with his arms and then put his hands in his pockets.

"Well, um, thanks," Lauren said. "For everything."

"You, too. All right, then. Have a good trip. Be safe."

And he was gone.

The moment the door shut behind him, Lauren heard herself give a strangled gasp. She felt like she'd just carved out her own heart with a bowie knife.

She wanted to go after him, stop him, wrap her arms around him, bury her face in his denim jacket, but she didn't move a muscle.

This was growing up, all right, and it really sucked.

ALEX MADE IT halfway down the cleared path from the bunkhouse to the driveway in a sort of stupor. Numbness gave way to hurt, then to anger. And then he turned around and walked right back to the bunkhouse.

He came in without knocking. Lauren was standing exactly where he'd left her, with her arms at her sides and a blank look on her face, like nothing was going on, like she hadn't just shattered him into a million little pieces and ground the pieces underfoot.

"I don't believe it," he said. "It wasn't all me. You felt it, too. I know you did. When we—when we kissed—"

"You mean when you kissed me."

"You kissed me back! I know you felt it, too. And now you expect me to believe… what? That you were just toying with me? That it didn't matter to you? That you just changed your mind? Like Evan?"

In an instant her face was transformed, twisted with fury. "How dare you say that? I am *nothing* like Evan."

"Well, you're acting just like him."

"Stop it, Alex. You're being a spoiled child. You and I are not married, okay? Evan was my husband. He made a vow to me, and he broke it. He cheated on me and abandoned me. This thing, you and me, is not the same."

"So you admit that there is a thing, a you and me."

She sighed and shut her eyes. "Okay, we kissed. And we had some good times. You are a very attractive and intelligent man."

"Don't do that. Don't patronize me."

"What, how am I patronizing you?"

"Talking about me that way, like I'm a location or a food. Like something you're going to blog about. Something to just enjoy in the moment and move on."

"You have a lot of nerve, you know that? You have no right to act so injured. It's not like we slept together, Alex."

"No, we didn't. And I took some flak for that. But I was careful not to compromise you at Béxar, because I care about your reputation and wanted to treat you with respect. What is wrong with you, Lauren? Do you really think love is just about sex?"

The word *love* went off like a dropped bomb. Lauren looked stunned, frozen. Alex could have kicked himself. *Wow. Not holding anything back, are you? Throwing your dignity to the wind.*

Then he saw the colored clay tiles he'd arranged so carefully along the walls. "I just realized, you're abandoning the bunkhouse. You let me go through all that with the plaster samples, and then you tell me you're leaving. You got this whole project started, got Dalia to sign off on it, got her excited about it, which is not an easy thing to do, got *me* excited about it, and now you're just dropping the whole thing? How can you let people down that way? How can you do that to her? How can you do that to me?"

Lauren held her hands to her head. "Stop it! Stop putting all that on me. Stop trying to make me feel responsible for other people's emotions."

He laughed, a hard, rough sound. "Do you even hear yourself? *You sound exactly like Evan.*"

He saw the words hit home. She opened her mouth, then shut it hard.

"You know what?" Alex said. "*Never mind.* I don't know why I'm trying to convince you. If you can't see it for yourself then there's no point. If you want to go, go. The road—your freedom or whatever—clearly means more to you than I do. There's nothing more to say. I was wrong to ever think there was more to you than that."

He walked out. He heard the door slam behind him, but didn't know if he was the one who'd slammed it. Then he was in his truck, but he couldn't remember getting in. His heart pounded, and his thoughts felt thick, like he'd had a blow to the head.

He started the ignition, then struck the steering wheel with his fists. A wave of nausea rose in his throat.

He forced himself to breathe, in and out, in and out. He counted to a hundred. Then he carefully backed his truck and headed down the driveway.

Idiot.

He'd known better than to fall for Lauren, and he'd done it, anyway. It wasn't like he didn't have a lifetime's experience with flaky people; he'd suffered enough from his dad. And yet he'd offered himself up to have his heart trampled by a woman who couldn't care less about him.

The road blurred. He took a furious dash at his eyes with the back of his hand.

He drove out to the ranch without really deciding to do it, got out, walked. In the distance, some hardwoods made a dark smudge against the sky, marking the course of the creek.

He missed his grandfather so much now. The most reliable person in his life—and even he had let Alex down in the end.

This place was all he had now—and he didn't even have it, just the hope of it. He had to get it back—that's what he had to focus on now. If he lost it, then he didn't even know who he was anymore.

He was tired—tired to death of striving and hoping and waiting and losing. When would he ever catch a break?

CHAPTER SIXTEEN

I WILL NOT CRY, Lauren told herself, and she didn't.

She hated how quick she was to dissolve into tears. Sad movies, the opening bars of certain songs, even certain pet-food commercials could set her chin trembling and her eyes watering. It was disgustingly childish and silly, and she was going to get a handle on it.

She'd found an eHow article on how to not cry. Apparently it was all about controlling your breathing. Inhale for a count of three, hold for a beat, exhale for three. Sounded doable.

She practiced, then went to the house and told Dalia she was leaving.

Dalia was in her little home office doing bookkeeping. With a pang, Lauren saw how crowded the room was getting. The desk and file cabinets were humongous antiques; the printer stood on an old console table that was

overflowing with stacked papers; the book-
cases were all full. There were baby things
in the office, too. It functioned well enough
for now—Dalia was a minimalist at heart,
and efficient and organized enough to make it
work—but the space had its limits, and Lauren knew how welcome the prospect of a future bunkhouse office would have been.

Dalia froze for a moment, then closed her
bookkeeping file and turned to face Lauren.
"Does this have something to do with Alex?"

"Yes. I never should have gotten involved
with him. I knew it at the time—I knew it all
along—and I did it, anyway."

"Just how involved are you?"

"Barely at all, really...but too much. I guess
I was fooling myself that it didn't mean anything, that I was just spending time with
someone I liked as a friend and no one would
get hurt. But now things are at the point where
Alex wants more, and I can't give him that."

"Does he know about the baby?"

Lauren squirmed. "No. I guess I should
have told him right from the start, but it's
not an easy subject to broach. It's embarrassing. It's just one more sign of how out of control my life is right now. And the more time
passed, the harder it was to bring it up. And

now… I just can't. I like him—I really do—but things can never work between us. I've got to walk away while I still can."

Carefully Dalia asked, "Are you sure you have to walk away?"

Inhale, two, three. Pause. Exhale, two, three.

Dalia waited.

Part of Lauren wanted to plop down on the armchair, tell Dalia every last detail and beg for advice. Dalia was the most levelheaded person Lauren knew. She'd put everything in perspective.

But that wouldn't be fair to Dalia. It was already weird enough that Lauren had kissed Dalia's husband's brother. Talking things over now would only muddy the water. Dalia would feel like she should take sides; her loyalty would be called into question.

All of which was exactly why Alex should have been off-limits to begin with.

Besides, it was Lauren's life, Lauren's responsibility. Whether she was equal to the task or not, she was going to have to rely on her own wisdom.

When she was sure she had her voice under control, Lauren said, "I don't know how many times over the past months I've agonized over how much better my life would have been if I had just walked away after meeting Evan for the first time, or not even gone to that stupid concert. I kept visualizing myself going back in time and just steering clear of him completely. Train wreck avoided. Well, this is my chance to do the right thing *now*. It's going to be a wrench, but I'm going to grit my teeth and rip off that Band-Aid, and then it'll all be over, and Future Me will be safe from a whole mess of future turmoil that'll never happen."

"Evan was a cheater," Dalia said.

"Yes, but I couldn't see that, could I? So how can I trust myself not to see disaster coming again?"

"That's not—"

"I've made up my mind," Lauren said.

Dalia still didn't look convinced, but she said, "Okay."

Lauren tidied the bunkhouse as best she could. Everything looked half-finished and forlorn. Chester watched from a windowsill, making the Contented Cat Face, showing off what a good house cat he was.

She carried him outside and set him on the porch. The key turned in the lock with a hard, dry little click.

Something hurt her throat. She swallowed hard. *Inhale, two, three. Pause. Exhale, two, three.*

SHE WOULD LEAVE TODAY. It would be a bit rushed, loading Vincent and getting him ready for the road, but she'd had lots of practice. She could handle some frenetic activity. What she could not handle was to spend one more night in this town.

The faster she moved, the less room there was for thought. Within a shorter time than she would have believed possible, she was standing on the driveway, saying goodbye to Tony and Dalia.

Dalia gave her a fierce hug.

"I'm sorry about the bunkhouse," Lauren said into Dalia's shoulder. "I'm sorry I got you to bump up your internet coverage for nothing."

She kept remembering what Alex had said, about what a flake she'd been to her friends. He was right, of course. But what could she do? She was leaving now in order *not* to be a flake. She couldn't undo past flaky actions; she could only wait them out and endure the consequences, and that would take a while.

But if she had no flaky behavior going forward, things would straighten out eventually.

"Don't worry about that," Dalia said. "Now, you call me when you reach your stopping place for the night, okay? Keep me posted on where you're heading, when you leave and when you get there. And *take care of yourself*."

Lauren knew this was code for "get prenatal care." And if Dalia was saying it in code, that meant she still hadn't told Tony about the pregnancy, and Lauren was glad. It wasn't like Tony would have looked down on her for being pregnant, but the pregnancy itself wasn't the issue. The issue was…well, it was complicated. First, she'd been stupid enough to get knocked up by someone like Evan in the first place, when any clear-thinking person could have seen he wasn't going to last the duration. Then she'd kept the pregnancy secret, lying to herself that it didn't matter because she wasn't staying in Texas long, even though she could see perfectly well that Tony was trying to set her up with his brother. And finally, in spite of her own better judgment, she'd gotten involved with Alex, anyway.

Basically she'd kept the secret long enough for it to take on a life of its own. Tony would know the truth soon enough, but for now Lauren was grateful to have one fewer awkward thing going on. The whole situation was awkward enough as it was.

Tony looked troubled, and his resemblance to Alex seemed a lot stronger than usual. The shape of the eyes was the same, and the jawline. Both men were big and tough, but with something achingly sweet and young about them.

She hadn't expected Tony to see her off. She wondered how much Alex had told him. Probably not much. Still, Tony had to be a little sore about the whole thing. But here he was, apparently willing to give her the benefit of the doubt, or at least wish her well.

"Oh, hey, I got you a little something for the road," he said. "It's in my truck."

Tony's idea of a little something for the road was the most Texas gift basket ever: pecans, salsa, chips, buffalo jerky bites, margarita taffy, sparkling grape juice from a Texas vineyard, chili mix, armadillo caramels, an Alamo chocolate bar, Texas-shaped crackers, Texas-shaped pasta, cilantro pesto, Texas flag dish towels and Texas flag coasters, all in an actual Texas-shaped basket.

Inhale, two, three. Pause. Exhale—

It was no use. Lauren cried hard. Tony looked almost frightened. He muttered something about getting the basket stowed for her and hustled it into the van, just behind the driver's seat. He took his time, which gave Lauren a chance to hug Dalia again and blow her nose.

Lauren rubbed Durango behind the ears. He looked up at her and whined.

She had to leave now. Every second was making it harder.

She climbed into Vincent Van-Go and drove off. She didn't look back.

CHAPTER SEVENTEEN

SPARKS FLEW FROM the wire brush on the drill as Alex scrubbed rust from the brake calipers of a Dodge Challenger. A sudden influx of cars to be repaired meant Manny had a backlog of work. That suited Alex fine. He needed something to do with his hands to keep his mind from idling.

Not that things had been going all that well in the shop today. While troubleshooting an intake gasket on an idling Crown Victoria, he'd sprayed carburetor cleaner with what turned out to be too free a hand around the intake, causing the engine compartment to burst into flames. The fumes of the carb cleaner must have gotten sucked into the distributor cap and touched off by the ignition spark, with the flames quickly spreading to all the oil and grease accumulated under the hood. Some prompt squirts from the fire extinguisher had taken care of the blaze, leaving Alex to ponder the flammability of carburetor cleaner and wonder whether mechanic work was a safe occupation for a guy who'd just had his heart ripped out and handed to him on a trash-can lid. But what else was he going to do? Brood in his apartment, going back through Lauren's Instagram for the zillionth time? No thanks. On the balance, flammable liquids and heavy machinery were probably his safest bet.

He couldn't stop thinking about her. He felt bruised inside, pulverized. He couldn't believe she'd blown him off that way—and yet it had been exactly what he'd expected from the start.

So he'd made a mistake. Now it was time to move on.

If only it was that simple.

He couldn't think straight. He felt like he'd left part of his brain somewhere.

He shut off the drill and wiped the loosened rust from the calipers with a damp rag.

"Alex. That you under there?"

It was Tony's voice, and from the sound of it, he'd probably been waiting awhile for the drill to stop. Patience was not one of Tony's virtues. Alex was lucky his brother hadn't tried rocking the body of the car to get his attention.

"Yeah, it's me."

"Well, come out. I want to talk to you."

Tony was mad, and not just about the wait. Alex could tell, because Tony was using that voice.

In many ways Tony was a weird candidate for older brother. He wasn't a studious person, or diligent, or steady, or particularly responsible. Alex was more like a firstborn. Tony would have done better as the baby of the family, with his charm and carefree ways. But he had his moments, times when he'd suddenly rise up out of his free-wheeling, fun-loving disposition and get all puffed up with righteousness and big-brotherly authority. You never knew what might set him off. Dumb stuff, usually, like his bottle of hair product being moved aside in the bathroom cabinet. It was totally random and really annoying.

Alex rolled his way out from under the car's body on the creeper.

Sure enough, there Tony stood, bowed up and indignant, looking about three inches taller and twenty pounds heavier than usual, like an avenging angel on steroids.

"What's up?" Alex asked. If he kept cool, the whatever-it-was would probably blow over pretty soon. Tony's temper was impressive while it lasted, but it never lasted long.

Alex wasn't feeling very cool right now, though. He felt more like an ignition flame waiting to come across some carb-cleaner fumes.

"That's what I want to know. What's up with you, man? What's your problem?"

"What do you mean, 'what's my problem?' What's *your* problem? You're the one with the attitude. I'm just minding my own business trying to get some work done."

"Don't play dumb. I want to know what happened between you and Lauren."

Wow. Besides a broken heart, I get my older brother on my case about it. Bonus.

"Look, Tony, I've got a lot to do today. After this brake job I've got to overhaul a transmission. I don't have time for this right now."

"No. You don't have time for anything but work and your dress-up history games. There's no room left in your life for anything that might get in the way of those things."

Alex rolled back under the car and started spraying caliper paint. "You're way out of line, man. You don't know what you're talking about."

"Then tell me. Why did Lauren leave?"

"Because she's a flake. All in the moment, *living the experience and not able to stick to* a task and see it to completion. She's childish and shallow and thrill-seeking. She can't see anything that isn't right in front of her face."

"So that's it, huh? You think she's not good enough for you? Not a suitable wife for someone who wants to be a rancher?"

Alex rolled back out again, stood up and reached for his water bottle. "We're too different for it to work."

"Oh, wow, what an insight. When did this wisdom come to you? I notice she wasn't too flaky for you to get involved with to begin with."

"I didn't think it through, okay? I shouldn't have done it. I see that now. I saw it at the time, but I couldn't stop myself. But it's over now before any more complications can mess up my life."

Tony grabbed his arm. *"Don't call it that."* He was so mad he was shaking, and for a second Alex thought his brother was going to hit him.

Alex was mystified. "Call what that?"

"The baby, moron. Don't call the baby a complication."

Everything went blank. Alex felt his mouth opening and closing soundlessly, like a fish out of water.

"Yeah, that's right," Tony went on. "I saw the expectant-mother packet in her van, in the holder thing behind the driver's seat. It's the same kind Dalia got at her first appointment, and it had Lauren's name on it. I just... wow. I always knew you were stubborn, and fixated on the family land and Texas history in a borderline unhealthy way. But I always figured you'd snap out of it when you fell in love. I didn't think you'd just use a woman and then cut her loose. I mean, it makes *me* feel like crap, because I actually wanted the two of you to get together. I knew she'd been done wrong by that scuzzball ex-husband, and I felt bad for her, and wanted her to find a good, kind, decent guy. And who better than my own brother? I thought you were that, at least."

Alex's voice started working at last. "Lauren's pregnant?"

He pulled his arm free and started walking around the garage with his head in his hands. She was pregnant? And she never told him?

Suddenly a lot of things made sense.

"Alex, I—I'm sorry, man. I just assumed

you knew. It never occurred to me that she didn't tell you."

Tony really was sorry. Alex knew that. As angry as he'd been before, he was twice as sorry now, and willing to do any generous or helpful thing possible. Alex could ask for the actual shirt off his back right now and Tony would give it to him without a moment's hesitation.

"I'm sorry," he said again. "It really sucks, not telling you."

"It's not my baby."

Pause. "It's not?"

"No."

Another pause. "Are you sure?"

"Yes, I'm sure! And thank you very much for assuming the absolute worst of me."

"Dude, I'm sorry. Really I am. It's just... well, you have spent a lot of time together lately, and I could tell there was something there. And if it's not yours, then whose is it?"

"Has she taken off yet?"

"She left about an hour ago. I'm so sorry. I wish now I'd come sooner. It's too late."

"Maybe not."

Alex peeled off his nitrile gloves, picked up his phone and started tapping.

"There. She's on Old Meyer Road, just past the bridge."

"Whoa, what is that? Some sort of stalker app on your phone?"

"No, we just turned on our locations and shared them with each other, when we went to the Béxar reenactment. I can see wherever she is as long as she has her phone."

He unzipped his coverall and started to shimmy out of it. It clipped him pretty tight in the shoulders, and getting it off took a certain finesse, but today he had no patience. He tried to use the sole of one work boot to kick off the other and ended up falling over.

"Whoa, are you okay? Is that how you take that thing off? How are you even alive?"

Alex looked up at Tony from the floor. "Quit being a smart aleck and help me."

It wasn't much better with the two of them pulling at cross purposes, but eventually Alex was upright and free of the coverall, in just his Under Armour boxers and tank. He stumbled to his locker and pulled out one of the shirts hanging inside.

"If I head east on the loop, I can probably intercept her. It might take a while to catch up, but I'll be monitoring her progress, and I know the roads around here better than she does."

"I don't know, man. That sounds kinda creepy. Maybe you should just call her."

"No. Some things you have to do in person."

"Well, if you're going to do it in person, then wear the other shirt, the blue one. And take your hair out of the ponytail."

"Why?"

"Just trust me. Whoa! Whoa! You're getting your buttons all messed up. Come here."

Tony got him buttoned up, took off his safety glasses and looked him over. Then he smiled and gave him a bro hug with two thumps to the back.

"Thanks for coming," Alex said. "Even though you did place my behavior in the worst possible light. If you hadn't, I wouldn't have known."

"You're welcome. Godspeed, brother."

Alex got into Rosie and drove away.

CHAPTER EIGHTEEN

THE COUNTY ROAD stretched straight away to a vanishing point, with open fields lying on either side. Lauren could see for miles in every direction. There wasn't another vehicle in sight...except for the mud-spattered Dodge crew cab parked crossways in the road, blocking her way.

A man leaned against the truck, legs crossed at the ankles, arms folded over his chest. He could have been posing for a cowboy calendar, with the vast sky stretching above him and the cloud shadows rolling across the ground.

She'd walked away from him once, and it had taken every ounce of self-denial in her system to do it. And now here he was again.

She thought about turning Vincent around and going right back the way she came. Instead she pulled over, turned off the ignition and got out—not because that was the most efficient way of dealing with the situation, but because he looked so unbelievably good that she couldn't not go to him.

He walked over to her—long, firm, purposeful strides. He was wearing a sky-blue shirt that brought out all the coppery tints in his skin, and as if that wasn't enough, his hair was loose. He did not stop or slow down until he was close enough for her to see the dark brown flecks in his amber-colored eyes.

"Why didn't you tell me?" he asked.

There was no need to ask what he meant. Somehow, some way, he'd found out about the baby. Now he wanted an explanation, and in all honesty she owed him that much.

"I should have, I know. I was wrong not to. It wasn't fair. But I couldn't see that then. I was barely admitting it to myself. I wasn't ready to tell other people. I didn't know what to do. I didn't mean to deceive you. I just didn't think it would be an issue. I never expected—"

"That's not what I mean. It was your business, I get that. It's not like you were obligated to let me know you were pregnant right from the get-go, just in case I got attracted to you. But why didn't you tell me later, once we started, you know, getting close? Why didn't you tell me at the River Walk? You knew I cared about you. We could have talked it over like adults."

"What was there to talk about? I'm the one who has to deal with it. I'm the one who's pregnant with my moron ex-husband's baby. I'm the single woman who's living out of a van and has to figure out a way to provide for a child."

"But why leave at all? Why not stay? Stay in the bunkhouse. We'll finish the work on it, the two of us. Then you and the baby will have a place to live that isn't a van, and you'll have access to a good doctor, and it'll be the same doctor for the whole pregnancy instead of a different one in each town you drive through. And I'll be there. And when the time is right, things can move forward with us."

"What does that mean?"

"It means we get married."

For a moment she couldn't believe she'd heard right. He'd actually said "get married," and he looked dead serious. Something caught at her heart, and all the colors in the wintry landscape brightened, as if a cloud shadow had just rolled past.

But she'd felt such things before, shock waves and thrills and ecstasies and all nature bursting into song. She couldn't trust them. That was why she had to get away, to put distance between herself and Alex so she wouldn't be at the mercy of her feelings—her frothy, unreliable feelings that had led her wrong so many times before.

"I'm sorry if that freaks you out," Alex said. "But I mean it. I'm willing to wait. I know it must feel weird, after Evan. We'll go slow, build up trust. I'll be patient. And in the meantime I'll be as close as you want, as close as you'll let me be."

So much open space all around her, and suddenly Lauren couldn't breathe.

"So, what, I'm just supposed to give up my whole way of life? Stop traveling and settle down in a small town? Turn my custom van into a soccer-mom van?"

The words rang hollow in her own ears, and she could see from Alex's face that he wasn't fooled.

"You just said yourself that you were the one living out of a van, like it was a bad thing. Now you're saying you won't give it up?"

"I don't know what I want to do. I don't *have* to give it up just because I'm pregnant. Lots of van-life people have kids that they travel with."

"But that's not what you want, not really.

You never expected to live out of a van forever. That's the whole reason you came here in the first place when you found out about the baby. You wanted a place to belong. You wanted good people around you, and a regular roof over your head, and so you came here, to this place. That's no accident. That's why you started working on the bunkhouse. You wanted a community, a real live, flesh-and-blood community that stays in one place."

"Stop doing that."

"Doing what?"

"Talking about me like you know me. Boxing me in."

"Boxing you in? How? By putting a roof over your head? That's bull. You drive away now, you still live in a box. It's just a box on wheels, whose transmission could go out a hundred miles from nowhere."

"That's *my* problem, not yours or anybody else's."

"No. It's not just your problem anymore. You've got to stop thinking of just yourself. You have a baby to watch out for now."

"You think I don't know that? Everything I'm doing now is for the baby."

"How? That doesn't even make sense. You're talking in circles. Listen, we can do this. I have a good job—two good jobs. You have a job you can do from home. We have a place to stay."

"Yeah, on someone else's land. I think Dalia's going to want her bunkhouse back at some point."

"Well, then, we'll deal with that when it comes. We'll figure out our options. I have savings. I have a nest egg."

"For a different nest! That money is for your grandfather's land, not for setting up housekeeping with a pregnant wife."

"So maybe getting the land back will take a little longer. That's okay. I've waited this long, I can keep waiting."

"No, you can't, Alex. That land is the focus of your whole existence, the land and its history. You live like a monk, working two jobs and saving your money, toiling and saving to get it back. You think you're going to give that up for me, and for a baby that isn't even yours?"

"Is that what this is about? You think I can't do it? You think because this baby isn't my biological child, that I can't be a good father?"

"No."

"You think I'm no better than that punk Evan?"

"No!"

"You think I'm like *my* father?"

"No! You'd be a wonderful father, Alex. You'd work yourself to the bone to give the baby everything you never had, all the security and stability and comfort that you were starved for all those years. And you'd give up your own dream in the process, and then one day you'd wake up and realize I wasn't worth it."

His eyes opened wide. "So that's what this is. You're not afraid of getting boxed in. You're afraid of boxing *me* in."

His face turned blurry, and her eyes burned. *Inhale, two, three—*

"I've got to go."

He touched her shoulder. "No. Don't do it."

"You can't stop me."

"Listen to me, Lauren. I love you. That's what it all comes down to. I love you and I want to be with you. Do you love me?"

She tried to turn away, but he held on.

"Look at me, Lauren. Look at me!"

The tears fell, then her eyes cleared, and she saw him looking down at her, so honest and strong and kind that the sight of him made her ache. There were tears in his own eyes. He wasn't just offering; he was fighting for the chance to give her everything he had to give.

Then he kissed her.

The kiss was not like any of their kisses on the River Walk. Those had been soft and tender and natural. This was hungry, needy, desperate.

It felt so good to be needed like that.

There had never been anything like this with Evan, not even close. Always with Evan there had been this element of theatricality, like he was the romantic hero in some movie Lauren was watching. This was different. Raw, real.

Then Evan blinked out of her mind completely like a burned-out light bulb. This was the only man who mattered, the only man in the world.

She plunged her hands into his hair, just like she'd been longing to ever since she'd first laid eyes on him in the goat pen at La Escarpa. His arms went around her, lifted her, turned her. He was so big and solid.

And then, somehow—she didn't know how—she ended it.

She'd never done anything like that before, never had the strength.

She laid both hands on his chest. She could feel the pounding of his heart.

"Goodbye, Alex."

She pushed away from him. His hands tightened on her arms, not hard, not hurting her, but firmly, and she twisted free like he was someone to get away from. He let her go then, hands held up in a gesture of compliance, face shocked.

She got into her van and started the ignition.

He was still right there, so close she could see the shadows beneath his cheekbones and the cleft in his chin. She backed up, did a U-turn.

Alex was right. He was the one talking like a grown-up, being reasonable and responsible. He wasn't guilty of anything but loving her and wanting to take care of her.

But she could be a grown-up, too. She could take care of him, put him first.

She couldn't outargue him. But she could leave.

"Rerouting," said the voice on her phone.

ALEX STOOD IN the middle of the road watching Lauren's van go away from him.

She's going to stop. She's going to turn

*around and come back and get out of that
van and run into my arms, and we're going
to be together.*

He kept thinking it as the van grew smaller
and smaller, and finally disappeared at the
horizon in a cloud of dust.

He stood there a little longer, and a little
longer.

She didn't come back.

She was really gone.

It was over. There was nothing more he
could do. He couldn't make her stay with him.
He couldn't go on following her like some
kind of nut. She'd told him to leave her alone.
He had to do that.

He'd offered all he could, done everything short of physically restraining her, and
it wasn't enough. She didn't want him. He
had lost.

A vehicle appeared on the horizon, heading his way. His heart gave a throb so painful
that he made a little gaspy sound in his throat.

But it wasn't Lauren's van.

He got back into his truck and moved it
onto the shoulder, slowly, like an old man.
He felt dead inside.

Then his phone went off, and his heart did
the painful throb thing again.

He looked at the screen. It was Claudia.

He leaned his head back against the headrest and took a few deep breaths before answering.

"Hey, Claudia. What's up?"

"Hello, *mijo*. I have bad news."

He knew what it was, knew what was coming even as he was thinking *oh, God, oh, please, oh, no—*

"I heard from the judge today. He's going to close the probate and award your father the land. I'm sorry, Alex. There's nothing more I can do."

CHAPTER NINETEEN

ALEX HATED DRINKING ALONE.

Alcohol was for social settings—for music and dancing, sporting events live or televised, national holidays, family celebrations. Alcohol took the edge off, made things smoother and easier, made himself and other people smarter and more appealing. Words and dance steps came quicker and better; anxiety and tension dissolved, leaving clarity, lucidity, wisdom, charm, dashing good looks and a better singing voice. What was the point of any of that without other people around?

He could have gone to a nice friendly bar, like Tito's, and told his troubles to whoever was available. Maybe not his Lauren troubles, but his land troubles for sure. Everyone would sympathize. And when the bar closed, there was no reason he should go home alone. He could get company. Lots of women would be glad to have him, and he knew he was looking good because Tony had chosen his shirt.

But the only woman he wanted to be with had given him the heave-ho. He'd offered her everything he had, everything he was, and it wasn't good enough. She'd climbed into her van and left him standing like an idiot in the middle of Navarro Road.

Just for an instant, as he'd made his plea out there between their two parked vehicles, he'd come within a hairbreadth of offering to go traveling with her. He hadn't said it, but he'd thought it. And not five minutes later, he'd found out that he'd lost the land. It was as if fate had called his bluff.

So, yeah. He'd done enough talking already today. He'd more or less asked Lauren to marry him, and she'd turned him down. And now he'd never see her again. Even her little location blip was gone from his phone. The closest he'd ever get to her from now on was looking at her Instagram. As weeks and months passed it would fill with pictures of new places she was visiting without him. Eventually there would be pictures of the baby—a baby that would have called him Daddy if he'd had his way, but would grow up a stranger to him now.

And meanwhile, the land his ancestors had worked for the past two centuries would be carved into tracts for crude modern housing, to be bought up by a bunch of transplanted Californians.

He didn't want sympathy, and he didn't want company. He wanted oblivion.

So that's how he came to be here, sitting on the rusted seat of a defunct tractor in front of his grandparents' house, drinking tequila straight from the bottle.

Lauren had basically said she was leaving him to protect him—that it would be foolish of him to give up his dreams for her, and one day he'd wake up and realize she wasn't worth the sacrifice, and blah, blah, blah.

But that was bull. *This isn't about you, it's about me.* Yeah, right. Just a token handout, a tossed crumb, a cop-out meant to allow him to salvage some self-respect.

"You're not afraid of getting boxed in," he'd told her. "You're afraid of boxing *me* in."

And she hadn't denied it.

But when he'd said, "I love you," she hadn't said it back.

Still. He'd kissed her, and she'd kissed him back. And that memory was the worst torment of all.

He took another swallow of tequila. There was no worm in his bottle, no salt on his palm; he wasn't some punk on spring break. The bottle was about half-full…or was it half-empty? And how many shots was that equal to? Not that it really mattered. The whole point of drinking from the bottle was to not keep track, to drink until you just couldn't anymore.

The limestone walls of his grandparents' house were streaked with red clay soil from where the rain had bounced up from the hard ground. The whole exterior needed a good pressure washing, and the clapboard lean-to addition had needed repainting since before Alex had his driver's license. Every spring his grandmother had been full of hope that this would be the year the house got fresh paint, and every winter had found the boards a little bit shabbier. There was always something else to spend the money on—a tractor repair, feed during a drought. By the time she'd died, there'd been more bare wood than painted wood. By the time his grandfather died, even the last flakes of paint had gone.

Tears stung Alex's eyes. Why hadn't he just bought the paint himself and done the work? His grandfather wouldn't have permitted it, of course, but he could have come in the middle of the night and gotten it done before anyone could stop him.

But what did any of that matter now? The house would be knocked down and all the boards and stones would be taken away.

Alex's phone went off for like the millionth time that evening. He felt a wild surge of irrational hope that it was Lauren calling, followed by a dreary letdown when he saw Tony's name on the screen. He knew he shouldn't hope, but he couldn't stop himself, and the hope was all mixed up with dread, because the odds were a hundred to one that he was about to be disappointed.

He could turn off the phone, but then if Lauren actually *did* call, he wouldn't know it.

Modern conveniences were such a curse. If you were a nineteenth-century vaquero and your woman turned you down cold, that would be the end of it. She might write you a letter or track you down in person one day, but you wouldn't be waiting every second for that to happen. You couldn't look at her Instagram, either.

Calls from Tony had been alternating with calls from his mother. He kept hitting Reject. He knew Claudia must have told them about the land, and he didn't want their sympathy.

They would mean well, but they would tell him to let it go, and he simply could not bear to hear those words right now. Besides, they didn't really *know*. The land had never belonged to his mom's family, never been in her blood. And Tony had never loved the land like he did, besides which he already had La Escarpa. Claudia had struck the proper tone, but even she could only sympathize so much.

Everyone was always talking about how there was no use chasing something that wasn't meant to be and how you had to bow to the inevitable. But was it really inevitable? The Alamo had been a lost cause from the start, but it ended up being the rallying point for the Texas Revolution—well, that and Goliad, which had been an even worse disaster. Bowie bayonetted on his sickbed, Fannin shot in the face, defenders and prisoners slaughtered without quarter—the carnage had been sickening, but it wasn't for nothing.

What Alex needed now was a gesture. Something to make people take notice.

Would it accomplish anything? Maybe, maybe not. But he wouldn't go down without a fight.

What should he do? It wasn't like there was an actual bulldozer heading his way to knock down the house this very night. That would be kind of nice, actually. He'd prefer a concrete conflict to this hopeless legal wrangling. An adversary he could meet face-to-face.

No, he didn't have a human enemy he could go at with musket and cannon and bowie knife. But he had an idea.

CHAPTER TWENTY

JUST SHY OF a sign that read Leaving Limestone Springs—Come Again Soon, Lauren pulled in at a gas station and started filling Vincent's tank. Considering how long she'd been on the road, she hadn't made much progress. Ever since meeting Alex on Navarro Road, she'd been driving aimlessly around town, wasting gas.

A restaurant stood in the next lot—Cocina de Pecarí. The front of the restaurant was decorated with a brightly painted mural of what looked like a javelina wearing a sombrero and an apron, tossing a tortilla and having a wild time.

A family was going in, a mother and father and a little toddler boy. The parents were holding the little boy's hands, and he kept picking up his feet and swinging in their grasp, and laughing this gurgling belly laugh that shook his whole body.

And suddenly Lauren was crying.

She got back into Vincent and drew the curtains over the windows. She cried hard—great, heaving, hyperventilating sobs. Images flooded her mind, of her baby, and Alex, and Alex with the baby, and Alex making pico de gallo in Dalia's kitchen with two little children toddling around, Lauren's daughter and Dalia's son, and Alex at Béxar, carrying a little girl dressed in one of Claudia's outfits.

She cried until the sobs ran out. Then she blew her nose, took her phone out of its holder and called her dad.

She hadn't talked to him in weeks—eight weeks, to be precise. Since just before the pregnancy test. She'd texted to tell him she was going to Dalia's, and again when she'd arrived, and a few times since, but she didn't trust herself on the phone with him.

"Hey, honey! It's good to hear from you. How are you?"

He sounded so cheerful and pleased, and Lauren wished she could just have a nice normal conversation with him.

"Hey, Dad. What are you doing? Are you working?" *Operating any power tools?*

"I was just about to lay some tile, but it can wait."

"Good. I have to tell you something."

There was a pause. Then he said in a calm neutral voice, "Okay."

For a moment Lauren couldn't get her own voice to work.

"Dad, I'm pregnant."

He let out a long sigh. "Thank God. I thought you had cancer."

"*What?* Why would you think that?"

"Well, I knew something was wrong, something other than the divorce, something you were afraid to tell me. You weren't calling, and you weren't taking my calls. That's not like you. I've been waiting for the blow to fall for weeks now."

"I'm sorry. I guess that does make my bad news seem a little less bad."

"Honey, a baby isn't bad news. So, um… how far along are you?"

"It's Evan's," she said, sparing him the math and the delicate questions. "He came back for a weekend in August—and then he left again. I should have known better, but I didn't."

"Does he know about the baby?"

She gave a short, dry laugh. "Yes. I called him just after the ultrasound. I didn't want to, but I thought he should know. And he made it perfectly clear that he couldn't care less. He actually blocked my number after he hung up. Whole conversation took about two minutes. Honestly, I think it's for the best. It'd be bad for the baby, having him come in and out of our lives. He's toyed with my emotions enough. I would hate to see him do that to my child."

"I think that's wise. So you've seen a doctor?"

"Yes. Everything's fine. I'm due in May."

"Good. I'm glad you're near your friend Dalia."

"Dalia's been great. But I can't stay here."

"Okay. Do you want to come home? You know you'd be welcome."

"I know. But I don't really have a destination in mind right now. I just have to leave."

"Why do you have to?"

She took a deep breath. "This is going to sound like the flakiest thing ever, but… I met someone here. I mean, I didn't *just* meet him. It's someone I already knew…well, a little bit. I didn't suddenly take up with a complete stranger again."

"Who is it?"

"Dalia's brother-in-law."

"Ah. I see how that could be awkward if things went south. But if you have to get away, then better now than later, a clean break. You don't need to be involved with someone who's bad news."

"It's not like that. Alex is actually a really good guy. Solid, dutiful, traditional. Hard-working. Good with people. Funny and kind. In a lot of ways he reminds me of you."

"And does *he* know about the baby?"

"He just found out today."

"And? Did it scare him off?"

She laughed. "He kind of asked me to marry him."

"Oh, really?"

"Yeah. And he said if I wasn't ready for that, he would wait, and just be there for me."

"And what did you say to that?"

"I said no. I packed up Vincent and left. I'm on the road right now. Not literally driving this minute, of course. I'm parked. I just filled up with gas."

He was quiet a long time. "Well, honey, I don't know what to tell you. I don't know this guy, or how you feel about him or how he feels about you. But I worry about you sometimes. There's this thing I've read about with people your age, this FOMO, which stands for fear of missing out. Have you heard of that?"

She smiled. "Yeah, I've heard of it."

"Apparently social media feeds into it a lot. You're always seeing these carefully curated posts and images of other people doing fun and interesting things, and that gives rise to this pervasive, ongoing anxiety that something exciting is happening somewhere else. And in your case, I think you're also kind of haunted by the things your mother missed out on in dying so young. Don't get me wrong. You know I've always been supportive of your desire to travel. And I know you've truly loved it, and you've had some incredible experiences on the road. But I have to wonder sometimes if part of it isn't driven by fear. You want to experience things intensely, but there's a paradox in that because you're so consumed with the *next* experience that you can't really settle down. That whole 'living in the moment' can actually rob you of the moment."

He sighed. "I'm not doing a good job explaining this."

"No, I understand. And…you're not wrong. But it isn't just the stuff Mom missed out on. It's the stuff you missed out on by being tied to me."

"What are you talking about? I loved being your dad. I wouldn't trade a minute of it."

"I know that, and you were the best father to me. But I remember how it was when I was growing up. You went on dates once in a while, you even had a few girlfriends, but none of them seemed to take. You were a young, good-looking man, sweet and funny and hardworking, with so much to offer. But you spent all those years single—decades, really, all through your twenties and thirties—and now you're, what, fifty-two? And you've been single for all but a few years of your adult life. And it's all because of me."

"You think it's your fault I never remarried? Honey, that's not true."

"It *is* true. Any woman in her right mind would have snapped you up in a minute, if you'd been unencumbered by a kid."

"No. You've got it all wrong. Sure, it's challenging, dating as a single parent. Some people are put off by the presence of a child, but those aren't the right people. I think in my case, knowing I had you to look out for gave me a lot of clarity. I didn't waste time on relationships that I knew on some level weren't going to work out."

"That's what I'm trying to do here. But I don't feel like I have much clarity."

"Is it possible that you're giving up too

soon? Some things worth having just take time. They have to be worked for. You can't have them right away, and you can't drive to them in a van. Listen, honey. I love how bold and eager you are, and how you're willing to go after what you want. But if you keep chasing experiences, you're going to cut yourself off from other experiences, like belonging."

"That's pretty much what Alex said."

"Well, he sounds smart. Look, I'm not telling you that you should be with this guy. But don't go away just because you're afraid of being tied down, or of tying him down, or of not knowing what's coming."

"But what if I stay, and I get close to him, and the baby does, too, and then it doesn't work out?"

"Then it'll hurt. But you can't insulate yourself from emotional risk. You can't work yourself to a place where nothing can touch you anymore. Or maybe you could, but that would be the worst thing of all."

"I don't know what to do. I'm afraid of messing up. There's so much I've got to figure out. I don't know how to be a mother. I'm four years older than you were when I was born, and I don't know anything."

"I didn't know anything, either. I messed

up a lot as a parent. I felt young and inadequate all the time, and I didn't know how to be a father any more than you know how to be a mother. I just did it, anyway."

"I guess that's what I'll have to do. Learn as I go."

"You're going to do great. And I'll help any way I can. You can still move back home if you change your mind, and I'm available anytime you want to draw on my font of parental wisdom. After all these years I actually do know a thing or two about raising kids."

A knock sounded at Vincent's window. Lauren pulled back the curtain and saw a confused-looking woman who was undoubtedly waiting on the gas pump. Lauren mimed "sorry," then said, "I've got to go, Dad. I'll call you later. Thanks. Love you."

"Love you, too."

She got out and returned the nozzle to the pump. There were some incredible food aromas coming out of Cocina de Pecarí. Suddenly she was ravenous. Her stomach had been tied up in knots all day, but now she felt limp and wrung out, and ready for some enchiladas. It was almost six o'clock, and she hadn't eaten anything since sometime yesterday. Her erratic eat-and-sleep schedule wasn't going to cut it anymore. She had to get proper rest and nutrients and all that.

She got a small table near a booth where the couple and the little boy were sitting. The boy was in a booster seat. A baby at another table sat in a high chair, and was being fed a mashed paste of rice and refried beans. How old did a kid have to be before you could spoon-feed it beans and rice at a restaurant? Dalia would know.

She ordered some green enchiladas with charro beans, then started in on the chips and salsa. The salsa was good, but hot. She imagined Alex sitting across from her, loading his chip with mounds of salsa like he had at the River Walk.

Then her enchiladas came, and for a while she took a break from thinking and just ate.

The restaurant seemed to have a lot of regulars. A couple of cops were sitting at the bar, eating nachos and drinking coffee and chatting with the staff and other customers. If Alex were here, he'd be greeting people and making comfortable small talk the way he did. Probably he knew half the people in this place.

The waitress brought her check. "Here you go, *mija*."

As Lauren was counting out her cash, the cops got a call on their radio. Lauren tuned in partway through.

"…report of a Hispanic male in a mariachi suit, chained to a gate at 412 Corbett Road, shouting taunts at passing motorists. Subject is armed and appears intoxicated or emotionally disturbed."

"Copy. We're en route."

The two cops looked at each other.

"Maybe he's intoxicated *and* emotionally disturbed," said one.

"Sounds like a humdinger either way," said the other.

"Corbett Road," said the waitress. "Isn't that the old Reyes place?"

"I believe so," said a cowboy at the bar. "But it's pretty much shut down since the old man died."

Back in Vincent, Lauren pulled up her navigator app. What was the street number? Was it 412, or 415? The patrol car was already gone.

She typed in Corbett Road and figured she'd know the right spot when she saw it.

CHAPTER TWENTY-ONE

SHE KNEW IT, all right. First, by the flashing lights of the parked patrol car, and then by the sight of Alex, chained to the front gate and jeering—there was no other word for it—at the two officers from the restaurant.

Oh, no. Alex, what are you doing?

She felt better once she got close enough to make out what he was saying. It was inflammatory stuff, all right, but nothing personal. He seemed to have them confused with evil land developers, or Santa Anna's men.

"Hello, officers," she said. They were wearing dark blue uniforms, unlike the earth tones she usually saw on sheriff's deputies, and the patrol car said they were county constables. In her travels Lauren had encountered lots of different types of law enforcement. She'd been surprised to learn just how much regional variation there was throughout the United States.

But there were some things all law-enforcement officers had in common—like that effortless authoritative vibe that always made Lauren want to stand up a little straighter and watch her words. These officers had that in spades. They looked guarded and reserved and grim. But just minutes earlier she'd seen the tall bearded one giving out play badges to little kids at the Cocina de Pecarí, and the stocky one with the shaved head had stirred his coffee with a candy cane.

Then she got a good look at Alex.

He was in full historical costume, hat and all, but his neck scarf looked skewed and the buttons weren't right on his waistcoat. His hair hung loose over his face, and his eyes glared with defiance and alcohol.

She couldn't see a weapon on him, but the dispatcher had said he was armed. With Alex that could mean anything from a flintlock carbine to a bowie knife, or even the Glock he kept in Rosie's glove compartment.

Lauren had witnessed a lot of conversations among van people about guns, both online and in person. Many van nomads kept guns for self-defense and refused to travel to states that didn't allow that. She didn't keep a gun herself—she doubted she'd be able to keep cool and fire it in an emergency, so she figured she'd be better off without it.

The online conversations tended to get heated, and she'd kept out. But the subject interested her, so she'd paid attention. She knew that Texas was among the freer states regarding the Second Amendment, and she knew Alex was licensed to carry. But she also knew that if he was carrying while drunk, he was in trouble.

Well, it couldn't be the Escopeta, because the Escopeta was too big to hide. Then she saw a curved gunstock sticking out of his belt. It might be the old defunct pistol Ron had given him for a restoration project.

He'd done a thorough job securing himself to the gate. It looked as if he'd taken a length of heavy chain and wrapped it around his waist, the bar of the gate and one thigh, making multiple passes, and had secured the links at both ends with a big padlock.

Apparently it was a keyed padlock. At least, there was a key hanging from a little stretchy bracelet around Alex's wrist.

He saw her, and his eyes widened.

"What're you doing here?" he called. "It's not enough you rejected me twice and ran my heart through a meat grinder? You gotta come here and rub it in? What're you gonna do, take pics? Put 'em on your Instagram? 'This screwup tried to get with me and now the Mexicans are taking him prisoner! Hashtag later, loser!'"

No doubt the officers were confused at being called Mexicans by an obviously Hispanic man. The bearded one's name tag said Kowalski; the bald one's said Hendersen.

"Ma'am, do you know this person?" Officer Kowalski asked.

"Yes. He's, um—he's a family friend."

"Family friend!" Alex repeated in a slurred shout. "Ha! Is that what you call it?"

"Alex," Lauren said. "Can you tell me what's going on here?"

"Heck, yeah. These *federales* are tryna seize my grandfather's ranch. They already overthrew the Constitution and now they're trampling property rights. You know what, Lauren? You go ahead and take those pictures and put 'em on Instagram. Hashtag liberty or death! Hashtag you'll never take me alive! Hashtag you'll have to rip me limb from limb and crush me with your tyranny bulldozers! Hashtag my blood will feed the revolution!"

The officers' expressions became a tad grimmer. No doubt they'd just pegged Alex as a conspiracy-minded nutball who wanted to overthrow the federal government.

Alex began to sing. Loudly. About the Alamo.

"Officers," Lauren said, "this is not what it looks like. This man is a law-abiding, patriotic, community-oriented citizen. He's not an anarchist. He's just a Texas history buff who's had a bad day and too much to drink, and now he has you confused with Santa Anna's forces."

"He said we overthrew the Constitution," said Kowalski.

"He means the Mexican Constitution of 1824."

Alex's voice rose as he sang something about a ghostly bugle and a roll call in the sky.

The two officers looked at each other. Then Kowalski said, "Ma'am, of course we'd like to see this situation resolved with a minimum of fuss. But this man is clearly intoxicated. He's being a public nuisance, distracting motorists. And he's armed."

Lauran nodded. "Yes. Yes, I understand. But may I ask, am I correct in thinking he's on private property right now? And if so, does that make a difference?"

They all looked at Alex, still singing. The gate was in fact set several yards back from the road.

"But *whose* private property?" asked Officer Kowalski.

"Well…that's currently being contested," Lauren said. "The last owner died, and this man is one of the potential heirs."

"If that's true," said Officer Kowalski, "then it would fall to the executor as to how to proceed with any charges against this individual."

"That sounds like a lot of paperwork," said Officer Hendersen.

"Not for us," said Officer Kowalski.

"What if I could get him to leave the premises peaceably with me?" Lauren asked. "Could we maybe let it go?"

Hendersen looked thoughtfully at Alex. "You know, I had an ancestor who died at Goliad," he said.

Alex broke off his song partway through a line about Santa Anna on his prancing horse, or something. "Wha-a-at? You guys are Texians? How come you're dressed like *federales*?"

"They're spies, sent by General Houston," Lauren said. "Some of Captain Seguin's men.

They infiltrated Santa Anna's camp two nights ago and they just made it back. Santa Anna's bulldozers broke down in the snow and ice. It'll be weeks before they're fit to travel again. I've got a message for you from headquarters."

Lauren thought she'd done pretty well on the spur of the moment. Alex looked confused, but at least he didn't call bull on the whole story. "Wh-what is it?" he said.

She stepped across the metal pipes of the cattle guard, crouched beside him and put her mouth to his ear.

Then she pulled the pistol out of his belt and quickly moved away again.

"Hey!" Alex said indignantly.

She handed the weapon to Officer Hendersen. "I recognize this pistol," she said. "It's just a shell. There's no flint, the firing pin is missing and the frizzen is all worn away."

She had no idea she'd picked up so much about firearm anatomy. Ron would be proud.

She went back to Alex and took the stretchy key chain off his wrist. "All right, *teniente*. Let's get you unbound."

The padlock opened easily, and the chain fell apart and clanged to the cattle guard. She started disentangling Alex from its links.

He'd done a real number on it, all right, securing it over and around himself and through the gate again and again.

"Hey!" he said again.

"Sorry, *teniente*. We've got to get you out of here. You're needed back at Béxar."

But Alex wasn't fooled anymore. "You're not with Houston. You don't even live in Texas. You're from *Pennsylvania*."

He spat the word out like an accusation.

Time for a change of tactics.

"Alejandro!" she said. *"Oculta tu trasero en la camioneta en este momento!"* Get your butt in the van this minute!

He sat up, startled into attention.

"¡Ándale!" she said.

He got unsteadily to his feet and stumbled toward Vincent, muttering something that sounded like *"Sí, Abuela."*

Officer Hendersen handed Alex's pistol back to her, chuckling. "You've sure got his number."

Officer Kowalski still looked grim, but all he said was "Get him home, ma'am, and let him sleep it off."

"Yes, Officer, I'll do that. Thank you *so* much for understanding."

She turned on the ignition and took off down the road.

She'd never been to Alex's apartment. She didn't even know where it was. All she knew about it was that everyone she'd ever heard speak of it, including Alex himself, called it his *crappy* apartment, so consistently that she thought of it as Alex's crappy apartment.

Alex was slumped against the passenger window, possibly asleep. He was a big man, and heavy. Lauren imagined parking in his parking lot and wrangling him out of the van and through the front door, under the watchful eyes of his neighbors. Then what? Would she leave him there? Camp out in his crappy living room? Did he even have a living room, or was it an efficiency?

She made a U-turn and drove back to the ranch gate. The patrol car was gone.

I said I'd take him home, and I am. This is his home.

She had a bad moment when she saw that the lock on the gate was a combination one, but when she asked for the combination, Alex rattled off the four digits without hesitation. His birthday, maybe? That would make him twenty-seven, one year younger than Lauren. It made sense. She and Dalia were the same age, and Tony and Dalia graduated the same year, and Alex was Tony's younger brother. But it shocked her somehow, and made her feel strangely protective of him. He was just a baby.

The combination worked.

She couldn't tell much about the house by moonlight, except that it was a plain rectangular stone structure with a shrunken, dingy, forlorn look. It had probably been a nice place once.

Lauren found a spot to park, next to what she hoped was a machine shed. She took her flashlight and went in search of a place to plug in, hoping the power was still on. Wonder of wonders, she found a 30/50 amp hookup…and it worked!

Back in the van, Alex hadn't moved. Lauren undid his seat belt and spun his seat around to face into the van.

Then she stood a moment and stared.

He was out cold, and he was big. How was she going to move him? How should she even begin?

Well, she'd solved boulder problems bigger and more unwieldy than Alex. She could solve him, too. She just needed to find a handhold and get started.

She slid one arm behind his back and took hold of his belt. With the other hand she picked up his arm and draped it over her own shoulder. She laid her cheek against his chest, planted her feet shoulder-width apart and braced herself.

One, two—

"Lauren? That you? What're you doing here?"

Tears stung her eyes. His voice sounded so groggy and...young. Had he really forgotten everything that had just happened?

She wrestled him out of his seat and hauled him upright. "Come on, stand up. I'm moving you to the back of the van."

"No, no. Tell me. What're you doing here? Why'd you come back?"

"Because you were in trouble and you needed help."

"How'd you know? Did Claudia tell you?"

"Claudia? No, why? What would Claudia tell me?"

He slumped against her, backing her against the van. Her face was pressed against his chest.

"I lost the land, Lauren. The judge is gonna give it to my dad. I tried, I really tried. But I lost. It's over."

He was heavy, and a full head taller than she was, and now he was sobbing in her arms like a child.

"Shh, it's okay. Everything's going to be fine. Come on, now. You're going to lie down and sleep for a while. It's way past your bedtime. You'll feel better in the morning."

Unbelievably, he let her lead him to the back of the van and take off his jacket. He was none too steady on his feet, but she managed.

"Alejandro, *siéntete,*" she said.

He sat obediently on the edge of the mattress, and she started to unbutton his waistcoat.

"What're you doing, woman? Aren't you even gonna buy me a drink first?"

He sounded so indignant that she could barely keep from laughing.

"Oh, I think you've had quite enough to drink for one night. Here, let's get your arms out. That's it. Now your shoes."

Raising one leg made him unsteady, even in a seating position, and he started to fall over on her.

"No, you can't pass out on me, you're too big. Lie down on the bed."

She was surprised by how cool and composed and take-charge she sounded. Alex obeyed without question. She drew off his long black boots—no easy task, with him little better than dead weight—and pulled off his linen stockings. Then she picked up his legs by the ankles and hauled them onto the mattress. His eyes were already shut again, and his breathing was slow and even.

He rolled onto his side and let out a long sigh.

"All righty then," she said.

She covered Alex with her comforter and turned off all the overhead lights except one, then took a cushion and a chenille throw to the passenger seat and settled in for the night.

CHAPTER TWENTY-TWO

ALEX WOKE TO a dry mouth, a splitting head-ache…and something soft and fluffy and sweet-smelling pulled up to his chin. He opened his eyes to a dim, narrow room. It wasn't his apartment, and yet there was something familiar about it, and about the red comforter covering him.

He shut his eyes. He tried to think, but his head wasn't working right. The last thing he remembered clearly was finding a twenty-foot tow chain in his grandfather's machine shed and taking it to the gate, along with what was left of his bottle of tequila. After as much as he'd consumed, the idea of chaining himself to the gate had seemed brilliant. He'd had a vague notion of bulldozers on their way to knock down his grandparents' house and rip out the fencing and tear up the fields, and the only way to stop this was to fasten himself to the gate.

After that things went all swimmy. He

thought he remembered headlights and tail-lights up and down the road, and shouting out challenges at the drivers—or were they the Mexican army?

He also thought he might have done some singing.

There was something else in the hazy part of his memory, something about Lauren. But that part was a dream…wasn't it?

He opened his eyes again. Thin wintry sunlight outlined shapes that could only be magnetic window covers. This was definitely Lauren's van.

He held very still—partly because of his head, and partly because he wasn't sure even now what was real and what wasn't. Whether this was real or not, it was nice. And once he got up and started talking, things would not be so nice or so simple. Dream or not, he wanted to keep this part going as long as possible.

"Good morning."

Alex's heart leaped into his throat.

"Wh-where are you?" he asked. His voice was like metal wheels on gravel.

"Over here. In the passenger seat."

She stirred a little. In the semidarkness, covered by a blanket, she'd blended right in.

"How do you feel?" she asked.

He sat up cautiously, enough to prop himself on one elbow. "Not great."

She got up, wrapped the blanket around her shoulders and went to the little fridge.

"Um…" Alex cleared his throat and made a back-and-forth motion with his hand between the two of them. "Did, uh, did anything…?"

She smiled as she took out two bottles of kombucha. "No, Alex. I did not take advantage of you last night while you were drunk."

"Oh. Okay." He felt stupid for asking. "I didn't think so. I mean…well, I'm guessing I was not at my most attractive last night."

Lauren chuckled. "Oh, I don't know. You do have a lovely singing voice."

Oh, no.

"That 'Ballad of the Alamo' song—was that Johnny Cash?"

He cringed. "Marty Robbins."

Welp, that was it, then. The last nail in the coffin. If she hadn't already rejected him soundly however many hours ago, she'd for sure be done with him now.

Only what was he doing now, on the mattress in her van? What was she doing here at all?

The questions must have showed on his

face, because she said, "We can talk later. Right now you need to get some fluids in you and rest some more. Do you think you can sip some kombucha?"

"Yeah."

She found some pill bottles, poured out some pills and handed them to him, along with the kombucha.

"Take these."

He swallowed them down. "What are they?"

"Ibuprofen and prenatal vitamins."

"Hey," he protested, but weakly.

"Don't knock it. Right now you need all the help you can get. Now lie down again."

He did. She sounded very in control, and that was comforting.

Then she pulled the comforter back up around him, laid a hand on his forehead and smiled down at him. Her hand felt soft and cool.

"Go to sleep, Alex."

He shut his eyes. For a moment he thought she kissed his cheek, but that couldn't be right, and, anyway, he was already half-asleep again.

He had a lot of questions, but his head hurt

too much to bother about them right now. He did feel better, though. Taken care of.

It was a nice change.

WHEN HE NEXT WOKE, his head no longer throbbed. He was even hungry. And he could smell something foodlike.

In fact, he could smell mesquite fire and… wait, no. That couldn't be right.

He sat up cautiously, then stood. He was a little weak in the legs, but his head and stomach were okay. Lauren was nowhere in sight.

A toothbrush still in the package was lying at the edge of the sink, along with a small tube of toothpaste. Alex brushed his teeth at the little van sink and felt better still.

He opened the door of the van—

And stopped in his tracks.

Outside, a camp was set up. White twinkle lights sparkled on the outside of the van, and a mesquite fire was indeed burning in a portable firepit. Two camp chairs sat close to the fire; a quilt was spread out on the grass. Lauren was setting up some dishes at an enamel folding table, which also held bags and cartons. An extension cord ran from the van to his grandfather's workshop.

Alex recognized the table and firepit from

Lauren's Instagram. He also recognized the logo on the food packaging.

"Cocina de Pecarí! I *knew* I could smell their fajitas, but I thought I was having some sort of aroma hallucination. Oh, man. My mouth is literally watering right now."

"Good! I had dinner there last night, so knew they were nearby, and it turns out they deliver. I'm glad you like the place. I thought you might."

"It's my favorite restaurant. It's actually where I wanted to take you."

She looked embarrassed, and he wanted to kick himself for mentioning their date that never was. It was mean and ungrateful, especially after she'd gone to so much trouble to look after him. It wasn't like she owed him anything.

"Thanks for getting the food," he said. "And for the toothbrush."

"No problem. I always keep a few spares. Would you like to use the outdoor shower? It's easy to set up."

"Thanks. I do feel pretty gross. I'll have to put the same clothes back on, though, so I don't know how much of an improvement it'll be."

"I have a shirt you can wear. And I found a

pair of jeans hanging on the clothesline. They look like your size."

"Oh, those *are* mine. I left them here last week."

"That sounds like an interesting story."

"Not really. I drove straight out here after work to feed cattle. I brought an older pair to change into and forgot to take the nicer ones back with me. Oh, and that reminds me—I didn't drive drunk last night. I brought the tequila out here, and I had my reenactor clothes with me in the truck, so I didn't have to go home for them. I was gonna have them cleaned, after Béxar. So, yeah. Just wanted you to know that. I was an idiot, but I wasn't a *reckless* idiot."

She set up the shower between the opened back doors of the van. A shower curtain protected the inside of the van, and another ran across the back.

The water was surprisingly hot. It felt good against his skin, but he didn't linger. The air was mild enough, but not so warm that it was comfortable being naked for very long. Anyway, he could smell the fajitas, and his stomach was rumbling by now.

He made a quick but thorough job of it,

then toweled himself off and pulled on his jeans.

The shirt she'd left for him was lime green, with a picture of a van driving on a ribbon of highway underneath the words *Van Life*. It looked like something Lauren would buy, but it was man-sized, way too big for her.

He carried it back to the camp area.

"Is this Evan's shirt?"

She made a face. "Ew, no. It's mine. I bought it big to sleep in."

Her glance trailed down his bare chest and abs. It soothed his hurt pride a little. He might have made a drunken idiot of himself, but at least she thought he had a nice body.

But he couldn't go around stripped to the waist like some punk. He put on the shirt.

"There. Do I look like a hipster?"

She laughed. "Oh, yeah. Like a real van-traveling man."

It felt good to be hungry. It felt even better to eat. They didn't talk about last night, not yet. They talked about a hundred other things—Alex's memories of the ranch, places Lauren had traveled. Alex had feelings of deep contentment, and simmering excitement, and unreality. Weirdly enough, this was pretty much what he'd planned for the date he'd wanted to take her on.

Why had she come back? He was burning to know, but he didn't want to mess up the good feeling by asking. He was content to... well, live in the moment. He wasn't going to trouble himself with what it all meant, or even with what lay in store for the land. Right here and now, he was with Lauren at his ancestral home, and that was something to cherish.

But when the food was all eaten and the fire was dying down, his loss hit him full force. It felt like grief, like someone had died.

"I'm sorry about the land," Lauren said, and he realized he'd been staring out over the fields. He must have told her what happened last night—how coherently, he didn't know. But he thought he remembered something about it, and about crying like a baby in her arms.

"I can't believe it's gone," he said. "I can't believe I lost. I told Claudia I was prepared for the possibility, but I wasn't, not really. I always believed somehow that if I just stalled the judge long enough, and worked hard enough, things would somehow be okay. Faith would have its reward." He picked up a stick and tossed it into the fire. "Stupid."

"There's nothing stupid about it. You loved the land and you wanted it. That's perfectly natural. And you did your best, so you have nothing to regret. So...what happened exactly? I'm a little short on details."

He dropped onto the quilt and stretched out on his back with his hands behind his head. "There aren't many details to be had. Yesterday, after we...after you drove away, I got a call from Claudia. The judge has decided to end the probate. It's over. My dad gets the land, the ranch gets razed, the nearest casino gets a fresh infusion of cash and Tony and I get screwed."

"I'm sorry," she said again.

He didn't know if she meant she was sorry about the land, or sorry about breaking his heart, or both. He was afraid he might have made himself sound kind of pitiful.

"I know I'm acting like an entitled brat," he said. "It's not like anything was actually taken from me. The land was never really mine to begin with. It was my grandfather's. And he had a right to do what he wanted with it...even if what he wanted was to give it to my father to be frittered away. It's just not what I expected, and not what my grandfather said he would do. He always said he'd take care of me and Tony, and I believed him. That part hurts as much as the loss of the land itself, the fact that he didn't do what he said."

"People always think they have more time, so they put off important things. And it can't have been easy, disinheriting his only son. It's understandable that he dragged his feet. Still, it sucks for you and Tony. You must have felt pretty beat down. And not just yesterday. Your whole life you've been let down by people who should have protected and provided for you."

His eyes stung. "Pretty much. But not you. You put your own plans on hold, and showed up when I needed someone, and took care of me. I had no right to expect that of you. I didn't think I'd ever see you again." He turned to face her. "How did that happen? How did you even know?"

"Well, I didn't, at first—or at least, not about the land. While I was at Cocina de Pecarí, those two cops were there, and they got a call about some whack job in costume chained to a ranch gate, shouting 'remember the Alamo' at passing cars. Who could that be but you?"

He writhed.

"How'd you get me unchained? I thought

I did a pretty good job securing myself to the gate."

"You left the key to the padlock around your wrist, genius."

He laughed, and the laugh turned into a groan. Then he rolled onto his stomach and hid his face with his arms, like he used to when he was little and playing with his dogs.

"Well, it's a good thing you did," she said. "I got you unchained, and that was the end of it. The cops didn't even cite you. They seemed relieved the whole thing was over."

They weren't the only ones. He might easily have ended up in jail if she hadn't intervened. He could just picture his mug shot, with his Tequila-ravaged face and rumpled Siege of Béxar outfit.

"I'm sorry, Lauren."

"For what?"

"Everything. Making a spectacle of myself, being a sanctimonious jerk. All those things I said to you about responsible behavior, and a few hours later I'm a sloppy drunk on the verge of a public-intoxication charge."

He heard her stirring, then felt her sit beside him on the quilt. She laid a hand on his back.

"You didn't say anything that wasn't true,"

she said. "You were right about me. I was running away because I was scared—too scared to see what an amazing thing you were trying to do for me. You were willing to take this major detour in your life for my sake, willing to take me with all my baggage—with my baby. And I panicked. I threw it all in your face. I blamed you for Evan's mistakes—but you're nothing like Evan. Everyone who knows you knows that. You're good and hardworking and conscientious—you care about people. You're passionate about everything you do. Whether it's Texas history or family land or old furniture, or me. When you care about something, you're all in."

His heart pounded against his ribs. What was she saying?

Her fingers combed slowly through his hair, making his whole body tingle.

"I love you, Alex."

He rolled over. She was looking down at him, her eyes dark and huge in her heart-shaped face, the long waves of her hair trailing to his chest.

"Y-you do?"

She laughed, and he did, too.

"Sorry," he said. "I just… I can't quite believe it."

"Believe it."

He closed his hand over hers and held it to his lips. "Well, I love you, too. But you already knew that."

"Yes. And if your offer still stands, I'm in."

"Which offer?"

"To move forward and see what happens."

"Oh."

She frowned. "What do you mean, 'Oh'? Is that not okay?"

"Oh, no, it's fine. I mean it's more than fine. Only… I thought maybe you meant my other offer. I thought maybe you were going to say you would marry me."

She laughed again and dropped her head to his chest.

"What's so funny?" he demanded.

"You are. You're the most amazing man I've ever met."

"Well, then. Marry me."

"I can't marry you—not yet. I barely know you."

"You know me plenty. What about all those things you just said, about me being such a solid guy and a good provider and all?"

"That doesn't mean I can marry you just like that."

"Sure it does. Just like that."

She shook her head.

He raised her chin, making her look at him. "At the very least," he said, "you can kiss me."

SHE KISSED HIM.

It was like falling down a well. His arms went around her, surprising her with their strength and speed. Then everything spun, and she was on her back with Alex on top of her, supporting his weight on his elbows.

His lips grazed her jawline.

"Marry me."

Her breath caught in a gasp, and tears started in her eyes.

"I love you, Lauren. I need you. Marry me."

"Okay."

He rose with a start, gazing down on her with his hair hanging loose and his arms braced on either side of her and a look of startled joy in his face.

"Really?"

The tears spilled out the corners and down her temples.

"Really."

He put his head back and let out a yell.

It was the kind of yell that might have been suitable for celebrating at a rodeo, or ringing in a new millennium, or going into battle, or celebrating victory at San Jacinto.

He yelled again.

Lauren shrieked with laughter, holding on to him. "Quiet! The neighbors are going to call the cops."

"Neighbors? Baby, ain't nobody here but you, me and a herd of Brahmas."

"Well, the next county, then. People can probably hear you there."

"I hope they do."

He yelled a third time, louder than ever. Lauren was laughing so hard she couldn't breathe.

Alex dropped beside her on his back, breathing heavily. "When is the baby due?"

"The fourteenth of May."

"Awesome! That's the same day the treaties of Velasco were signed."

"Well, then! You'll never forget her birthday."

"Her birthday? It's a girl? You know already?"

"Yes, I found out at my first appointment."

"When was that?"

"Monday. Yesterday."

"Whoa, is this just Tuesday? So much has happened."

"I know."

"All right, then. We're having a girl. When's our next appointment?"

He sounded so crisp and businesslike, so natural and self-assured with his "we," that Lauren had to kiss him again.

"What was that for?"

"For being adorable."

"I'm not sure that's the right adjective for me."

"Oh, it is. Believe me."

He laced their fingers together.

"Five months," he said. "Five months from now I'll be a husband and a father."

"Five months ago, could you have believed we'd be together now?"

"Heck, no. And I know you couldn't have. Hey, does Evan know about the baby?"

"Yes."

"And?"

"Let's just say I don't think he's going to be beating down my door anytime soon for parental rights."

"Good." Then, deadly serious, he added, "I want my name on the birth certificate."

The words warmed her through.

"I want that, too."

Then she sighed.

"But?"

"But I'm scared. What if Evan starts getting random fatherly fits and showing up and being disruptive? I almost wish I hadn't told him at all. But that wouldn't be right. And even if he keeps away, what if the baby wants to meet him someday? I mean, don't get me wrong. You will be such a better father than Evan could ever be. But still—"

"Blood is blood," Alex interrupted. "Yeah, I get that. Well, let's just let it be for now, and then take it year by year. As far as I'm concerned, that baby is mine. But her feelings should be respected as well, once she's mature enough to handle the situation. At some point, if she's curious about Evan and wants to find out about him or meet him, I won't stand in her way. But there's no need to clutter up her childhood with him. I mean, really, it's not like we could keep it from her even if we tried. Sooner or later she'll be able to do the math on our wedding date, and notice that she's a whole lot whiter than our other kids. But as far as when to deal with that, and how, we'll just wait and see."

This was all so calm and sensible that Lauren immediately felt better.

Alex started to get up, but Lauren held on to him.

"Don't go."

"I'm just gonna put more wood on the fire. I'll be right back."

"Promise?"

"Promise."

She watched him build up the fire. He was so beautiful, he made her throat ache.

"This whole camping-with-the-van scenario is not bad," he said. "We've got all our stuff right here in a rain-proof storage and transportation unit. And when we're ready, we just pack up and move somewhere else."

"Am I hearing right? You're praising the van life?"

He sat back on his haunches, gestured to his shirt and stared into the middle distance. "Don't forget, I'm a van-traveling man now."

She giggled. "That shirt is hilarious on you. You do fill it out nicely, though. A lot better than I do."

"Oh, I doubt that."

He came back to the quilt and lay down behind her, cupping her back with his torso.

"But seriously," he said. "Do you want to go on traveling, the two of us?"

"We're getting married, remember?"

"Yeah, but that doesn't mean you have to give up traveling. Lots of married couples do it, you said. With babies, too."

She rolled over and looked at him. "Are you saying you *want* to live in a van?"

"I'm saying that if you want to go on traveling, I'm game. Why not? At this point I have nothing to lose. Heck, maybe the timing is right. I've lost the land. I wouldn't be giving up anything but a crappy apartment."

"That's not true. You'd be giving up a whole community of people who love and respect you."

"Well, I'm willing to try it. I know it means a lot to you."

"Thank you for that. But I honestly don't want to go. You were right about why I came here. I did want to belong someplace, and this is a good place to belong to."

She smoothed his hair and tucked a strand behind his ear. "One day I do want to go traveling with you. See some more of Texas together, and show you some of the places I've visited. But I think my days of actually living out of a van are done."

"I don't know what we'll do about a place to live and a livelihood and all that, now that I have no land and no prospects."

"We'll be fine. We can stay in Vincent until we figure out something else. We both have jobs—lots of jobs. You said so yourself. You know engines and carpentry and ranching. La Escarpa is getting to be a lot for Tony and Dalia to manage. You can help them. I can, too. Privately owned farms and ranches are going to have to evolve to survive. We can all figure that out together."

"Yeah," he said. But he couldn't keep a note of sadness out of his voice.

She traced his jawline with her fingers. "I know it's not what you wanted. You wanted your own ranch. This ranch."

He nodded. "Six generations this place has been in our family. Six generations. Do you know how special that is? And now it's over. My dad's going to sell the land. Men are going to come here with heavy equipment and knock down the house and level the ground and carve it into single-family housing tracts, and in a year's time there'll be nothing left to show that any Reyes ever lived or died here."

She thought about that awhile. Then she got to her feet and held out her hand to him.

"Come on."

"Where are we going?"

"We're going to do this date properly. You

wanted to show me the land, right? Well, here we are. Show me."

He shook his head. "When I said that, I still had hope. I wanted you to see the place and fall in love with it. I wanted you to be able to envision a future here, with me. Now it'll just be sad, like saying goodbye."

"It might be sad, but it's time to say good-bye, Alex. The backhoe people will come whether you say goodbye or not. And if you don't, you'll regret it. Put on your boots, *te-niente*. We're going for a walk."

LAUREN TOOK PICTURES at every spot Alex told a story about, and just about every spot they saw had some story connected to it.

"This is where the chickens scratched. This is where my grandmother used to feed the barn cats. She'd pour the cat food in that beat-up old pan. That's where we would pen the cattle and give them their worming med-icine. We used to have this one dog, Paco, that would play hide-and-seek with me, and he would always hide behind that bush right there. Even in the winter, when it was cut back and I could see his hound self sticking up behind the little stump, he'd huddle back there thinking he was all hidden. I'd always play along and act like I couldn't see him. And this is the rock where Tony chipped my tooth when we were wrestling."

As he talked, he grew visibly more relaxed. It was as if all the bitterness was washing away, leaving only the sweetness of the memories behind.

"I wish we had more time," he said. "I wish I could show you the back pastures and the old creek bed where the fireplace stone came from. Every square foot of this place has a history. But we don't have much daylight left."

"Is that an old tractor over there by the yard fence?"

"Oh, yeah. I used to play on it all the time when I was a kid."

"How come it got left out like that?"

"I don't know. Seems like it was already broken-down before I ever came along. It's been sitting there not running for as long as I can remember."

"Is it valuable?"

"It might have been once, if it had been taken care of, or even moved to a barn. But it's too far gone even for restoration now. Just a heap of rust."

He chuckled.

"What is it?"

"Oh, just thinking. One time when me and Tony were out here for the weekend, my grandparents gave us some money for school clothes. It was just after my dad had lost big at an Oklahoma casino and we were pretty cash-poor. But my dad found out, and he took the money. And after that, whenever we got back from visiting my grandparents, he'd ask if they'd given us any money, and if they had, he'd take it. Well, I couldn't just *lie*, you know. And my grandfather knew that. So he started leaving envelopes of cash in the old tractor's exhaust pipe, under that little rain flap. That way he wasn't *giving* it to me, see. I'd just found it. And when my dad asked if they'd given me any money, I could honestly tell him no."

"Clever. Get up there. I'll take your picture on it."

He did. He looked incredible sitting there with his hand on the wheel and that far-seeing look in his eye.

Then he said, "Now you get on, and I'll take *your* picture. You'll look better on it than I ever did."

She showed him how to work her camera,

then climbed onto the seat and put her hands on the wheel.

After he'd taken a few shots, she said, "I'm going to take this little rain flap."

"Take it? Where? What for?"

"For you to hold on to. It's small and nifty-looking, and it has good memories associated with it."

"Like you and your dad used to do? That's not a bad idea. But will it come loose? The screws are probably rusted through."

She tested it. "Yeah, I don't know. Maybe if we had some tools. Some screwdrivers and saw blades and things."

"I'll be right back."

She kept working at it while he was gone. By the time he got back, she had the flap open and was scrabbling around inside with her fingers.

"There's something wedged down in the exhaust pipe," she said. "Some sort of tube."

"The exhaust pipe *is* a tube."

"Yeah, but this is something else. Here, hand me that big screwdriver."

She stuck the screwdriver down the exhaust pipe, stuck the edge into the thing and started dragging it up. After a few tries, she managed to get a corner worked up far enough to grab and pull.

It was a rolled-up manila envelope.

She spread it flat on her lap. There were words written on the front. The ink had faded, but she could make them out.

The last will and testament of Miguel Reyes.

LAUREN SMOOTHED THE stiffly rolled packet flat on her lap and froze.

"Alex. Alex, look."

She gave it to him. He saw the scrawled line of familiar handwriting, read it and looked back at Lauren.

"Open it," she said.

The flap was sealed shut. He slit the envelope open and took out some folded sheets of yellow paper. His hands shook.

I, Miguel Reyes, of Limestone Springs, Texas, on this date—

"It's dated two days before he died," Alex said.

Lauren got down from the tractor. "What does it say?"

He kept reading, aloud this time.

"'…am of sound mind, and am writing this holographic will with the intent of setting forth my wishes for the disposition of my estate after my death. I expressly revoke all prior wills and make them invalid and without binding legal force.' Then there's a description of the land. Then it says 'I hereby leave this property—'" he took a shuddering breath "'—to my grandsons, Antonio Ignacio Reyes and Alejandro Emilio Reyes. To my son, Carlos Antonio Reyes, I leave nothing.'" He swallowed hard. "'I regret that it this is necessary, but his reckless behavior has given me no choice. I have determined to provide for my grandsons, and I am confident that they will respect their heritage and make me proud, as they always have.'"

He lowered the paper. He felt light-headed.

Lauren took the will from his hand. "Is this even legal?" she asked.

"I don't know. I gotta call Claudia."

BUT IT WAS Lauren who actually talked to Claudia. Alex was too delirious to make coherent sentences.

"Oh, yes, a handwritten will is certainly valid in Texas, as long as it's done right,"

Claudia said. "It has to be handwritten in its entirety by the decedent, and he has to say he's of sound mind, and the probate court has to believe that he is. Then he has to demonstrate testamentary capacity, which means he understands the value of his property and the natural objects of his bounty—family members and such. He should expressly revoke any earlier wills, and set forth his property, and say whom he's bequeathing it to. If someone's being left out, he should say why—otherwise that person might challenge the will by saying he wasn't of sound mind. He has to sign and date, and draft a self-proving affidavit, which makes it so he doesn't have to have any witnesses to testify that the will is in his handwriting."

"This has all that. The wording seems pretty legit, like he was following some sort of template or form."

"He might have just looked it up online. It's like Miguel to want to do it himself."

All this time Alex was pacing around with his hands laced behind his head, breathing raggedly, like he was cooling down after a run. His eyes were glassy, and he had a stunned smile.

"She says it sounds like everything's in

order," Lauren said after she hung up with Claudia. "She'll check it out and take it to the judge. It's not a slam dunk, but things look good."

Alex put his arms around Lauren and held her tight.

"He didn't forget me," he said. "He took care of me and Tony, just like he said he would. He didn't forget."

"No. But why'd he put the will in the exhaust pipe? I mean, I get that that's where he used to leave money for you so it'd be safe from your dad, so I guess there's a certain poetic justice in it, but what the heck? How were you supposed to guess a thing like that?"

Alex released her and took a look around. "Let me think. He would have made the will at night, after supper and evening chores. Then he'd want to take it to town early the next day, first thing after morning chores. He hated going to town, and when he had to do it he always did it as early in the day as possible to get it out of the way. He'd have come down the path, out the front gate. And then—"

He stopped and looked at her. "My dad. My dad came to see him that morning. It was right after those thugs smashed my truck, and he wanted to borrow money to pay back the loan shark. So my grandfather would have seen my dad's car coming down the drive. He didn't have time to reach his own truck, and he didn't want to be caught with an envelope in his hand that said last will and testament. So he stuck it in the exhaust pipe. Then my dad told him about the loan shark and how the thugs were coming after me now. And so my grandfather agreed to pay back the loan shark, but personally. He wasn't going to just give the cash to my dad. So he went to the bank—loan sharks don't take personal checks, I'm guessing—and took out the money. I'm on that account, and I remember the big withdrawal he made that day. Then he drove to wherever the loan shark had his storefront or whatever. It must have been a long drive. And by the time he got back, he had evening chores to do. And after that— after that, he made out the gift deed, giving his truck to me. And then the next morning is when I found him."

He leaned his back against the tractor and stared off into space.

"He knew," he said. "He knew he didn't have much time left. He—he was doing the best he could."

Lauren leaned next to him. He put his arm around her and kissed the top of her head.

"Thank you," he said.

"For what?"

"For saving my ranch. Don't you realize that's what you did? If I hadn't come back here with you, I never would have found it. I never would've looked inside the tractor's exhaust pipe. There was no reason to."

"I hadn't thought of that. But it was your doing, too, you know. We wouldn't have been anywhere near the tractor if you hadn't been willing to say goodbye."

"That's true. I was ready to let go. But I'm glad I don't have to."

CHAPTER TWENTY-THREE

"I DON'T UNDERSTAND how you've managed to live in this tin can for as long as you have," Dalia grumbled. "There's hardly room to turn around."

"Well, there aren't usually three grown women and an infant in here getting ready for a wedding," Lauren said.

Having Claudia and Dalia together in Vincent Van-Go was an exhilarating experience. They were both such ruthless, efficient, take-charge people that it was a wonder the van could hold their combined energy and not burst.

Dalia was in charge of makeup, and Claudia was on wardrobe and hair. They barked orders to Lauren one after another. *Hold still. Turn your head. Look up. Look down. Close your eyes. Hold your breath.* Between the two of them they had Lauren looking so good she hardly recognized herself.

Little Ignacio watched from his infant seat

on the mattress, round-eyed, his shock of thick dark hair sticking straight up.

Lauren turned sideways to look at herself in the full-length mirror that had been moved into the van from Dalia's bedroom. "How pregnant do I look?"

"Not very," Dalia said.

"What do you mean, not very? What kind of a maid of honor are you? You're supposed to say not at all. Really, in this dress I don't think I show."

The dress had been Claudia's contribution, and she'd insisted on making it as a gift. Lauren couldn't even imagine the cost in terms of materials and labor. The design was from the eighteen-twenties, a transitional period between the neoclassical-influenced Federalist style, with its high waistlines and columnar silhouette, and the full-on Victorian, with its wide skirts, big sleeves and tiny corseted waists. It was more fitted than Lauren's first historical gown, the one she'd bought from Claudia at the festival, while still accommodating to a second-trimester shape.

It was soft ivory in color, and off-the-shoulder, with light drapes of tulle around the neckline, gathered at intervals with tiny clusters of silk flowers. Delicate embroidery edged the hem.

"You don't," Dalia said. "But as skinny as you are overall, the only reason you wouldn't have a dress fitted through the waist would be if you were pregnant. That's just common sense. It is a terrific look, though."

"Pregnant or not, you look gorgeous," said Claudia. "You're going to blow Alex's mind."

Claudia seemed almost as happy about the wedding, and about the saving of the ranch, as Lauren and Alex were. There were still some legal things to sort through, but the handwritten will appeared to be in good order, and Claudia said she thought it was only a matter of time.

With the estate reopened and things moving along, Alex was allowing himself to talk about things like fixing the fence here or taking out some mesquite brush there. His ultimate goal was to be able to ride a horse in a clear path around the perimeter of the fencing. Some of his reenactor friends had volunteered to help with the work, evidently thinking fence-mending and brush-clearing sounded like fun.

Once the property was secured, it would take time to get the house ready to move into.

In the meantime, the bunkhouse would be Alex and Lauren's home. Dalia had wanted to do all the bridal prep there, but Lauren had said no. The bunkhouse was for her wedding night. Getting ready for the wedding had to happen in Vincent. So what if it was a little cramped? The van had been her home for so long that she wouldn't feel right getting ready anywhere else.

They'd had two months to pull the wedding together. Lauren had felt a little funny about that at first. It wasn't even a full year since her first wedding, let alone her divorce. But Alex had wanted it settled and done, with the two of them in their own home well before the baby came.

He'd also wanted a real wedding, not just a trip to the justice of the peace, as Lauren had suggested. And when she'd realized how much it meant to him, she'd given in, and contented herself with resolving to make this wedding all about him. She'd already been a bride once, but he'd never been a groom. She would give him the beautiful wedding he deserved, surrounded by the people who loved him. It didn't matter about her.

But she'd ended up being overwhelmed by how the community's affection for him had enveloped her as well—not just as Alex's wife, but for her own sake.

"Carlos came by earlier," said Dalia.

"Did he? What did he say?" asked Claudia.

"I don't know. I just saw him talking to Tony. He didn't stay long."

Carlos had not responded well to the appearance of the new will. He'd done everything from accusing Alex of forging the whole thing to pleading with his sons to divide the property with him voluntarily—which, considering what short shrift he'd given Alex when Alex had offered to *pay* him for a portion of the land, was really adding insult to injury.

Lauren couldn't tell whether she was relieved or sorry that Carlos hadn't stayed for the wedding. He'd been invited, which had been a tough call to make. If he had come, he might have been perfectly charming, or he might have ruined the day. There was just no telling. But in the end Alex had decided to err on the side of magnanimity and send him an invitation.

"I feel sorry for him," Lauren said.

"It's his own fault," said Dalia. "He's hurt his family again and again, and he's never even sorry. He just tries to shift the blame and justify himself. He's had more second chances than he had any right to expect and squandered them all."

"Oh, I know. But don't you think it must be awful for him, to realize at his age just how bad he's messed up? Crouching down in that corner he painted himself into, cramped and cut off, and knowing he has only himself to blame? His charm isn't going to save him forever. He's not going to be able to pull a rabbit out of a hat."

"I agree it would be awful to realize all that," Dalia said. "But I doubt he does."

A knock sounded on Vincent's door, and her dad's voice said, "Lauren, honey, it's time."

Lauren took one last look at herself. Claudia had done her hair in ringlets, with a high gathering of curls at the crown and a few tendrils hanging loose at the hairline and neck. A strand of Lauren's mother's pearls completed the look perfectly—and, according to Claudia, period-appropriately. Her skin looked creamy and smooth, and her eyeliner was perfection itself. No one did eyeliner like Dalia.

Claudia opened the van door. Lauren's dad stood waiting, beaming and immaculate, in a dark green frock coat borrowed from Ron the gunsmith. He was such a youthful father to a grown-up daughter, so trim and handsome.

They had to exit the van in single file. Her dad held out his hand and helped Claudia down, then Dalia with Ignacio in her arm, then Lauren.

"Here, give me the baby," Claudia said.

Dalia handed him over and picked up Lauren's bouquet and her own from the little enamel table beside the van. The bouquets were rounded bunches of pink floribunda roses from an antique rose that had been growing on an arbor at La Escarpa for as long as anyone could remember.

Suddenly everything seemed to be happening fast. Claudia disappeared down the aisle with Ignacio. Dalia gave Lauren her bouquet and squeezed her hand. The guitar music shifted subtly into the Spanish ballad chosen for the processional, and Dalia headed down the aisle, back straight, head high.

Lauren took her father's arm and started walking, past the improvised seat rows decorated with native cedar and holly, past the various guests, some in historical dress and some not, past the grape trellis and the ivy-covered stone wall to the arbor, where the antique rose was blooming like crazy.

Zander, playing guitar, winked at her. As Alex had said, "He may be a punk, but he sure can play."

Alex stood waiting, stiff and tall in his new black breeches and jacket and silk stockings, with a clenched jaw and a face tight with the strain of holding it all together, except his eyes, which glowed like sunlit amber.

Jay performed the ceremony, using a seventeenth-century reproduction of the *Book of Common Prayer.* The words of the old marriage service were beautiful and dignified. *With this ring I thee wed, with my body I thee worship, and with all my worldly goods I thee endow.* How could any modern wording possibly improve on that?

From the moment their eyes locked until the kiss, it felt as if she and Alex were in a warm bubble together, with everyone else present but peripheral. Tony, as best man, looked a little self-conscious in his own historical outfit; Dalia seemed perfectly comfortable in hers. Durango, spruced up and clean with a spray of holly in his collar, sat bolt upright just outside the arbor; Dalia had told him to stay. Cats ambled in and out at their leisure.

Only afterward, when the ceremony was

completed and they turned around, did Lauren see Claudia standing near her dad, where her mother would have been. She must have done it by accident; the rows were a little haphazard, and people were informally grouped.

They looked good together.

LAUREN WAS GIVING Chester a nibble of cheese off her plate when Alex stole behind her and whispered into her ear, "I love all these people, but I can't stand this anymore. I have to get away from here. I want to take you into the bunkhouse this minute. Or take you in the van, or the rose arbor if no one's there. Basically I just want to take you."

A delicious shiver ran down her spine. "I think it would be wrong to ghost our own reception."

Alex brushed her ringlets back and dropped a light kiss on the curve of her neck. "We don't have to ghost it completely. We could just sort of absent ourselves for a while. We could do it right now. No one's watching us. We could be locked in the bunkhouse inside of two minutes."

Lauren set her plate down, turned to face him and put her arms around him. "Oh, no. We're not leaving and coming back again.

Once I have you alone behind closed doors, I'm not stepping outside until sometime next week."

She felt his muscles tighten, and he drew in his breath with a hissing sound.

"Please, please, can we go right now?" he asked.

She thought fast.

"We've had a chance to greet all the guests. We just have to say goodbye to your mom and my dad, and Tony and Dalia."

"That sounds risky. We might get bogged down."

"We won't let ourselves. How long does it take to say 'thank you, I love you, goodbye'?"

"Let's find out."

THE BUNKHOUSE WAS QUIET, peaceful, and spotlessly clean—and Lauren and Alex had it all to themselves.

The harvest table in the dining room held an arrangement of bare twigs and leafless holly thick with berries. An old Spanish cupboard that Alex had restored stood in the kitchen, topped with a blue-and-white pitcher and two green glass wine jugs, all found inside the bunkhouse when Lauren was first cleaning it out. A fire burned in the hearth—the hearth she and Alex had remade together.

"What is that in your hand?" Lauren asked.

Alex looked at the small gift bag. "Oh. It's from my dad. He left it with Tony. I was talking to Tony and somehow I ended up holding it."

"What is it?"

"Ugh, no telling. Do we even want to know? I haven't exactly been his favorite person since...well, ever."

Lauren took it from him. "It feels light."

"Could be a hateful letter."

"Or maybe it's a peace offering."

She reached inside and pulled out something red and white and soft.

"A little Christmas stocking. Look, there's money inside. Tens, twenties, fives, ones. It looks like a wad of random bills. And here's a note."

"Is it hateful?"

"No. It just says congratulations on your marriage, and that there are a lot of back payments included here."

Alex took the note and read it. They looked at each other, both mystified.

Then Alex smiled and said, "I know what

it is. It's the money he would have spent on scratch-offs."

"You're right! It *is* a peace offering."

"I guess. But I'm not sure. It might turn out to be some subtle passive-aggressive thing."

"Maybe you shouldn't overthink it. You know what they say. Best not to look a gift horse…"

She smiled. "I know just what to do with it."

She took one of the wine jugs down from the cupboard. "We'll put it in here. It'll be the start of your horse fund."

"Brilliant! What a brilliant woman I've married."

He put the bills in the jug, and Lauren added the penny from her shoe.

"Lot of empty space left in that bottle," Alex said.

"We'll add to it as we're able," Lauren said. "Spare change and windfalls."

Alex set the jug back onto the cupboard, then held out his hand to Lauren and bent at the waist in a courtly gesture so graceful and perfect that it made her ache.

She took his hand, and he led her down the hallway.

There were various objects hung on the

wall that Lauren had found in or around the bunkhouse: a small rusted gear of some sort, an iron horse that looked like it might have topped a weathervane once, a random letter *R*. The *R* was a mystery. After unearthing it, she'd expected to find more letters in the area that spelled out a word, but no others had ever appeared, so *R* it was. *R* for restoration, for romance, for Ramirez, for Reyes.

In the baby's room, the cradle Alex had made stood ready, carved and polished to perfection. He'd started it for his nephew, in case Calypso the cat refused to vacate the antique heirloom original, but a month or so before Ignacio's birth, Calypso had found a cashmere blanket in the linen closet and started bedding down there instead. So now Ignacio had the heirloom cradle, and the reproduction waited for Lauren's baby. A soft blanket, crocheted by Tamara, was waiting inside—yellow, like the *esperanza* blossoms that would be covering the shrub outside the door by the time the baby was born.

They'd talked about naming her Esperanza, but they weren't sure yet. Esperanza was a lot of name. They might call her Peri, or maybe Essie. Or maybe they'd go with the anglicized version, Hope.

Alex pushed open the door to the master bedroom. Twinkle lights glowed above the solid oak headboard of the sleigh bed.

"We did a good job with the place," Lauren said.

There were still details to be sorted out, like some empty gilt picture frames Lauren wanted to arrange on the living-room wall, and what kind of rug to put in the bathroom, but that was true of any house. For now they were both content to be here, and dream and plan the restoration of Alex's grandparents' house and ranch.

"Yes, we did. And so did our cowboy."

The imaginary cowboy had a full-blown story by now—a bizarre, convoluted, somewhat contradictory story that was constantly being added to or amended. On the spot, Alex made up an appendix about the guy bringing his new bride there for the first time.

"And that was all very nice for them," he said. "But they're not here now. We are. I'm not the imaginary cowboy, or even Alejandro Ramirez. I'm just me, and you're you. And this is our home, not anyone else's."

"Don't you mean our home for now?"

He raised her hand to his lips and kissed the palm. "I mean exactly what I said. Wherever you are is my home—*mi alma, mi vida, mi corazón.*"

My soul. My life. My heart.

She cupped his cheek. "And you are my adventure, Alejandro."

He leaned into her touch. "I love it when you call me that. I always have."

"Everything sounds better in Spanish, doesn't it?"

"Sí. Ahora deja de hablar y bésame."

Yes. Now stop talking and kiss me.

So she did.

* * * * *

Get 4 FREE REWARDS!

We'll send you 2 FREE Books
<u>plus</u> 2 FREE Mystery Gifts.

Love Inspired books feature uplifting stories where faith helps guide you through life's challenges and discover the promise of a new beginning.

FREE
Value Over
$20

YES! Please send me 2 FREE Love Inspired Romance novels and my 2 FREE mystery gifts (gifts are worth about $10 retail). After receiving them, if I don't wish to receive any more books, I can return the shipping statement marked "cancel." If I don't cancel, I will receive 6 brand-new novels every month and be billed just $5.24 each for the regular-print edition or $5.99 each for the larger-print edition in the U.S., or $5.74 each for the regular-print edition or $6.24 each for the larger-print edition in Canada. That's a savings of at least 13% off the cover price. It's quite a bargain! Shipping and handling is just 50¢ per book in the U.S. and $1.25 per book in Canada.* I understand that accepting the 2 free books and gifts places me under no obligation to buy anything. I can always return a shipment and cancel at any time. The free books and gifts are mine to keep no matter what I decide.

Choose one: ☐ **Love Inspired Romance**
Regular-Print
(105/305 IDN GNWC)

☐ **Love Inspired Romance**
Larger-Print
(122/322 IDN GNWC)

Name (please print)

Address   Apt. #

City   State/Province   Zip/Postal Code

Email: Please check this box ☐ if you would like to receive newsletters and promotional emails from Harlequin Enterprises ULC and its affiliates. You can unsubscribe anytime.

Mail to the **Reader Service:**
IN U.S.A.: P.O. Box 1341, Buffalo, NY 14240-8531
IN CANADA: P.O. Box 603, Fort Erie, Ontario L2A 5X3

Want to try 2 free books from another series! Call 1-800-873-8635 or visit www.ReaderService.com.

*Terms and prices subject to change without notice. Prices do not include sales taxes, which will be charged (if applicable) based on your state or country of residence. Canadian residents will be charged applicable taxes. Offer not valid in Quebec. This offer is limited to one order per household. Books received may not be as shown. Not valid for current subscribers to Love Inspired Romance books. All orders subject to approval. Credit or debit balances in a customer's account(s) may be offset by any other outstanding balance owed by or to the customer. Please allow 4 to 6 weeks for delivery. Offer available while quantities last.

Your Privacy—Your information is being collected by Harlequin Enterprises ULC, operating as Reader Service. For a complete summary of the information we collect, how we use this information and to whom it is disclosed, please visit our privacy notice located at corporate.harlequin.com/privacy-notice. From time to time we may also exchange your personal information with reputable third parties. If you wish to opt out of this sharing of your personal information, please visit readerservice.com/consumerschoice or call 1-800-873-8635. **Notice to California Residents**—Under California law, you have specific rights to control and access your data. For more information on these rights and how to exercise them, visit corporate.harlequin.com/california-privacy.

LI20R2

Get 4 FREE REWARDS!

We'll send you 2 FREE Books plus 2 FREE Mystery Gifts.

Love Inspired Suspense books showcase how courage and optimism unite in stories of faith and love in the face of danger.

FREE Value Over $20

YES! Please send me 2 FREE Love Inspired Suspense novels and my 2 FREE mystery gifts (gifts are worth about $10 retail). After receiving them, if I don't wish to receive any more books, I can return the shipping statement marked "cancel." If I don't cancel, I will receive 6 brand-new novels every month and be billed just $5.24 each for the regular-print edition or $5.99 each for the larger-print edition in the U.S., or $5.74 each for the regular-print edition or $6.24 each for the larger-print edition in Canada. That's a savings of at least 13% off the cover price. It's quite a bargain! Shipping and handling is just 50¢ per book in the U.S. and $1.25 per book in Canada.* I understand that accepting the 2 free books and gifts places me under no obligation to buy anything. I can always return a shipment and cancel at any time. The free books and gifts are mine to keep no matter what I decide.

Choose one: ☐ **Love Inspired Suspense Regular-Print** (153/353 IDN GNWN) ☐ **Love Inspired Suspense Larger-Print** (107/307 IDN GNWN)

Name (please print)

Address   Apt. #

City   State/Province   Zip/Postal Code

Email: Please check this box ☐ if you would like to receive newsletters and promotional emails from Harlequin Enterprises ULC and its affiliates. You can unsubscribe anytime.

Mail to the **Reader Service:**
IN U.S.A.: P.O. Box 1341, Buffalo, NY 14240-8531
IN CANADA: P.O. Box 603, Fort Erie, Ontario L2A 5X3

Want to try 2 free books from another series? Call 1-800-873-8635 or visit www.ReaderService.com.

---

*Terms and prices subject to change without notice. Prices do not include sales taxes, which will be charged (if applicable) based on your state or country of residence. Canadian residents will be charged applicable taxes. Offer not valid in Quebec. This offer is limited to one order per household. Books received may not be as shown. Not valid for current subscribers to Love Inspired Suspense books. All orders subject to approval. Credit or debit balances in a customer's account(s) may be offset by any other outstanding balance owed by or to the customer. Please allow 4 to 6 weeks for delivery. Offer available while quantities last.

Your Privacy—Your information is being collected by Harlequin Enterprises ULC, operating as Reader Service. For a complete summary of the information we collect, how we use this information and to whom it is disclosed, please visit our privacy notice located at corporate.harlequin.com/privacy-notice. From time to time we may also exchange your personal information with reputable third parties. If you wish to opt out of this sharing of your personal information, please visit readerservice.com/consumerschoice or call 1-800-873-8635. **Notice to California Residents**—Under California law, you have specific rights to control and access your data. For more information on these rights and how to exercise them, visit corporate.harlequin.com/california-privacy.

LIS20R2

THE WESTERN HEARTS COLLECTION!

19 FREE BOOKS in all!

COWBOYS. RANCHERS. RODEO REBELS.
Here are their charming love stories in one prized Collection:
51 emotional and heart-filled romances that capture the majesty and rugged beauty of the American West!

YES! Please send me **The Western Hearts Collection** in Larger Print. This collection begins with 3 FREE books and 2 FREE gifts in the first shipment. Along with my 3 free books, I'll also get the next 4 books from The Western Hearts Collection, in LARGER PRINT, which I may either return and owe nothing, or keep for the low price of $5.45 U.S./$6.23 CDN each plus $2.99 U.S./$7.49 CDN for shipping and handling per shipment*. If I decide to continue, about once a month for 8 months I will get 6 or 7 more books but will only need to pay for 4. That means 2 or 3 books in every shipment will be FREE! If I decide to keep the entire collection, I'll have paid for only 32 books because 19 books are FREE! I understand that accepting the 3 free books and gifts places me under no obligation to buy anything. I can always return a shipment and cancel at any time. My free books and gifts are mine to keep no matter what I decide.

☐ 270 HCN 5354   ☐ 470 HCN 5354

Name (please print)

Address   Apt. #

City   State/Province   Zip/Postal Code

Mail to the **Reader Service:**
IN U.S.A.: P.O. Box 1341, Buffalo, N.Y. 14240-8531
IN CANADA: P.O. Box 603, Fort Erie, Ontario L2A 5X3

*Terms and prices subject to change without notice. Prices do not include sales taxes, which will be charged (if applicable) based on your state or country of residence. Canadian residents will be charged applicable taxes. Offer not valid in Quebec. All orders subject to approval. Credit or debit balances in a customer's account(s) may be offset by any other outstanding balance owed by or to the customer. Please allow three to four weeks for delivery. Offer available while quantities last. © 2020 Harlequin Enterprises ULC. ® and ™ are trademarks owned by Harlequin Enterprises ULC.

Your Privacy—The Reader Service is committed to protecting your privacy. Our Privacy Policy is available online at www.ReaderService.com or upon request from the Reader Service. We make a portion of our mailing list available to reputable third parties that offer products we believe may interest you. If you prefer that we not exchange your name with third parties, or if you wish to clarify or modify your communication preferences, please visit us at www.ReaderService.com/consumerschoice or write to us at Reader Service Mail Preference Service, P.O. Box 9062, Buffalo, NY 14269. Include your complete name and address.

50BWH20

Get 4 FREE REWARDS!

We'll send you 2 FREE Books plus 2 FREE Mystery Gifts.

FREE
Value Over
$20

Both the **Romance** and **Suspense** collections feature compelling novels
written by many of today's bestselling authors.

YES! Please send me 2 FREE novels from the Essential Romance or
Essential Suspense Collection and my 2 FREE gifts (gifts are worth about
$10 retail). After receiving them, if I don't wish to receive any more books,
I can return the shipping statement marked "cancel." If I don't cancel, I will
receive 4 brand-new novels every month and be billed just $7.24 each in the
U.S. or $7.49 each in Canada. That's a savings of up to 28% off the cover
price. It's quite a bargain! Shipping and handling is just 50¢ per book in the
U.S. and $1.25 per book in Canada.* I understand that accepting the 2 free
books and gifts places me under no obligation to buy anything. I can always
return a shipment and cancel at any time. The free books and gifts are mine
to keep no matter what I decide.

Choose one: ☐ **Essential Romance** ☐ **Essential Suspense**
(194/394 MDN GQ6M) (191/391 MDN GQ6M)

Name (please print)

Address   Apt. #

City   State/Province   Zip/Postal Code

Email: Please check this box ☐ if you would like to receive newsletters and promotional emails from Harlequin Enterprises ULC and
its affiliates. You can unsubscribe anytime.

Mail to the **Reader Service:**
IN U.S.A.: P.O. Box 1341, Buffalo, NY 14240-8531
IN CANADA: P.O. Box 603, Fort Erie, Ontario L2A 5X3

Want to try 2 free books from another series? Call 1-800-873-8635 or visit www.ReaderService.com.

---

*Terms and prices subject to change without notice. Prices do not include sales taxes, which will be charged (if applicable) based
on your state or country of residence. Canadian residents will be charged applicable taxes. Offer not valid in Quebec. This offer is
limited to one order per household. Books received may not be as shown. Not valid for current subscribers to the Essential Romance
or Essential Suspense Collection. All orders subject to approval. Credit or debit balances in a customer's account(s) may be offset by
any other outstanding balance owed by or to the customer. Please allow 4 to 6 weeks for delivery. Offer available while quantities last.

Your Privacy—Your information is being collected by Harlequin Enterprises ULC, operating as Reader Service. For a complete
summary of the information we collect, how we use this information and to whom it is disclosed, please visit our privacy notice located
at corporate.harlequin.com/privacy-notice. From time to time we may also exchange your personal information with reputable third
parties. If you wish to opt out of this sharing of your personal information, please visit readerservice.com/consumerschoice or call
1-800-873-8635. **Notice to California Residents**—Under California law, you have specific rights to control and access your data.
For more information on these rights and how to exercise them, visit corporate.harlequin.com/california-privacy.

STRS20R2

Get 4 FREE REWARDS!

We'll send you 2 FREE Books plus 2 FREE Mystery Gifts.

Harlequin Special Edition books relate to finding comfort and strength in the support of loved ones and enjoying the journey no matter what life throws your way.

FREE Value Over $20

YES! Please send me 2 FREE Harlequin Special Edition novels and my 2 FREE gifts (gifts are worth about $10 retail). After receiving them, if I don't wish to receive any more books, I can return the shipping statement marked "cancel." If I don't cancel, I will receive 6 brand-new novels every month and be billed just $4.99 per book in the U.S. or $5.74 per book in Canada. That's a savings of at least 12% off the cover price! It's quite a bargain! Shipping and handling is just 50¢ per book in the U.S. and $1.25 per book in Canada.* I understand that accepting the 2 free books and gifts places me under no obligation to buy anything. I can always return a shipment and cancel at any time. The free books and gifts are mine to keep no matter what I decide.

235/335 HDN GNMP

Name (please print)

Address   Apt. #

City   State/Province   Zip/Postal Code

Email: Please check this box ☐ if you would like to receive newsletters and promotional emails from Harlequin Enterprises ULC and its affiliates. You can unsubscribe anytime.

Mail to the Reader Service:
IN U.S.A.: P.O. Box 1341, Buffalo, NY 14240-8531
IN CANADA: P.O. Box 603, Fort Erie, Ontario L2A 5X3

Want to try 2 free books from another series! Call 1-800-873-8635 or visit www.ReaderService.com.

*Terms and prices subject to change without notice. Prices do not include sales taxes, which will be charged (if applicable) based on your state or country of residence. Canadian residents will be charged applicable taxes. Offer not valid in Quebec. This offer is limited to one order per household. Books received may not be as shown. Not valid for current subscribers to Harlequin Special Edition books. All orders subject to approval. Credit or debit balances in a customer's account(s) may be offset by any other outstanding balance owed by or to the customer. Please allow 4 to 6 weeks for delivery. Offer available while quantities last.

Your Privacy—Your information is being collected by Harlequin Enterprises ULC, operating as Reader Service. For a complete summary of the information we collect, how we use this information and to whom it is disclosed, please visit our privacy notice located at corporate.harlequin.com/privacy-notice. From time to time we may also exchange your personal information with reputable third parties. If you wish to opt out of this sharing of your personal information, please visit readerservice.com/consumerschoice or call 1-800-873-8635. **Notice to California Residents**—Under California law, you have specific rights to control and access your data. For more information on these rights and how to exercise them, visit corporate.harlequin.com/california-privacy.

HSE20R2

Visit
ReaderService.com
Today!

As a valued member of the Harlequin Reader Service, you'll find these benefits and more at ReaderService.com:

- Try 2 free books from any series
- Access risk-free special offers
- View your account history & manage payments
- Browse the latest Bonus Bucks catalog

Don't miss out!

If you want to stay up-to-date on the latest at the Harlequin Reader Service and enjoy more content, make sure you've signed up for our monthly News & Notes email newsletter. Sign up online at ReaderService.com or by calling Customer Service at 1-800-873-8635.

RS20